CW01024852

THE
GENTLEWOMAN
SPY

Kit Scarlett Mysteries
Book One

Adele Jordan

SAPERE
BOOKS

THE GENTLEWOMAN SPY

Published by Sapere Books.

24 Trafalgar Road, Ilkley, LS29 8HH

saperebooks.com

ISBN: 978-1-80055-715-4

For my Mum, Kathryn, who decided not to correct my English homework, because it was written a little differently.

CHAPTER 1

Edinburgh, Scotland 1584

"Of all the castles in the whole of Scotland, it had to be this one, didn't it?" Kit Scarlett muttered to herself as she looked up at the wall above her. The grey slate cliff stretched tall, so far above her head that she felt rather like a mole in comparison. Atop the cliff itself in the centre of Edinburgh city, the yellow curtain wall circled the keep of the castle, stretching into the sky as though it were not far off touching the clouds.

Kit looked around herself, glancing up and down the path she was standing on that hugged the castle foundations, but no one was coming. She was hidden from the town nearby by a clump of dense trees as she sidled along the rock face, searching for a way into the castle. There was only one way in as far as she could see, and that was to climb the cliff face, a task she'd rather not do.

"Remember why you're doing this," she urged herself and reached for the rock. She was a good climber, she'd done it before, it was just the challenge today was taller than usual.

Her dark red leather gloves allowed a good purchase on the wall. She dug in with her fingers and began to climb, using the wrinkled gamache-style boots on her feet to launch her body further up the rock.

Sir Francis Walsingham had told her the castle was supposedly impenetrable, but that was for anyone going in through the front gate. If she wanted to get in, then she knew no guard would even think to look this way. For who would be foolish enough to scale a wall this size? She wondered that herself when she got halfway up and paused, with her feet balancing precariously on a sliver of rockface.

Determined not to fail, she swallowed past her fear and tilted her brown hat a little further back before clambering up the cliff. What was at first sheer and steep began to level out into curves of rock, dappled with grass, moss and lichen. Scrambling across the stone was made easier by the men's hose she preferred to wear, reaching out across each crevice with her long legs, unencumbered by a dress or petticoat.

As she neared the bottom of the yellow-stone wall that marked the boundary of the castle, she could hear sounds above, of guards moving about within the castle. She fell still and hid her body amongst the tufts of grass, trying to blend in with the rocks.

When no shouts of alarm went up, she peered out from her hiding place toward the top of the wall.

Edinburgh Castle dominated the landscape for miles around. Being set so high on the hill, the stone structure stood rather like a carbuncle on the lush green landscape. Supposedly nigh-on impossible to attack, they had only a handful of guards keeping watch over their prisoners these days. They never guarded themselves from attack. They were more worried about their prisoners escaping, rather than someone trying to break in.

Yet that was why Kit was here. She was the lone figure trying to break in to see a prisoner, to retrieve a message that was meant for the very man that had sent her here, Sir Francis Walsingham.

Queen Elizabeth's spymaster was the one who had watched over Kit to this point. He had trained her, for as long as she could remember, preparing her for days like this.

"The most secret of intelligencers, Kit. That's what you will be."

Walsingham's words rang out in Kit's mind, the memory of what he'd said before she had left London for Scotland coming through strongly. He had trained her, tested her, and now she had passed, at last permitted to go on such tasks that crossed the span of the country. Though Kit couldn't help wondering if this challenge was another test set by Walsingham, to see if she was truly ready.

As two guards passed along the top of the curtain wall, their hats just visible above the edge, Kit took her chance. She stood up from her crouched position and clambered up the top of the hill before it levelled out completely. As before, she began to climb, but the stone wall was smoother than the cliff face and not so easy to traverse. When her boots slipped off the wall, casting loose stones through the air, she had to cling onto the flimsy purchase she had on an outstretched stone with both hands, swinging her legs in the air wildly.

"Did ye hear something?" a voice came from above the castle wall.

Kit swung her legs back toward the main body of the wall and pressed herself against it, hiding her body between the shadows. Above her, on the top of the wall, she heard a guard moving about, the footsteps heavy. Overhead, two crows took flight off a tower and passed near to her arms.

"It's just the crows, that's all," another Scottish accent answered the first. They walked on, leaving Kit enough peace to reset her footing against the wall and climb again.

The more she climbed, the sorer her hands beneath the leather gloves became, but she fought through the pain, gritting her teeth. It was imperative to make it into the castle without anyone seeing her, and it had to be today.

She glanced back, looking to the sun on the horizon. It was beginning to drop in the sky, signalling an hour or two of sunlight more at most. She didn't have long left.

With renewed vigour, she pulled her body up against the wall, reaching for the top of the battlements and peering over the edge of the stone. There was no one about on the curtain wall. Either side of her, the stone floor stretched out, empty, turning orange with the setting sun.

She clambered over the top, landing soundlessly on the stone and pulling her hat lower down over her face to hide her features. The easy part was done, actually getting into the castle. The somewhat more interesting part lay ahead, walking through the castle undetected.

She hugged the edge of the stonework as she headed toward a turret built into the wall. As she neared an open door, she could hear someone moving about inside. They were humming to themselves, a soft sort of bumbling tune, suggesting they were alone. Peering round the corner proved her suspicions right. A man was alone, pacing the small octagonal space wearing a guard's uniform. With his back turned to her, Kit had one opportunity to get the jump on him.

She stepped into the room, tiptoeing as fast as she could through the tower room whilst casting a gaze around for a weapon she could use. An empty beer bottle was discarded on a table. She took it quickly and approached the man before striking him across the back of his head, just hard enough to stun him.

The humming tune stopped as the man dropped to his knees and slid to the floor.

Kit checked the wound first, seeing he would be fine, before pulling off his hat and his doublet. Large and gaping, the doublet fitted easily over her own. Her brown cap she stuffed in her pocket before placing the guard's hat on her head, bearing the unicorn of the Scottish royal insignia.

As she stood straight, she caught a glimpse of her reflection in murky glass, latticed with black lead. Her short dark auburn hair was barely visible now beneath the large hat, yet her features still gave her away. The large bronze-coloured eyes and the small mouth were too feminine for her to impersonate a man so easily.

She returned to the guard who was still out cold and took the black scarf from his neck, wrapping it around her own and covering her mouth with it too. Satisfied when her true features were covered, she winked once at the reflection and hurried out of the room, heading for the spiral staircase.

The trick was to make it look like she belonged.

When she reached the ground and strode out of the tower up to the main cobbled path through the castle, she adapted her walk, spacing her feet wider apart. It was a skill she had been practicing since she was a child, and had perfected over the years, walking convincingly as a man. As she passed other guards going about their business, they all nodded to her in passing, not one realising she was a woman in disguise.

Walking through the middle ward of the castle, she headed straight for the dungeons. The chart of the castle was hidden in a secret lining within her own doublet, but she had already memorised the layout to not draw suspicion to herself.

She slipped between the central keep and into the upper ward, on the tallest part of the hill, before heading through the castle square and toward the towering building where their prisoners of war were kept.

At the gate, one soldier stood, almost napping in his duty as he leaned against the wall. He lifted his head up, startled by her approach.

"Who ye here to see?" he asked, blinking bleary-eyed.

"Prisoner Harold MacArthur," she said, mimicking the guard's Scottish accent. Her already husky voice she made deeper, to perpetuate her deception.

"Why?" the guard asked, tilting his head high in suspicion.

"Orders from above," she gestured upward with her words. "Aye, the General still wants his answers."

"Torture did not do much."

"Then there is nay harm in letting me ask, is there?" she asked, keeping the fake accent in place. The guard seemed to give up his resistance as he reached for the wooden door beside him and turned the key in the lock.

"Then I wish ye luck," he murmured, tugging on the door and swinging it open. It flung to the side with a whine, revealing within a dark corridor and a stench so strong that Kit's eyes watered.

"Thank ye," Kit said tightly and hurried inside, burying her nose further into the scarf in the effort to avoid the smell. Sweat hung in the air, as did the aroma of damp. The worst part was the lingering odour of excrement.

As the door swung shut behind her, locking her into the prison, she flinched, just once. It was a momentary realisation of what her fate could be someday, if she put a foot wrong in her task.

She brushed off the feeling and walked confidently through the corridor, heading toward the spiral staircase that led down to the dungeon cells. With each harried step she took on the stairs, the stench grew worse, to the point that she wrinkled her nose to try and stop herself from gagging.

At the bottom floor, the staircase opened out through an archway into a cavernous cellar. The underground dungeon had lofted white curved ceilings, either side were hundreds of cells. Each cage was so tiny that they were not big enough for more than one prisoner.

Kit walked slowly down the centre between them, looking around at each face that stared back at her in wonder. Many had been tortured, with the lines of scars on their faces and blood on the clothes so abhorrent that Kit looked away. She was looking for one man in particular. Someone she had only met once before.

At the far end of the dungeons, she found him. He was curled up into a ball at the far side of his cage. The only light that fell on him was from a tiny window set high in the stone wall, casting his face mostly in shadow, but Kit recognised what she could see, from the man's hulking form down to the long narrow nose. He'd changed much though, with fresh cuts on his face, a greying beard scruffily growing across his jaw and his clothes torn open from being flogged.

"MacArthur?" she whispered his name as she reached the cell. He was blocked in by iron bars formed in a cross-hatched pattern. He looked up, frowning at her.

"Who are ye?" he asked, his voice dry and croaky from thirst. She didn't answer, instead, she lifted her hat a little higher and pulled the scarf down from her face, revealing herself to him. "What are *ye* doing here?" he said in sudden panic, scrambling forward across the dungeon floor like a dog hunting for food. His hands latched onto the iron bars between them, revealing knuckles that were cracked and bloodied.

"He wants his message," Kit answered as she crouched down to reach MacArthur's level.

"Course he does," the man muttered, shaking his head. "Does he not have a plan for me?"

"You must wait," Kit said, lapsing back into her normal accent. "He'll open negotiations to get you out, but until then…" she paused and beckoned to him to hand something over. "I am sorry." She truly meant the words. Had she been able to run the day her way, she would have broken MacArthur out of the prison, yet Walsingham had warned her it was too dangerous. For now, she was only permitted to retrieve one thing: the message.

"So God mend me," MacArthur muttered under his breath as he reached down to the belt around his waist. He began a string of other curses that Kit ignored and looked around the dungeons instead. Many men were just like MacArthur here, bloodied and hurt, all because they had something their imprisoner wanted.

"Is there anything I can do for you?" Kit said. Her words sparked something, as MacArthur reached out toward her through the iron bars and grabbed onto the guard's doublet she had stolen, tugging on it tightly.

"Ye can get me out of here!" he seethed in a whisper, his yellowing teeth moving manically with the words.

"I would if I could," she murmured softly, watching as her statement took the wind out of him. He muttered curses again before he returned his attention to the belt around his waist.

"What I have done for that man," he scoffed amongst the curses, "and he leaves me here to rot."

"He's not leaving you here," Kit said strongly. She would never hear a word said against Walsingham, she couldn't bear it.

"He is."

"He's not," Kit's whisper was sharp. "This is about more than you and me, and you know it."

MacArthur begrudgingly nodded as he held the belt up a little, into the light so she could see.

"In here," he pointed to the threading of the belt. Quickly, he threaded the belt through the holes in the bars. She slid a hand into her own belt and took out one of the two daggers she always kept at her side. Carefully, she placed the tip of the blade into the threading and sliced through it. With a few threads torn, a gap opened within the belt, revealing a piece of parchment inside.

She slipped her hand in and pulled out the parchment. Crumpled from its time in prison, it was beginning to yellow, but the name written across the front was plain to see. *Taurus*.

"Thank you," Kit said softly and slipped the parchment under her glove, hiding it against her palm before handing the belt back to MacArthur through the bars.

"He's leaving me here, is he not?" MacArthur asked, the small eyes had water in them, as he stared back at her.

"He wouldn't do that," she assured him and placed a hand over the bars. He met her touch briefly, just one of mutual friends following the same cause. "Until next time, MacArthur."

He nodded to her, before she stood up and walked back through the dungeons, this time refusing to look at the other faces around her as she hurried toward the spiral staircase. She had obtained what she had come for. Now she had to get out, before anyone realised she had been in. She pulled her hat lower and tugged the scarf back up around her face to hide it before she took the steps two at a time, reaching the top corridor quickly and heading toward the locked door. Two knocks against the wood and the door opened, where the same guard who had let her in before still stood.

"Any luck?" he asked as she stepped out.

"Nay," she said, using the fake Scottish accent. "I'll report back." She nodded her head in goodbye, just as the guard did the same. He took up his sleepy position leaning against the wall, leaving her the freedom to cross the courtyard, heading back out to the lower wall.

As she walked, she clenched her hand around the parchment in her hand, feeling it crumple between the lining of her glove and her palm. She hoped Walsingham would be pleased.

She slipped under the portcullis that bordered the upper ward before walking straight into something. No, someone.

"Ah, watch where ye are going," a deep voice rang out as she stumbled back.

"Aye, I'm sorry. I'm always in a rush to get places," she hurried to explain, looking up at the face of the person she had walked into.

It was a soldier, not a guard after all. With his badges clearly pinned to his waistcoat and a strip of plaid flung over his shoulder. His weapons were displayed around his belt too, rather than hidden. The crossbow and the rapier in particular made her mouth dry. She had no such heavy weapons to protect herself today, and the daggers would do little when faced with that crossbow.

"Ye should be more careful," the soldier warned, crossing his arms over his chest and drawing her eyes up to his face.

He was unusual looking. His cropped black hair and trimmed beard were well groomed, but it was the scar across his right cheek that was particularly unusual, with the sharp green eyes staring so strongly at her that she feared the hat and scarf would not be enough to convince him she were a man.

"I should be, and I will be," she said quickly, trying to walk around him. "I do apologise, sir, I hope ye will forgive me." Her words were jumbling together in her haste to be away. "If ye will excuse me, I should get back to work." She turned, looking away from him and preparing to stride away when she felt something on her shoulder. It was his hand.

"Halt," he barked, tugging her back an inch to give him the room to walk around her. She cast her gaze downward, hoping the brim of the guard's hat would hide her eyes.

He silently stopped in front of her, giving her a perfect view of the buckskin boots he was wearing. She frowned, for they were not usual attire for a Scottish soldier. She felt a pull on her hat, and the brim was lifted. She looked up, her eyes finding his as he adjusted her hat.

"Release my hat, sir," she pleaded and stepped back, out of his reach. He didn't give up. He stepped forward again and tugged at the scarf, revealing her face completely to him. She watched as his eyes widened.

"Ye're nay guard."

"Sound the bell!" a roar called up from the curtain wall a few hundred yards away. It was another guard's voice. "There's a guard been injured, and his uniform has been stolen. We have an intruder."

CHAPTER 2

Kit took another step back, as the soldier moved toward her. Around them, the shouts were growing louder, each guard calling to the other.

"I found our intruder!" the soldier bellowed. Heads turned in their direction from across the square behind her and down to the curtain wall.

She dived to the left, but the soldier reached out and grabbed her arm. She snatched the dagger from her belt and swiped out at him, aiming perfectly for his forearm. He cried out in pain, releasing her and giving her the moment of freedom she needed.

Kit ran down across the cobbled path, heading to the outer stretch of the curtain wall. Already she could see the guards hurrying to lower the main portcullis in the gatehouse, but she wasn't going to be so reckless as to leave by the proper exit.

Other guards sprinted toward her, but she was fast and light on her feet. She outran them, dashing far in front of them as she headed back toward the turret set in the curtain wall. As she reached the bottom of the turret, the door opened and another guard stepped out, with his rapier drawn.

Kit grabbed the large hat off her head and threw it at his face. Momentarily distracted trying to knock it away, he fumbled, lifting his rapier in the air. It gave her the opportunity to swipe her dagger across the back of his knuckles, forcing him to stumble away and drop the rapier. She snatched up the weapon.

Kit dived into the tower just as she could see more guards advancing. She closed the door behind her and rammed the guard's rapier through the door handle and into a crack in the stone wall beside it, wedging the door in place. It would buy her a few minutes at least, if not many.

She ran up the spiral staircase, reaching the top quickly where she found the same octagonal room she had been in before. The guard she had struck earlier that day was still out cold on the floor. In spite of the need to escape, she hurried toward him, quickly checking for a pulse. He would be fine, for she could feel the pulse was strong. She turned to leave him as something caught her eye wrapped around his belt: a long rope. She hurried to untie it and looped it over her shoulder, taking it with her.

Kit hurried back out along the ramparts of the castle wall, far above the other guards down below. She could see fifteen of them, gathered by the bottom of the turret, each one trying to break down the door she had jammed shut. At the front was the soldier who had discovered her, ramming his shoulder repeatedly against the door with his forearm bleeding where she had cut him.

"Up there!" a guard called, pointing to her place on the wall.

Crossbows and arbalests turned in her direction. As bolts were fired, she dropped down to the floor, laying perfectly still on her front in the effort to hide from their fire. Bolts and arrows landed in the cracks of the stone wall beside her, whilst others missed completely, disappearing over the crenellations.

As the fire stopped and the guards reloaded, she jumped to her feet and sprinted to the same spot where she had climbed up, peeking down over the wall. From this height, the drop seemed even taller than before.

She glanced between the drop and the rope in her hand.

"I must be mad," she muttered to herself as she grabbed the rope and began to tie it round one of the stone crenellations in the top of the wall. More bolts were fired, just as she crouched down to the floor. She waited for the next break in the fire as she wrapped the other end of the rope around her waist. As the arrows stopped, she stood up and pulled herself cleanly over the wall, hesitating only long enough to see the guards break through the door at the bottom of the turret.

Her time was up.

She sent a silent prayer to heaven before she took hold of the rope, looping it around her arm to give her some leeway and began the jump down.

The drop was sudden and fast, causing her feet to skid against the wall in the effort to slow her fall. She heard the wind whipping past her, and her ankles collided with outstretched rock, until she lashed out with her gloved hands and managed to grab onto one of the clumps of rock. Breathing heavily, she looked around her body, aware of how much further she had to go. She was only halfway down.

She hurried to climb down the rest of the way, using the rope as just a support in case she fell. That was until the rope would go no further. One glance up proved her suspicions. The guards had reached her part of the wall and were pulling on the other end of the rope, trying to draw her back up. The rope tightened around her waist because of their pull, making her yelp and cling against the wall at the sharp pain.

She tugged against the rope, but to little avail. With more than one guard pulling the other end, she found herself drawn up a few footholds in the cliff face. She whipped out the dagger from her belt. Using one hand to cling onto the rock, she began to saw through the rope.

It was difficult and clumsy, as the guards pulled on her tether another time, she had to pause as she was drawn upward, scraping her cheek against a nearby rock. With the rope half cut through, she was hanging only by a few threads. She sat her weight back, fighting against their pull and sawed through the last of the rope. As it snapped, she held tightly onto the wall with the other hand, stopping herself from falling.

One glance up showed she was now free, with half of the rope travelling back up to her pursuers, and the other half hanging down around her waist. She clambered down the rest of the wall as fast as she could. As her feet touched the floor, she knew she didn't have time to catch her breath. She thrust the dagger back into her belt, threw off the rope and ran along the path through the trees.

She tore off the guard's jacket, tossing it into the branches nearby in the hope it would be a distraction, then she continued sprinting, through the trees and the formal gardens of the castle, heading toward the main part of the town.

She had already mapped out the journey she was to take exactly, having memorised it from the chart hidden in her jerkin and walked it twice in the early hours of the morning. She barely had to think as she sprinted between the trees as she knew the way so well.

When Edinburgh town began to appear through the tree trunks, she slowed her pace, looking back over her shoulder. None of the guards it seemed had been foolish enough to follow her descent down the cliff face, but she didn't doubt they would search the town for her, as soon as they managed to lift the portcullis in the gatehouse again.

She reached the first timber buildings and slowed her pace entirely, pulling the scarf back up around her mouth to hide her features. It was a busy day, market day, with the square covered in all sorts of stalls. Some were bakers, with the scent of fresh bread hanging in the air. Other stalls sold clothes with leather gloves and belts, and some sold confits, with sugar in the air that tingled the edge of Kit's nose.

She pushed past them all, trying to disappear in the crowd and between the people as she headed toward the bundle of horses gathered at the far side of the square. Amongst the steeds and mares, at the very edge was the horse she had bought for a few coins the day before. A small chestnut with an agile build, she chose the horse as the ideal animal in case she had to run back to her escape point.

That was now necessary.

Kit grabbed her horse off the stable boy that had been holding him, being sure to throw him a small coin for his trouble before launching herself up into the saddle and turning the horse around in the street.

The steed trotted down the road, but she came to a halt just a few seconds later as others appeared at the far side of the road. Within the shadow of the castle, guards had appeared atop their own horses. At the very front was the soldier she had met. When his eyes found hers, he pointed her way.

"By this light, they're eager in their work," she muttered in anger as she urged the horse to do a quick circle. Together, they cantered away through the street, heading toward the other end of Edinburgh.

The path was not easy, with the roads dense and packed with not only people wandering up and down, but carts and carriages too. She had to avoid them all, the nimble horse made its way down the centre of the road, avoiding the circumventing carriages and the passers-by.

Walsingham had once called her the finest horsewoman he had ever seen. She smiled at the memory, hoping it was true today, for she needed the skill if she were going to escape. As she reached the far side of the town, she glanced back to find that the guards had been unable to follow her in her mad dash, that was all except one.

The soldier was still behind her.

She turned forward again and bent further down over the horse's head, urging him on. The horse snorted in complaint but as she hitched her ankles into his sides, he rode forward, nevertheless.

With the road ahead filled with carriages and carts, she had no choice, she pulled the steed up onto the path and overtook them all, forcing pedestrians to jump back in fear.

"Out of the way!" she called, her eyes flicking between each face as they leapt back. Some jumped into doorways, others toppled into each other.

At the end of the path, she found a butcher's stall, with meat laid out across the surface and hanging from a plank of wood on meat hooks. The frightened faces of the men behind the stall showed there was no way they could get out of her way in time.

She tugged harshly back on the reins of the horse, slowing him up. He came to a halt, whinnying loudly into the air, just as she looked to see the soldier had not given up, but followed her path.

"God have mercy," she whispered and directed the horse back into the path. They darted between carriages and carts with some difficulty, but as they reached the edge of the town, the heavy traffic began to slip away and in its place was a long open road.

One glance at a nearby road sign proved exactly where she was. She wasn't far from her escape route.

She took a road that headed north-east, toward the coastal port of Leith on the edge of Edinburgh and urged the horse forward. They developed a rhythm, with her looking back every so often to see the soldier was not giving up. The distance increased between them, but he never dropped out of sight. He was evidently determined to catch her.

As the road slipped downward, sloping into the camber of a hill, she was finally afforded a view of the ocean stretching out ahead. This far up in the country, it was windy beyond the coast, with great waves leaping high in the air and the sea itself appearing grey rather than blue at all. Even the clouds overhead swarmed above, threatening rain at any moment.

She rode toward it, despite the threat, knowing it wouldn't be long before the horse tired and gave up completely.

As the townhouses of the port began to slip away, revealing the edged wall along the side of the city that separated it from the ocean, the dockyard came into view. There were great galleons for trade docked with their large white and red sails rolled away. Between the ships were smaller dinghies and sloops too. One such sloop had its sails unfurled, waiting for her. The sails were blue, as was their agreed silent signal.

At the edge of the promenade, the dock hut stood to the side, with the dockmaster standing in front of it, checking people as they walked in. Kit didn't have time for such formalities. One look back proved that the soldier was gaining ground on her.

She rode forward, bypassing the dockmaster and nearly knocking him from his feet. He shouted and called for her to stop, but she ignored him, keeping her eyes on the sloop up ahead. She lifted her arm and waved madly at it.

Even at this distance, she could see they took her cue, as they began to release the boat from its ties to the dock and set sail. Within seconds, she would be with them, but she had to lose both the horse and her pursuer first.

In the centre of the dock, she pulled the horse sharply to a halt and jumped down from the saddle before pulling on its reins, turning it around and tying its reins up behind its head. One harsh slap to its rump and the horse drove forward, back in the direction from which they had come and straight toward the soldier that was chasing her.

Kit only paused to note the look of fear in the man's face and the way he fumbled with the reins of his own horse before she turned and fled toward the ship. She jumped down sections between the wooden slats on the dock, until she was on the right level, crossing quickly toward the sloop.

"Kit? Let's go!" the captain was shouting to her, beckoning her on.

With horror, she stopped, inches from the edge of the wooden floor. In the haste to be gone, the ship was already a good two feet at least from the dock. Her eyes flicked down to the grey ocean beneath her feet, as her palms grew clammy, with the sweat building up along the back of her neck.

It was always the same when it came to the ocean or any body of water. It was the same feeling, the raised heartbeat pumping in her ears and the trembling legs. She blinked, trying to force the memory out of her mind that always plagued her.

She must have been a child when it happened, though she never knew how old. All she could discern from the memory was looking up through the water, being unable to breathe and get to the top. The sky above her was wobbling through the water surface and there was a figure watching her from it.

"Kit!" the captain shouted at her again. She opened her eyes, seeing the sloop only getting further and further from the dock. The distance to jump now was even more difficult than before.

She backed up along the dock, knowing she had no choice but to take the leap. She looked back as she heard voices crying out. Further down, the soldier must have escaped the scuffle with the horses, for he was on foot, racing toward her.

Kit bent her head and ran toward the sloop, leaping off just as she connected with the edge of the dock. She catapulted through the air, as two men from the boat's crew ran forward, hurrying to her.

She caught one of their arms with one hand whilst the other connected with the gunwales of the sloop. Her feet landed in the water, kicking about the cold ocean depths.

"We have you, Kit," the crewmate said as he tugged on her arm and pulled her over the bow of the boat. She tried not to think of the water she was so close to falling into. She was just thankful for the hard wood beneath her feet as she stood straight and tried to stop the trembling of her hands.

"Let's go!" the captain called as the sloop took the wind in its sails and stretched out, far away from the dock.

Kit looked back, just in time to see the soldier come to a hasty halt on the wooden slats, looking out to her. He had the crossbow around his belt still, he could easily use it at this distance and shoot her, she knew it, yet he didn't.

Instead, those sharp green eyes merely followed her as she left, staring after her.

"That was a little close, Kit," one of the crew laughed and clapped her on the back of the shoulder. "Who was that man?" he asked, pointing to the soldier that still hadn't moved. He continued to watch their retreat as they pulled out of Leith port.

"A soldier from the castle," she explained, though she couldn't take her eyes away from him. "He didn't shoot. He could have done, but he didn't. Why is that?" she asked, turning at last to the crewmate at her side.

"Let's just be thankful he didn't," he mused and clapped her shoulder again. "Come on, let's get you back to Taurus."

She nodded silently before looking again to the soldier. She couldn't resist the temptation and lifted a hand to wave at him in a kind of taunt. She saw the man cross his arms in response.

Desperate to think of something other than the soldier and the coldness of the water now seeping through her boots, she moved to the opposite end of the sloop, leaning against the side, and fiddled with the tiny piece of parchment that was still safe between the leather glove and her palm.

CHAPTER 3

Kit checked her pocket yet again, but the parchment was safely there. She'd carried it all the way from Edinburgh to London, first travelling by boat and then by horse. Now, she was walking between the streets of townhouses, searching for the building that always tried its best to stay hidden.

Within the tall walls near Tower Ward, the houses were narrower, with doors between timber beams difficult to discern. The white plaster and thatched roofs made all the houses jumble together into one clump, with the clothes hung at the windows the only thing distinguishing one home from the next.

Kit followed the route she had first learned when she was only a child, heading through narrow alleys and small lanes where pickpockets liked to frequent the back streets of Tower Ward and Seething Lane. Between two houses was a tiny gap, not big enough to fit a horse, but easy enough for a person to slip through. She hurried through, under a lofted timber archway, into a small courtyard that opened up before her.

On each side of the courtyard, the houses looked squashed together, each one practically impossible to know was there from the main road. In particular, Kit was heading for one house pressed in the corner between two other buildings, the door disguised as just another wall.

She knocked on the plaster door twice, waiting for a head to pop out of the window beside her.

"Kitty, you're back," a familiar voice greeted her. Kit turned to see the housekeeper hanging her head out of the window. The elderly face bore deep lines of age, though the eyes were still as animated as Kit could remember them being when she was a child. The woman's grey hair was curled around her forehead and ears before disappearing under a white muslin cap.

"It's good to see you too, Doris," Kit smiled as the woman waved at the door, showing she'd be there momentarily.

The fake wall opened up, revealing a long dark corridor beyond.

"You'll have to wait, Kit," Doris said, beckoning her inside and shutting the door again. "He has people with him." She slid back a multitude of locks. One was simply the turning of the key in the handle, but there were two strong bolts across, and another third bolt that dug down into the floor, plus a padlock across the handle.

"He has?" Kit asked, straining to see further down the corridor. At the far end of the mahogany hallway, she could see light pooling down the thin staircase that led up to the main chamber in the house. It was used as a study and place of work, though in truth it was large enough to accommodate every need. She continued to look, in the vain hope that she would see someone leaving his chamber.

"Some other people who work for him, more like you," Doris said and waved at the idea in something akin to dismissal. "Come this way," she urged Kit to follow her into the adjoining room, but Kit only went as far as the doorway, preferring instead to keep her eyes fixed on the corridor. She had come at the right time, the time that they had agreed upon. She didn't like the idea of things running late. It suggested things weren't as they should have been.

"Now, am I allowed to ask where you have been?" Doris asked as she moved to the fire on the far side of the kitchen, placing a hot water cauldron over it. As she looked back, Kit grimaced, giving the only response she was permitted to give. "God's mercy, he is a secretive man. I pray every day that I can learn something of where you have been."

"I think that's how he likes things." Kit looked out into the corridor another time. "How has everything been here?"

"Busy, very busy," Doris agreed with a nod. "The whole place was up in arms last night."

"Why?" Kit asked, turning back round.

"Something must have gone wrong," Doris said pointedly, pausing in her work and widening her eyes. "I don't know what," she held up her hands in surrender, "but something concerning all you lot running round. There was quite a to-do here last night. Arguments too. You should have heard the master's voice."

"He doesn't shout very often." Kit fidgeted on her feet at the idea. It was true, though there was a time when she could remember him shouting a lot. That was when she was little though. Back then, she didn't do what he said quite as much.

"Exactly," Doris said, gesturing with her arms animatedly. "Ooh, so upset he was."

Kit shifted on her feet, hoping that it was nothing to do with her. Her hand subconsciously went to the pocket where the parchment was. It was still there, perfectly hidden. Before she could ask any more, there were footsteps in the corridor. She peered down it, watching as two familiar faces crossed the open corridor, heading straight to the door and toward her.

One was Thomas Phelippes, the favoured cryptographer, the other was Jules Knepper, who always seemed to be at his side. The two men nodded in their direction before gesturing to the door.

"Do you need this many locks, Doris?" Phelippes asked, fiddling with the padlock.

"That's not my order but the master's," she explained as she went to unlock them all again. "You best go up now, Kitty."

She didn't need any more encouragement. Kit rushed across the corridor and headed straight for the narrow staircase at the far end before climbing quickly. At the top, the door had been closed, casting the tiny space where she was waiting in darkness. She knocked three times and barely had to wait for an answer.

"In," Walsingham's voice called.

Kit opened the door to find the cavernous room stretching out before her. At the far end Sir Francis Walsingham, spymaster to Queen Elizabeth, sat behind his desk with a multitude of papers beside him, on top of which a quill was delicately balanced. Behind him, there were shelves upon shelves of scrolls of parchment. To her left, windows stretched high into the rafters, casting the space in white light that revealed how dusty it was. The timber beams in the roof above them cast darkness in the space, making it seem a room of shadows.

To her mind, it seemed a rather apt place for the spymaster to spend his time when he was not attending the queen's privy council. Half in the shadows, and half in the light.

"Hmm, you're back," Walsingham's voice did not sound pleased. Kit found her smile faltering.

"Yes, I am. I haven't even had a chance to tell you what happened whilst I was gone. Best not to sound too sad just yet," she said and brought her smile back as she hurried across the floor with a lightness in her step. She crossed wooden floorboards that creaked beneath her, past armchairs placed near a fire, and delved into the pocket of her jacket before handing over the parchment.

Walsingham's thin face looked up from what he was doing. The always stretched-looking features seemed to narrow even more as they stared at the parchment in her grasp. His pink ruddy skin was visible just beyond the full beard and the moustache that were both excessively groomed. Those pink cheeks now seemed to redden a little more than normal.

"I thought you would be a little happy," she trailed off warily, losing the happiness she'd felt before as he took the parchment from her.

"I am." He calmly unfolded the parchment.

"Then … why do you not look it?"

"Because I have only just let you start going alone on these commissions and already you're leaving disaster behind you," he said as he pulled on a pair of spectacles that just balanced on the bridge of his nose.

"What makes you say that?" Kit asked, stepping back from the desk. "I thought I did rather well."

"Hmm," he made no more reply as he read the parchment.

She turned away and moved toward one of the tall windows that bore glass, staring at her reflection rather than the view of the other houses in the courtyard. She was wearing her man's clothes again today, her short auburn hair hidden by the hat and her dark red quilted jerkin pulled tightly around her torso. She adjusted the hat on her head as she waited for his response.

She had been so certain she had done a good job on this commission, now she was chewing her lip with worry.

"What does it say then?" she broke the silence after a minute, unable to stay quiet for much longer as she looked back to him.

"He uses a cipher," Walsingham said and laid the crumpled parchment flat down on the desk. "Fetch the Circadian Cipher map, would you?"

She stepped toward the shelves full of scrolls and charts, reaching up to the top shelf where the scroll was kept for this particular cipher before passing it into the spymaster's hands. He unrolled the parchment and laid it out beside the other, moving between the two with quick eyes to decode the letter.

Kit could still remember the first time Walsingham had shown her such ciphers. She had only been ten years old at the time, sitting in one of the attic rooms on the other side of the same house where he had laid out all the different scrolls of ciphers she would need to learn.

The room had looked like the inside of someone's mind, teeming with ideas and words. Some ciphers worked by using Zodiac signs as codenames, others worked by applying symbols to certain words. The one the current letter was using, adopted numbers instead of letters and had shifted all the letters in the alphabet up by five positions. It would take some time to decode.

As Walsingham worked, Kit paced around the room. She moved to an armchair by the fire, trying to sit and find comfort, but she was only there a few seconds when she jumped up, upset and feeling tormented by his previous words.

"I am guessing you are not going to tell me what it is I have done wrong?" she asked, as she crossed the room to stand on the other side of the desk. Walsingham returned her gaze with a sad sort of smile on his features.

"Well, you retrieved the letter, so I cannot be too upset, can I?"

"That did not answer my question," she pointed out, earning a light chuckle from him. It was rare to see him laugh at all.

"I hear you were discovered and not only chased from the castle, but halfway across Edinburgh too." Walsingham leaned forward across his desk, gesturing with the words. "All the way to the port in fact, with guards on your tail."

"Just one solider, actually," she murmured.

"And you think that makes it any better?"

"I'm not trying to make excuses," she said and walked away from him, despising this feeling of being inadequate in his eyes. "It wasn't without its hiccoughs, no, but I did the job, and I wasn't caught. Isn't that what matters?" she asked, darting her head back to him.

His narrow face turned back down to the translated parchment in front of him.

"It's good then that what MacArthur had to say was worth the mess you caused," he stated clearly, making her pace once more across the floor.

"What does he have to say?"

"It's news of a plot being put together in Scotland and in London," he said, pointing down at the parchment. "It seems they're trying once again to put the pretender, Mary, Queen of Scots, on the throne of England."

"But … I thought she was under house arrest?" Kit asked, pushing aside her irritation.

"She is," he confirmed with a nod. "At Sheffield Castle."

"Then how do they plot to put her on the throne?"

"MacArthur says the plotters intend to gather an army and…" he paused, his eyes slipping down the parchment.

"And?" she prompted him on. He hesitated for a little longer, then made a couple of notes on his parchment. As he crossed the quill back across the parchment, his eyes widened, and the letter dropped from his grasp. He had decoded the next part.

"And to assassinate Queen Elizabeth."

Kit did not have time to react. Walsingham was on his feet so suddenly that he sent his chair falling backwards, clattering against the wooden floor loudly. In his abrupt animation, some of the papers fell off his desk too. He marched up and down the space, running his hands across his face.

"By the mass, are these people incapable of showing fealty to our queen?" he called to the ceiling, complaining not to her but she rather suspected to God Himself. "She was placed there by God, no matter what they may think of her. She was ordained by Him for the position." His voice snapped at the end as he turned back and marched the other way. "They would murder her just because she is not the queen they want? It sickens me."

Kit said nothing, but she hurried to pick up the papers from the floor.

"Stop tidying up, Kit," he ordered.

She still placed the papers on the desk before she stood back, reaching for the decoded note. There was more to the letter than just the threat. MacArthur talked of a rumour he'd heard passed between men that some of the plotters met in an alehouse in London on Thursday nights to discuss their plan.

"This means hiding the Queen away again, she'll hate that," he said, practically speaking to himself as he turned then clutched his back, his age betraying his less than sprightly nature these days.

Kit reached for the fallen chair and put it back in place before stepping out to take Walsingham's arm.

"She despises being told what to do, and she hates appearing weak. What will she say to me now if I tell Her Majesty that she must hide indoors until I can be certain the danger will have passed? She won't listen to me. She'll do what she likes, regardless," he said with fervour.

Kit didn't bother answering him. She just steered him back to the chair. With each step he took, his back clicked again, and he flinched in pain.

"It's getting worse," he muttered.

"Here, sit." She helped him into the chair. As he sat, his head lolled onto the back rest and his face contorted in pain. "Where's the laudanum?"

"Top drawer." He pointed to the desk beside her. She hurried to fetch the small bottle he kept. These days, he took more and more to contend with the pain. In his fifties, his body was weakening faster than his mind and it seemed to Kit every time she came to see him, he was struggling more.

She found the small green bottle and pressed it into his hand. He tipped out a small black pill, made of opium and citrus juice. He popped it into his mouth before crushing it between his teeth and swallowing. Kit turned the bottle to read the label: *Stones of Immortality*. One glance at Walsingham showed that immortality appeared to be a painful state. She placed the bottle back in the drawer.

"You need a physician," she murmured softly, perching on the edge of the desk.

"I am quite all right." Though he kept his gaze on the ceiling and refused to look at her. "You don't need to worry about me, Kit." His voice softened, just as it would do every so often, betraying the fact that after so many years of living in and out of each other's pockets, they knew each other quite well. "This must be stopped." He gestured down to the parchment.

"Let me do it," she said, picking up the transcribed letter.

"You can't even sneak into a prison without being noticed." His soft tone vanished once again. "It will not work." His words only made her desperation to take on the commission even stronger.

"I am not so incapable," she declared and dropped the paper back to the desk. He chuckled, though he stopped a second later, reaching his hand behind his back as though the laughter had hurt his bones.

"Believe me, Kit, I know you're not incapable," he said quietly. "I just don't think you are ready yet to take on something like *this*."

"I can do it," she spoke strongly with feeling, leaning toward him and finally earning his gaze.

Before he could answer, there was a knock to the door of the chamber.

"Wait," Walsingham called to the closed wood, before flicking his gaze back to her, the beady black eyes were watching her closely.

His whole appearance seemed consumed in age these days. His need to always wear black that contrasted the bright white ruff around his neck made his cheeks appear even more hollowed and gaunt. The high hairline and greying hair too showed time was passing on. "There is only one way I'll let you go after this one." He spoke incredibly slowly, clearly thinking through the words as he uttered them.

"And that is?" she asked, feeling hope lurch in her stomach as she stood off the desk.

"If you have a partner with you," he said boldly with a smile.

"I do not need a partner." She folded her arms.

"It's not negotiable," he said again. "You want this commission, then you go with someone else."

"I…" she trailed off, fidgeting with her hands and the sleeves of her doublet. "Who would you even pair me with? I am not working with Knepper. Marlowe is a cad and a rogue, and Somers would not get involved in something like this."

"I had someone else in mind." Walsingham held up a hand, stopping her mid tirade before she could go on.

"Who?" she asked, holding her breath as she waited for her answer.

"Enter!" he called to the door and pointed to it for her to see.

Kit twisted her head round, looking to the door as it opened. A man with cropped black hair and a dark green doublet walked in, the face was familiar. Then his eyes widened as he caught sight of her, and Kit remembered exactly where she had seen him before.

It was the soldier from Edinburgh Castle.

CHAPTER 4

"The guard from Edinburgh," the soldier's strong Scottish accent echoed through the large room. "I was not expecting to see ye again so soon."

"What…" Kit turned away from the soldier, looking down at Walsingham in the chair. "What's going on?"

"Well —"

"Ye messed up the plan," the soldier said, interrupting Walsingham and striding forward into the room. She snapped her gaze toward him. As he pointed at her, she stepped out from the desk and went to meet him in the centre of the room, her hand automatically reaching for the dagger in her belt.

"Me?" she asked, startled. "Who are you?"

Evidently seeing her hand on her dagger, he pulled back the edge of his black cloak that was wrapped around his shoulders, his hand went straight for a rapier that he revealed at his belt.

"Stop!" Walsingham's voice bellowed through the room.

Kit didn't look back to him, she continued to stare at the Scottish soldier, wary and just waiting for him to make a move. He stared back at her, breathing heavily.

"Before you two kill each other, allow me to explain," Walsingham pleaded. "I don't particularly like the idea of asking Doris to mop up the blood from the aftermath."

"You know him?" Kit finally looked away from the Scottish soldier as his words began to register. "He works for *you*?"

"Yes, he does," Walsingham nodded once. "It was rather difficult last night when I had to explain to my friend here that you work for me too."

Kit snapped her head toward the soldier, watching as he still refused to move the hand from the hilt of his rapier.

"I do not understand," Kit spoke quietly. "He was a soldier at the castle."

"Ye think ye're the only one who can put on a uniform and look the part?" the soldier asked with a smirk. "At least mine was more convincing."

"I would have been fine if you had not seen me," Kit pointed out, her hand clenching around the dagger again. He must have noticed it, as she saw his rapier begin to slide out of its thin scabbard.

"I thought I told you two not to kill each other," Walsingham said, his voice tired. "Kit, step away, God save us."

Hearing the pure exasperation in his voice, she followed his order, backing up across the room until she was level with his desk once again. At this distance, the soldier released his hold on the rapier.

"Kit." Walsingham slowly stood to his feet, using one hand to support himself against the table and the other to hold onto his back. "This is Iomhar Blackwood. One of my Scottish spies."

Iomhar nodded his head, though he didn't offer a smile.

"Iomhar, this is Kit Scarlett," Walsingham explained.

"When ye first mentioned an intelligencer called Kit, I thought ye meant a man," Iomhar hesitated with the words, flicking his eyes back to Walsingham. Kit bristled instantly, shifting on her feet.

"It's a common mistake that's often made," Walsingham answered. Kit felt the glance he sent her way, pointedly staring at her clothes. "Katherine is her full name. Doris called her Kitty when she was young. Kitty then became Kit."

"I don't understand," Kit remarked, turning her eyes fully on Walsingham. "You sent two of us to meet MacArthur, didn't you?"

"I did." Walsingham leaned forward, clearly intending to hold her gaze. Despite it, Kit flicked her head away, frustrated by his decision.

"You were that confident I was going to fail?" she asked quietly.

"No, I wasn't," Walsingham said, moving to sit down again. There were cracks as he sat that may have come from either the chair or his bones, she wasn't sure which. "The message was important, and I couldn't afford to take the chance of anyone failing. The day after you were there, they moved MacArthur to the north coast. The challenge of getting this message from him then would have been nearly impossible."

Kit placed her hands on her hips, turning back to look at Walsingham.

"I didn't fail you," she spoke with strong feeling in her words.

"So I see." He held up the parchment in agreement. "It wasn't a decision against you. I had to hedge my bets. With two of you on the commission, it was more likely one of you would succeed. Though I heard from Iomhar last night when he reported to me that he chased you from the castle along with the guards who practically accepted him as one of their own."

Kit looked back to Iomhar, watching as he smirked. For the first time that day, she looked properly at him. Without the soldier's uniform, he was easier to discern.

The black hair and trimmed beard were not so neat today. The green eyes which were constantly alight, darting back and forth, sat within a strong face that contrasted the scar across his cheek. Today, the scar seemed almost silver in its marring of the skin.

Unlike most men in London who chose to wear the latest fashions of hose, jerkin and ruffs, he wore something altogether more informal. The dark green doublet matched his eyes, contrasting the black cloak around his shoulders, and was set above loose-fitting trousers that were tucked into his buskin boots. Seeing the boots that were scruffy and torn round the edges, Kit winced at the memory. She had remembered when she saw him in Scotland how odd a choice those boots for a soldier had been, it was because he was no soldier at all.

"Kit," Walsingham's voice brought her back to the present. "You want this commission, then your new partner is Iomhar."

"What?" Iomhar stuttered out the word before she had a chance to. He marched forward a few steps, drawing past the armchairs and the chests full of other loose papers to reach the desk. "Sir, I have nay wish to work with her."

"The feeling is mutual." Kit stepped back from the desk in order to put some distance between her and the Scottish intelligencer.

"I do not care how the two of you feel about it," Walsingham said pointedly, looking between the two of them.

"She's reckless," Iomhar was bold, "she did not care she caused a scene in the whole of Edinburgh. I cannot work with someone like that."

In spite of her own resistance to the idea, Kit couldn't help bristling. "There would not have been a scene had *you* not been there." Her words didn't even appear to register with him, for he just kept his eyes firmly on Walsingham.

"Find a way to work together," Walsingham ordered, rearranging the papers on his desk. He snatched up the translated note and handed it over for Iomhar to read. "They're going after our queen again."

Iomhar's expression darkened as he read the letter. "Is there any confirmed link with Mary Stuart?" he asked.

"Other than her name being mentioned, no," Walsingham shook his head. "Nothing to prove she's behind it. The two of you need to go to this alehouse mentioned. See what you can find out about the plotters that meet there."

"Sir, is there really nay one else —"

"That's enough," Walsingham said, interrupting Iomhar with surprising strength in his voice. "You're working with Kit. And Kit," he turned his head to her, "from now on, try not to cause so much ruckus in your wake."

She felt duly admonished under his stare and gave a soundless nod.

"Good, you may both go," Walsingham gestured to the door.

Kit glanced once Iomhar's way before heading to the door, with him following close behind.

As they descended the stairs back down to the main corridor, neither of them said anything. Kit kept fidgeting with her hands, struggling to move past Walsingham's reprimand. Once they reached the corridor, Doris appeared at the far end, waiting for them by the door to let them out.

"Are ye always so upset when Walsingham chides ye?" Iomhar's words brought Kit to a sharp halt. She spun round in the wide corridor to stare at him. He was still bearing the same insufferable smirk that he had revealed before.

"You misunderstand me," she lied. "I'm just upset that I have to work with you."

"Well, I do not like it either, but as far as I'm concerned, I'm happy to do anything to make sure this plot is stopped, so I'm willing to swallow my pride to work with ye."

"How noble of you," Kit scoffed as she snatched the translated letter out of his hand. They'd have to burn it soon, to make sure no one ever got their hands on it, but for now she could glean as much information from it as she could. "Why are you so keen to help?"

"What do ye mean?" Iomhar asked, frowning.

"Half the Scotsmen I have met are loyal to Mary Stuart. It seems you're not one of them," she said, looking up from the parchment to see him slowly shaking his head.

"She has not been Queen of Scotland for some time now. Her son is our king instead. As far as I'm concerned, my loyalty is to him and to the queen of England, not Mary Stuart." The way in which he elongated the syllables over Mary Stuart's name piqued Kit's interest. It suggested there was something else to his words, something he was not so willing to talk about.

She watched him for a minute, feeling the distrust build within her. She still saw him as the soldier that chased her down, that was the problem. She'd had no idea at the time that he was after the same message she had retrieved.

"I see," she said slowly, "then tomorrow we'll go to the alehouse to find the plotters."

"Aye." Iomhar snatched the parchment back from her grasp. "How does six in the evening sound?"

"Too early. We'll go for seven o'clock," Kit answered, trying to take the parchment back again, yet he held it out of her reach. "We'll meet at my lodgings. It's round the corner."

"The address?"

"Six Vine Street, top floor. Now, give it back."

A small smirk appeared on his face before he passed it over to her.

"Until tomorrow then." He turned to the locked door that Doris went to unlatch, slowly sliding all the bolts back into place. "Oh, and do me a favour," he glanced back to Kit just as the door opened. "Try not to cause so much of a scene this time."

Kit clamped her lips shut in the effort to stop herself from making a sharp retort just as the door closed behind him.

"Are you all right, Kitty?" Doris asked, her face a little worried.

"Yes," Kit lied, trying to ignore the irritation that had formed a tight knot in her stomach.

She walked past Doris and into the small kitchen, heading straight for the fire at the other side of the room where she tossed the translated letter. With the contents slowly burning to ash, there were now only three people in the world who knew of what MacArthur had to say in his message, and one of them she was unsure she could trust.

CHAPTER 5

In the attic room where she lived, Kit had paced up and down, half expecting to have worn grooves into the wooden floor from the number of times she had walked back and forth. She didn't have much furniture and the lodgings themselves were cheap and affordable. Set high within the rafters of the timber building, each window was slanted into the thatched roof, casting streams of light at diagonal angles across the dark space.

She passed the few bits of furniture she had, the two armchairs by a small fire, the table where she laid her things and the bed pushed into the far corner under the eaves of the roof, looking around at the room. What she lacked in objects, she made up for in neatness. Everything had its place, right down to the small mirror placed upon the stool beside her bed and the wardrobe in which she kept the few items of clothes she owned. On one side of the wardrobe were the dresses and gowns that Walsingham had purchased for her, on the other side were the men's clothes she preferred to wear.

She bent down to avoid hitting her head on the low-lying timber beams as she continued to walk around, turning her mind away from the room and toward her plan for that evening.

The alehouse mentioned in MacArthur's note was on White Lion Hill in Blackfriars, a part of town just outside of the heart of the city, where many a man could discuss a secret without being overheard. It had that reputation, for being on the wrong side of town. It was hardly the first-time dissenters had met in such a place. She'd heard of Jesuits and Catholic priests gathering there once, though that commission had belonged to another intelligencer, and no one was ever caught. The last time she had seen the alehouse, it was filled with pickpockets and thieves, so she did not relish the chance to go.

She turned back to the table where she had laid out what to wear for the night. She was already dressed in her usual hose and red jerkin, but across the surface there were other more useful things Walsingham had taught her to always carry. There were the two daggers she always wore at her belt; the handles were bronze and embellished with a corkscrew pattern. The blades themselves were short, but excessively sharp.

An implement she usually kept tucked away in a hidden pocket was a compass. A gift from Walsingham a couple of years before, though she rarely used it, for the spindle was always spinning round, restless. Beneath the surface of the compass was a tiny vial of liquid, black in colour. Poison. She'd never had cause to use it, neither did she ever intend to.

Beside the compass was the belt she always wore. Just as MacArthur had hidden his message in the lining of his belt, in the lining of hers were rolled up cipher charts, allowing her to write ciphers as needed to send back to Walsingham.

She started with the belt, wrapping it tightly around the waist of her doublet, before tucking the two daggers into tiny scabbards placed at either hip. The compass she slipped into a secret pocket within the doublet, then she reached for the dark red leather gloves she always wore and pulled them on too, completing her preparation.

One glance at the position of the sun in the sky beyond the window showed that it was still early. Iomhar would not be here for another hour at least. Tired of pacing for so long, she reached for an armchair placed near to the entrance, sitting down so that she could watch the door for his arrival.

Only, the exhaustion was catching up with her. She had travelled for so long these last few days to and from Edinburgh, she had slept very little because of Walsingham's words. Now, it felt too easy to close her eyes and steal a few minutes of peace.

Kit was no longer in her attic room. She was in the backrooms of Walsingham's house in Seething Lane, with her head bent over a small desk as she copied out the letters on the parchment, flourishing her quill as quickly as she could. The sand timer beside her on the desk was running fast. She could practically hear each grain as it slipped through the bowls of glass.

She scratched a line of ink under the letters to show she was finished and sat straight in her chair. Walsingham looked up from his place at the window. He was younger here. His hair wasn't quite so grey and the lines in his face weren't so haggard.

"You're getting quicker," he remarked as he crossed the room toward her, picking up the parchment to peruse it.

She stood to her feet, barely half his height. She turned to leave the room with her task complete when he called her back.

"Do it again," he said and put the parchment down on the desk.

"Again?" she asked, sitting down with a huff. "Why?"

"Because it has to be right," he said gently and pointed at the symbols she'd used in her code. He gestured to two symbols that were slightly skew-whiff. "Can you read these?"

"No," she sighed in acknowledgment.

"Then do it again," he urged, turning the sand timer back over. "Your time starts now."

She didn't like these lessons. They were the dullest. She preferred the more active lessons where she was taught to sword fight, climb rocks or use a dagger. Walsingham would often put her under the tutelage of his other

intelligencers for those lessons, but these lessons where it came to
cryptography, he always instructed himself.

She finished the code and drew another line underneath. This time when
Walsingham came over, he smiled as he read her text.

"Good," he said simply, yet the simple praise brought a big smile to her
face.

Kit's eyes flickered open. The memory left her as quickly as it
had come. She blinked a few times, when she saw a silhouette
moving between the low beams in her room, his face too much
in darkness to see who it was.

Someone was there with her.

CHAPTER 6

Kit launched for the figure. Without hesitation she reached up and wrapped one arm around his neck, with the other hand holding the dagger, she placed the tip at the top of his throat. It was the perfect threat, and her intruder fell still, his chin tilted up for if he moved at all, the blade could pierce him.

"Do not move," she ordered.

"Ye've already wounded me once this week, do ye really have to do it again?" Iomhar's distinctive deep voice rang out.

Startled, she released him, watching as he stumbled away from her, into the streams of light from the windows above.

"You broke in," Kit accused, gesturing to her door.

"Not exactly." With a hand on his throat, he rubbed the sore spot she had created. "There was nay answer when I knocked so I found a way to open the door."

"That's called breaking in," she warned, still holding the dagger out in his direction.

"Please do not use that again," he said tartly, pulling back the sleeve of his doublet to reveal a bandage on his forearm. "Once was enough."

"I had to find a way to make you release me back in Edinburgh, it was the simplest way." She placed the dagger back into her belt. "You shouldn't go sneaking around other people's lodgings if you don't want to get hurt."

"This is where ye live?" he asked, looking around.

"Yes, why?" She followed him as he began to examine the place.

"Hmm…"

"Hmm what?" She blocked him off before he could reach the wardrobe. She returned his stare, finding him bearing that same smirk she had seen before.

"Nothing," he said with a shrug. "I just thought Walsingham's favourite might live somewhere a bit more…"

"What?" she asked, watching as his gaze flicked between the simple bed and cheap furniture.

"Never mind." He shook his head, refusing to answer. "Shall we go?" He turned to leave, but she didn't follow. Only when he reached the door did he look back, noticing her position still on the far side of the room. "Something wrong?"

"You broke in," she kept her voice level despite her temptation to rile at him. "I have a good mind to go back to Walsingham and refuse to work with you."

"And he'll just say the same thing to us that he said before. Ye know it as well as I do." He turned and pulled open the door sharply.

She followed this time, hurrying to catch up with him after she locked the door tightly behind her. As they reached the street and began to walk toward Blackfriars, she felt Iomhar glancing at her every few seconds.

"You will find it easier if you look where you're going," she pointed out, striding ahead of him.

"I was just wondering if ye lift a dagger to everyone who steps through your door."

"Any intruder, yes," she confirmed. "When the intruder is you, then definitely."

"Aye, ye really do not trust me, do ye?" he asked, taking her elbow and pulling her back. Startled, she nearly struck out at him with her other hand. Lifting it high in the air, it made him retreat and release her arm. "Calm," he practically barked the

51

word in surprise. "Ye do not need to keep threatening to hurt me all the time."

"I do when I don't trust the person that I'm with." She watched his expression for his reaction. He didn't seem especially shocked, though the eyebrows knitted together.

"Ye have to trust me."

"What an odd statement," she nearly laughed in surprise. "Why? Why do I have to trust you?"

"Because we're working together." He took a step forward and gestured between the two of them. "The only way this is going to work is if ye trust me."

"My apologies, but I cannot do that," she said and turned away from him, continuing down the street. She walked past other groups wandering the streets, circling carts and carriages, and women dressed in ruffs so large they were twice the size of their own heads.

"Why not?" Iomhar asked, following her path through the people.

"Because there is only one person I do trust." She spoke more to herself than to him at all.

"Let me guess, would that be Walsingham?"

She chose not to reply. As they reached the Thames River, she turned instead, walking along the lane that ran parallel to it.

"It is, is it not?" Iomhar asked, catching her up. When still she didn't answer, he laughed. The sound was so sudden that Kit whipped her head back toward him.

"Why are you laughing?"

"It just seems rather ironic that the one person that ye would trust is the spymaster," he pointed out, still chuckling.

She chose not to answer him again. Instead, she pushed on, concentrating on reaching their destination.

As they found the alehouse, Kit found her pace slow, and her legs fell still beneath her. They were far off darkness and yet still the doors to the building were wide open, revealing people spilling out, with drinks in their hands that were sloshing over the rims of their tankards. There were plates of food too, with the scents of pigeon pie hanging in the air and some pastry even discarded across the cobbles that was now being crushed beneath men's boots.

The air stank of beer and sweat, making Kit recoil. When one man ran free of the door, clutching his hand over his mouth, both she and Iomhar had to leap away, just in time before he found a place nearby between two buildings to empty the contents of his stomach. At the sound, Kit turned away.

"Charming place." She wrinkled her nose with the words. To her surprise, she saw Iomhar smirk at her words. She looked back to the building, her gaze flicking between the black and white timber frame to the faces in the windows, all red from heat and alcohol. "It's too busy. It will be almost impossible to overhear a conversation in there without being noticed."

"Maybe it's not what we think."

"What do you mean?" Kit asked, turning to look at Iomhar.

"Alehouses have public rooms, right? For meetings," he pointed out, striding toward the alehouse and beckoning her to follow. He pushed through the groups of men that had gathered outside. Being so tall, his head was mostly above the others, whereas Kit was at their level, having to come face to face with each man that had beer dripping from their lips and pie clutched between their fingers. "All I'm saying is if I wanted to have a meeting about something like this, I'd make sure it was away from prying eyes. Especially somewhere as busy as this."

Kit knew he had a point, and nodded slowly as she followed him in. It was uncomfortable with the alehouse rooms so heated from the two roaring fires in the main front rooms and the sheer number of people inside. They had to squeeze between the groups of men that had gathered, leaving Kit to pull the brown cap down over her face, trying to hide her features from them. In the heat, she snatched off her gloves and shoved them in the pocket of her doublet.

"Two small beers," Iomhar called to the alehouse owner. The man nodded and swayed to the side, clearly as inebriated as his customers were. Within seconds, two tankards were dropped down on the wooden bar in front of Kit and Iomhar, with the beer sloshing over both of their hands. In time, they both tried to shake off the beer from their fingers and picked up the tankards. They said nothing, though they exchanged a mutual glance of disgust before trying to squeeze back through the crowds.

Kit was peering between heads, looking for any indication of a public room. At the back of the alehouse, between timber pillars, she could see a staircase leading up into the rafters. She stopped walking so suddenly, that Iomhar collided into her back, nearly sending her beer flying. He held up his hands in a quick apology.

"Ye're not going to pull out that dagger again, are ye?" he asked, only half-joking.

She shook her head and pointed at the staircase, beckoning him to follow.

The route was difficult with men so drunk that barely any of them could stand straight, choosing instead to lean on tables or on each other. As one man fell over, nearly knocking straight into Kit, she felt an arm drag her back. She was pulled out of the way just in time, as the man face-planted the floor, smacking the wood with his cheek.

Kit looked back to see Iomhar had hold of her arm.

"Thank you," she murmured tightly.

"Ye're welcome." He offered his first genuine full smile. She tore her arm out of his quickly, aware that he hadn't released it straight away and hurried on to the back of the room.

As she reached a table at the bottom of the stairs, she placed her tankard down on the table, just as Iomhar did too. She opened her mouth to say something when she found Iomhar placing a finger to his lips, urging her to be quiet. A second later, she realised why.

Behind him were two men, heading toward the stairs. They were speaking in hushed whispers, but she just caught the tail-end of their conversation.

"We're late," one of them muttered strongly in a Scottish accent. "By blood, hurry up," he demanded to his friend, who seemed more interested in trying to get a drink. The first man grabbed the second by his ruff and towed him toward the staircase, practically dragging him backwards up the steps.

Kit waited until they had ascended the stairs, listening as they disappeared out of view when a door closed. "Looks like you were right," she said, craning her neck to look up the staircase. At the top of the stairs there was a small landing and two closed doors.

"I know the Scottish one," Iomhar whispered quietly, earning her gaze again. "I've seen him before, on another commission."

"Where?"

"Taurus once asked me to intercept a message he believed was being delivered to Scorpio at Sheffield." He used assigned codenames now they were in a public place. Taurus was for

Walsingham, and Scorpio was for Mary, Queen of Scots. "I found nothing, but that man," he pointed up the stairs, "was trying everything he could to see Scorpio. He was thrown out the castle grounds in the end."

"His name?"

"Graham Fraser," Iomhar whispered. "When I asked about him, I could find nothing out."

"But it's a safe bet to say he's loyal to Scorpio's cause?"

"I'd wager me house," he nodded solemnly, drinking the beer before screwing up his face and placing the tankard back down on the table. "It's been watered down."

Kit duly pushed her tankard away too. "We need to find out what they're saying," she said, angling her head to look back up to the staircase.

"Ye're not thinking of going up there, are ye?" he said as his eyebrows shot up, almost disappearing into his hairline.

"How else are we supposed to find out what they're saying?"

"I'd prefer an idea where we're less likely to get caught." His words were sharp.

"For all we know, their meeting could be over within minutes," she urged, already circling the table and heading toward the stairs. Iomhar made a grab for her arm, but she pulled it out of his reach. "There's no need to worry."

"How can I not worry after Edinburgh?" he asked, his voice a seething whisper.

"Then you stay down here." She climbed the staircase and walked slowly, comforted that any noise of her climbing the steps was masked by the loud shouts of those far below. As she reached the top landing, she peered back down to see Iomhar walking up the stairs too, his face resigned.

"Changed your mind?" she whispered as he reached her side.

"If ye're caught, I figure ye might need some help." He crossed his arms with clear dissatisfaction.

"Keep watch." She took his shoulder and turned him to face the stairs as she leaned toward the two doors. Beyond one there was no sound at all, yet the second public room had muffled voices.

She strained to listen in for a few minutes. There was an argument at first, with men's voices bickering about some of their group being late. Kit pressed her ear to the door, the better to hear them, just as their conversation turned to the matter at hand. She heard Mary Stuart's name once or twice, followed by Queen Elizabeth's, but with the men talking so quietly and the noise below them in the alehouse being so loud, she caught just the odd word every now and then.

Iomhar stood behind her, shifting between his feet in clear discomfort. When his moving feet caused the stairs beneath them to creak surprisingly loudly, she waved a hand in his direction, demanding he stayed still.

"In two weeks," a voice said from inside the room, the English accent was plain to hear. "That's all we have left."

"It is not long," a Scottish voice answered him.

"It's all we need," the first man spoke again. "She'll be dead by then."

Kit pressed her ear even harder against the closed door. Two weeks wasn't very long. Whatever plan had been put in place to assassinate Queen Elizabeth, they had to be confident of their plot to have it culminate so soon.

"Deliver the message to your groups," the English man spoke again.

As a chair slid across the floor inside the room, signifying they were leaving, Kit jumped back from the door. She didn't have time to explain but grabbed Iomhar by the shoulder and began to push him down the stairs, away from the room. They took the stairs two at a time in their haste to be at the bottom, where they picked up their tankards from the table, both turning their heads away from the staircase.

"Well?" Iomhar whispered to her.

"Two weeks," she said, her voice barely audible at all. In response, Iomhar paled a little and his lips parted.

Behind her, she could hear voices on the staircase of the men leaving the room. Their voices were muffled by the raucous drunkards around them. As the men left, pushing between the different groups, she lifted her cap a little off her brow, the better to see what was happening.

Graham Fraser, the man Iomhar had mentioned earlier, seemed to hang at the back of the group, flanked by another man who was dressed finely indeed. The intricacies of his white ruff and the black and gold doublet suggested he was a man that did not belong in an alehouse such as this. He would not have looked out of place at Hampton Court, attending to the queen.

Together, Fraser and the well-dressed gentleman walked to the door of the alehouse, where the gentleman reached into his pocket and pulled out a sealed piece of parchment. He passed it into Fraser's hand who quickly slid the parchment into a pouch attached to his belt near his hip.

"We need to see what's in that letter," Kit said, pushing away from the table.

"Kit, wait!" Iomhar called after her, but she didn't. She was not going to waste time second-guessing herself when they had just two weeks until this group tried to kill their queen. No time could be wasted.

She slipped between the drunkards, heading outside. Fortunately, the crowd had gathered out the front too, meaning the density of people was so thick that no one appeared to bat an eyelid when their shoulders bumped against strangers.

Kit glanced back just once to see Iomhar was struggling to catch up with her. She looked round as Graham Fraser nodded his head to say goodbye to the gentleman. As the latter walked off down the street, Fraser turned to two other men that had been in the public room with them. As they talked, with their heads bowed together, she saw the opportunity she needed.

She strode forward as a drunken lad passed by her. She reached out her foot, latching it around the lad's ankle just enough to send him toppling over, into the direction of Fraser and his friends. The fallout was instant with Fraser and the others struggling to stand straight. He grabbed the lad under the arms and tried to heave him to his feet.

Kit passed close to Fraser's back and reached for the pouch where he had hidden the letter. Slipping her fingers inside unnoticed wasn't difficult in the chaos she had caused. Once the letter was out, she held it down close to her side and walked away, as quickly as she could.

Just as she broke free of the crowd and out into the clear cobbled road, Iomhar caught up with her.

"That was reckless. Did ye get it?" he asked, pulling on her elbow and drawing her to a stop.

"What do you think?" She held the letter up in front of her for him to see.

"It's gone," a Scottish accent yelled from the crowd.

Kit felt Iomhar push her hand down again, trying to hide the letter from view, but it was too late. One of the men that had been beside Fraser was staring their way and had seen the action.

"Over there!" he called, pointing straight at them.

CHAPTER 7

"I knew I should not have agreed to work with ye," Iomhar said as Fraser and the two men with him turned in their direction.

"You want to discuss that now?" Kit snapped as Fraser reached for something in his belt. In the lamplight from the alehouse, she saw the glint of a rapier.

"Time to run." Iomhar grabbed her arm and pushed her ahead.

Kit shoved the letter through the buttons of her doublet, hiding it from view as she sprinted away across the cobbles down the road. She could hear Iomhar running close behind her, his boots striking heavily on the ground.

They took a corner at the end of the road, giving Kit the brief chance to glance back to see if they were being followed. Fraser and his friends were in pursuit, running into the shadows so that their faces were no longer visible.

"Hurry!" Iomhar ordered, moving up to her side. She looked forward again, running with him along the next road. "This way."

"We'll be going in circles that way," she argued with him. "This way." She tore off in the opposite direction, turning left when he turned right. He had to run back on himself to catch up with her.

"Are ye trying to make this difficult on purpose?" he asked, panting heavily and speaking through heavy breaths.

"We'd get caught that way," she explained, refusing to look at him as she focused on her route. "We need to get out of Blackfriars."

She headed for the river, knowing that the area was particularly busy at this time of night and was their best chance of losing the men in a crowd.

"We should go the other way," Iomhar said, running alongside of her.

"We can't argue about this now."

"Well, we are, are we not?" He jumped ahead of her, turning their path so that they scampered off to the left.

"In God's mercy," she muttered, following him. She was struggling to argue whilst breathing so heavily.

They turned down a few different streets, but each time she glanced back proved their efforts were only getting them so far. Fraser and the other two men had dropped back a little way, but they weren't giving up the chase. In the moonlight, she could see their shadowed figures still following them.

"We can't run like this forever," Kit warned, just as they both turned into a narrow alleyway, the crevice appearing between two timber buildings. Iomhar was the one who skidded to a halt first, alerting Kit to what was ahead. She looked up, just in time to see the moonlight shining off a wall ahead of them. "Damn, it's a dead end."

"I noticed," Iomhar said drily, earning a dark glare from her. She didn't need to look back to know Fraser wasn't far behind. She could hear his footsteps and his shouts to his friends.

"Which way?" he called.

"Left ahead, into that alleyway," one of the others shouted back.

Kit looked at the wall in desperation. Built of stonework that was messy, with each rock at an odd angle, it was the perfect surface to climb. Not too high at roughly double her height, it was still a feasible escape route.

"Well, we only have one option," Kit said and hurried to the wall. She began to climb, clambering up the stonework as quickly as she could.

Iomhar cursed as he began to follow her, moving at a much slower pace.

"Can't you climb?" she asked, pausing as she reached the top of the wall.

"Not very well," he explained, only halfway up.

Kit glanced back to see Fraser and the others had now reached their alleyway and were just a couple of hundred yards away. "Go faster," she urged.

"I'm hardly taking my time about this!" Iomhar snapped back, reaching up. He was making progress, but it wasn't quick enough.

Kit panicked as she watched the three men run toward them. She looked down at the daggers in her belt, but they could do her little good now. She swung herself up onto the top of the wall, so she was sitting there with a leg dangling down either side, then she reached down toward Iomhar.

"Give me your hand," she ordered him. He looked reluctant at first, glancing up at her as he reached for the stones instead. "Do you want to get caught?" she asked, waving her hand madly at him.

He took it this time, grasping tightly onto her wrist. She heaved as much as she could, using her position on the wall to lever him higher. It was difficult and ungainly with him weighing more than her, but she managed to help pull him out of reach just as the others arrived at the bottom of the wall. They tried to grab Iomhar's ankles, but he was too high.

Kit released his wrist and dropped down the other side, looking round to find herself in a courtyard between a cluster of houses.

"Ye did not have to do that," Iomhar said as he jumped down too.

"Do what?" she asked, as the voices continued on the other side of the wall.

"Quick, follow them. We need that letter back!" It was Fraser's voice.

Iomhar strode forward, running across the courtyard to one of the houses, with Kit close behind. "Ye could have just gone ahead," he said as he reached for a door. The handle refused to move. It was fixed firmly in position, locked tight.

"And left you to them?"

"Many a man would have done." Iomhar looked back to her, the whites of his eyes visible in the moonlight. There was clear shock on his face, as though she had stunned him by her actions. She tried not to think about it too much. She hadn't hesitated in her decision, not for one second.

"You're not talking to a man, remember?" she said with a smirk, looking back to the wall as a head began to appear above it. "Knock down the door."

Iomhar stepped back before lifting his foot and kicking at the wood beside the lock. It splintered open and the door swung wide, ricocheting off the far side wall. He walked in first, with Kit behind, the sound of the door breaking had woken those inside and steps could be heard running down a set of stairs.

"Be quicker," Iomhar urged, sprinting through the house and reaching for the front door on the other side.

"As you said, I'm not going slow," she snapped, just as she flicked her head round to see a man running down the stairs. He was dressed in a nightshirt with a chamber pot held high in his hands like a weapon.

"Who are you? Why are you in my house?" he demanded, his voice bouncing off the walls.

"Apologies for the intrusion," Kit spoke hurriedly as she followed Iomhar out of the door. "I believe you might have a few more strangers in your house shortly." She pointed down the corridor through which they had just ran before closing the door on him.

It was only a few seconds before she heard the thud of the chamber pot being struck against someone's head.

"That might have bought us some time," Kit panted between the words.

"Not long enough." Iomhar gestured to a window where Fraser was currently climbing out of.

They glanced at each other before sprinting off down the road again. This time, neither of them spoke and they didn't bother arguing. They just ran as quickly as they could, over one set of cobbles and then onto a dirty track before they appeared near the river, close to the London bridge, with its towers silhouetted against the night sky.

"This way," Iomhar headed off in the direction of the bridge, forcing Kit to follow, her lungs burning in the effort of having run for so long.

As they reached the bridge, there were many people wandering to and fro, going between alehouses and out to see friends. They pushed through the groups, causing mayhem and uproar with people shouting after them, urging them to slow down.

"Is he still there?" Iomhar shouted back to her.

Kit glanced once to see Fraser's head through the crowd with one of his friends still at his side, the other was missing. "Two of them," she said and looked forward again.

As they reached the end of the bridge, the crowd began to disperse a little as Iomhar took them down back streets, jumping from one small lane to the next.

"I can't keep running like this," Kit's pace was slowing as her legs began to sting with pain. She tried to keep sprinting forward, but her body seemed to have a mind of its own, refusing to go any further.

"Then we hide instead," Iomhar answered, looking back as she started to slow. He stopped, his eyes widening at something.

"What?" Kit asked as she nearly collided with him.

"They're there," he pointed behind her, grabbing her arms to stop her from running into him. She looked back. Fraser and his friend were catching them up. "This way," he pulled her to the side, down another narrow alleyway, only this time, the path didn't open out into another road. Instead, they passed under an archway, before crossing into a courtyard then heading through a doorway and into a building.

Iomhar shut the door behind them, just as Kit realised where they were. Guffaws of laughter and applause made her whip her head round to see stalls set in a circle, full of an audience, with a stage set in front of them. On top of the wooden boards were two actors, dressed more like harlequins. One was falling over another as the crowd erupted in laughter.

"The theatre?" Kit asked, looking round in amazement. "Did you know this was here?"

"Seemed like a good place to hide to me." Iomhar pushed her forward and into the crowd that were standing in front of the stage.

Kit gagged against the stench that met her, for this was the area where those who could not afford to buy seated tickets were forced to stand. Pressed so tightly together, the stench of body odour was overwhelming.

"Strange, I never had you down for a theatre man," she said as she struggled to follow him through the audience.

"Ye do not know me very well, remember?" he called back to her. As they reached the middle, Kit looked back to the door they had come through, watching as Fraser and his friend emerged, darting their heads to and fro, looking for them.

"They're here," she whispered to Iomhar, just as the laughter stilled around them.

"Then pretend to watch," he turned her back to face the stage.

"You're too tall," she pointed to his head. "They'll notice you in this crowd." He crouched down in response, coming down to her level.

They both feigned interest in the performance, watching as the two harlequins completed their skit, much to the roaring delight of their audience as they laughed again. One of the actors was performing some grandiose monologue whilst the one behind him mocked him rigorously for it. The whole time, Kit was watching Fraser out of the corner of her eye. He was slowly moving through the seated actors, searching all their faces.

"They'll find us soon," she whispered to Iomhar. "They're looking through the crowd."

Iomhar glanced back at Fraser. "We get out of this crowd now and they'll see us," he said quietly to her. "We wait it out. It's our best bet."

She was not so sure and bit her lip as Fraser moved on, climbing between the different seats in search of them. That's when she realised she had lost sight of his friend. She whipped her head back and forth, trying to recall the features she had seen chasing them across the bridge. He was nearly bald with a hooked nose, but in the dim candlelight of the theatre, she was struggling to see much at all. The best light came from the open roof and the moonlight that shone through it.

"He's gone," she whispered.

"Fraser's over there," Iomhar pointed back over his shoulder.

"Not him, the other one," she answered, elbowing him with the words.

"I thought I told ye, ye do not have to keep doing that," he said, rubbing his ribs.

"Doing what?" she asked innocently.

"Ye know very well what," he tried to slyly search the crowd. His head stilled and his expression changed, alerting Kit to the fact that there had to be something wrong.

"What is it?"

"Duck," he ordered her.

"What?"

"Now!" he snapped the word quite loudly, drawing attention of those around. She did as he said and crouched down to the ground, then she heard a crack above her. She looked up to see the balding man had been standing right behind her. His arm was outstretched, as though he had gone to strike her, but instead he had been met by Iomhar's fist colliding with his nose. The crack had belonged to bone.

The man stumbled back, wailing and clutching at his bloodied nose.

"Someone call a constable!" an audience member shouted.

"Grab him!" Another tried to take hold of Iomhar, but he shook him off easily.

Kit stood straight, barely looking back to the injured balding man before she ran, pushing through the people.

"Fraser is following," Iomhar warned from close behind her.

The crowd were not so willing to let them through now that they had seen violence. It led to people trying to restrain them, but once Kit had shoved one young man into another, sending them toppling to the ground, a path carved itself through the people, no one else was willing to get in their way after that.

Unable to circle back round to the door through which they had entered, Kit aimed for another door entirely. She launched herself through it, with Iomhar closing it behind him before he threw himself against the door, using his weight to stop it from opening.

Fraser must have reached the other side seconds later, for Kit could see the wood bumping against Iomhar's back and he had to work hard to keep it closed.

"Get something to keep it shut," Iomhar waved a hand at her as he threw his weight against the door harder.

Kit looked around, seeing exactly where they had come out. It seemed to be a kind of props room for the theatre with many boxes strewn through the space and bundles of items tossed in each one, from fake weapons to costume jewellery. Beside the boxes were chairs and tables that had to be sometimes dragged on stage.

Kit grabbed hold of one of the tables and began to slide it toward Iomhar. She piled boxes of props on top, weighing it down further, before replacing Iomhar's place at the door with the table itself.

"That will not hold long," Iomhar muttered, as he slowly let the table take his position.

"Then run for that door," Kit gestured toward one of the two doors on the far side of the props room, picking it at random. "Now."

They both released the table and ran for the door. In their kerfuffle, it wasn't clear who was going through the door first, and they bumped shoulders as they moved through to the other side.

The next room was a dressing room with clothes, wigs and make-up strewn all over. Beyond the room was a curtain, showing ahead was the stage.

"We're trapped," Iomhar said, coming to a stop.

In the room behind them, Kit could hear the scraping of the table along the floorboards, indicating Fraser was nearly through. He could opt for the other door, or he could choose the same one through which they had come.

"Then we hide in plain sight," she moved toward one of the displays of clothes in the corner of the room and grabbed a massive cloak, pulling it around her shoulders.

"Ye are not serious?" Iomhar reached her side.

"Look the part, Iomhar," she declared with a smile and grabbed a woman's wig, flopping it down on top of his dark hair.

His eyebrows shot up in surprise. He was too busy looking at the long fake blonde locks to be prepared for what Kit did next. She grabbed a woman's dress and threw it into his arms, with the sudden toss he tumbled back on his heels, before falling into a chair nearby. Kit just had time to replace her own hat with a large tasselled one, when the door behind them opened.

Fraser hurried into the space, but before he could look their way in the corner of the room, his eyes were drawn to the curtain that led to the stage and the two harlequins that were walking off stage. In this dim room that was lit just by two candles at either side of the space, it was hard to see facial features at all.

"What are you doing?" one of the harlequins called to him. "You can't be back here."

"I'm sorry," Fraser said quickly, holding up his hands in an apology. "I was looking for someone."

"Actors only. Out!" the second harlequin took Fraser's shoulder and steered him back to the door through which he had come. As the door closed behind him, Kit looked at Iomhar with a great smile, watching as he tried to blow some of the blonde strands of dyed horsehair out of his face.

"I honestly did not think that was going to work," Iomhar breathed out the words, his eye peeking out from the mad locks.

"He wasn't looking properly," Kit said with victory as she tossed off the tasselled hat. "He saw two actors dressed up only, if he looked this way at all." She gestured to their clothes.

"Who are you two?" one of the harlequins turned to them.

Kit looked back to see the actors' narrowed glares now trained on them.

CHAPTER 8

"Actors only allowed back here!" the second harlequin bellowed once again, walking toward Kit and Iomhar.

"My apologies," Kit said quickly, pulling off the cloak. "It was imperative we hide from that man." She pointed at the door. "Let's just say he was intent on hurting us."

"In which case, stay as long as you want," the actor harrumphed with the words, sending a narrowed glare at the closed door. "He certainly did look like a brute." He put upon a dramatic shiver.

The other harlequin turned his attention to Iomhar, who was still sat in the chair with the blonde wig on, and a smile appeared on his face. "It suits you."

Iomhar immediately snatched the wig off his head and threw it back into a box nearby. "We're going now. Apologies for the interruption," he hurried with the words, jumping to his feet and dropping the dress too.

"If you fancy a career in acting, my friend, you know where to come." The harlequin winked at him as he picked up the blonde wig from the box. Kit had to stifle her laugh as she followed Iomhar out of the room.

"Thank ye," Iomhar said stiffly before hurrying through the door and closing it quickly behind them.

"I think he liked you," Kit whispered, unafraid to hide her laugh once they found the props room empty with no sign of Fraser at all.

"I noticed." Iomhar aimed for the other door in the props room. "An exit." Peering his head outside, he stayed there for a second or two more, glancing up and down the street before he took a step out. "I cannot see him, or the balding one."

"Good." Kit followed him out. Clouds were beginning to inch across the night sky, making it more and more difficult to see people's faces in the street. "We need to get somewhere safe." She glanced up and down as the darkness grew. "The night watchmen will be out soon."

"My lodgings are a long way from here," Iomhar said, coming to a stop in the centre of the road.

"Then we'll go to mine," Kit said, striding forward in one direction. "Where we can read this." She patted the place in her doublet where she had hidden the letter.

"After what just happened, I really hope whatever is in that letter is worth it," Iomhar sighed, shaking his head.

"It wasn't so bad," Kit pointed out.

"Not so bad?" Iomhar whispered harshly, snapping his head toward her. "Have ye forgotten it already?"

"No," she elongated the syllable. "It is sometimes necessary for things to get a little…"

"Reckless? Impetuous? Foolish?" Iomhar offered.

"I was going to say messy," her words were quiet, as they rounded the front of the theatre.

"I prefer my words," he said. Out the front of the theatre, lanterns had been lit, casting a lemon-coloured glow around the street. "Keep an eye out for Fraser," he warned as they passed the door.

Leaning against the door were two young women, both orange sellers with their baskets of oranges set down by their feet.

"I see some business," one of the women hurried forward. She took hold of Kit's arm, but Kit snatched it away quickly. "Not interested?"

"No thanks," Kit declared sharply, coming to a halt when she noticed the other woman blocking off Iomhar's path. She watched wide-eyed as the two women took hold of Iomhar's arms, trying to draw him back to the theatre.

"He's not interested in buying oranges," Kit huffed tiredly, watching them with folded arms.

"I do not think they want to sell me oranges, Kit," he said with a smirk.

"Indeed, we are not." One of the women smiled sweetly up at him. With horror, Kit could see far behind Iomhar in the shadows of the doorway to the theatre that two figures were appearing. They were too far back in the shadows for her to see their faces, but their silhouettes were clear, and one was clutching his nose.

It could well have been their two chasers.

"Not tonight, thank ye." Iomhar was trying to disentangle his arms, but the women were persistent.

"Sorry, ladies," Kit walked toward them, seeing only one way out of this that would resolve the situation quickly before the men looked their way. She snatched off her hat and shook her hair out. "He's taken." She pushed one of the women off Iomhar's arm and took her place, before dragging him forward. The woman whined and the other harrumphed as Kit pulled him away.

"I thought that was a boy," one muttered as they walked off down the street.

"He's taken?" Iomhar repeated with a smirk that was soon hidden by the darkness a second later as they walked away from the lamplights.

"What else was I supposed to say?" Kit asked, releasing his arm when they were some distance away. "I think Fraser and his friend were in the doorway. You were seconds away from being seen." She glanced back down the street, relieved the two silhouettes she had spied were walking in the other direction. They hadn't noticed Kit and Iomhar. "They're gone."

Kit's legs were burning by the time they reached the attic room of her lodgings. She unlocked the door and stumbled inside, reaching for the nearest chair in the darkness. Iomhar walked in beside her.

"Ye all right?" He gestured down as she flexed her leg muscles.

"I prefer climbing to running," she explained. "I'll be fine. I just need to rest up."

"Ye did not do too bad," Iomhar said, his figure moving in the darkness toward a candle that was on top of her fireplace. He opened a tinderbox and struck a light against a tallow dip.

"Thank you," Kit replied mockingly, sitting back in the chair. "Were you expecting me to do very badly?"

"After Edinburgh, well —"

"Don't answer that." She reached into her doublet to pull out the letter.

"I still think ye should not have taken the letter," he said as the flame filled the room with a soft orange glow. The light fell on his features, casting half his face in shadow and the other in an ethereal apricot tinge.

Kit froze as she looked at him. Momentarily, she felt she had seen him somewhere before, and not just in Scotland. An image flashed in her mind, of a statue with a face carved in marble. Then the statue was gone, like a flash of lightning, there one second and gone the next.

"Something wrong?" he asked, watching her with a frown.

"No," she said, looking away from him and shaking off the moment. She tried to recall what statue it was that had appeared in her thoughts, but she couldn't. She had no idea where she had seen it before but reasoned that Iomhar just happened to look a little like it.

"We should have told Walsingham what we heard and left the letter," Iomhar insisted, leaning on the mantelpiece beside the candle.

"That would not have done much good." She leaned forward and turned the letter over in her hands. "Do you really not think it was worth the risk?" she asked, looking up. "The queen's life is at stake here." To her surprise, he didn't answer. He looked away instead, his features tensed, suggesting he was deep in thought. "Well? Was it then not worth the risk?" she prompted him.

"Maybe, but now they know someone took their letter, they will be wary of what they do next," he answered slowly. There was something in his tone, something that suggested there was more to his thoughts, but she didn't press for more information. "Where did ye learn your skills, by the way?"

"What do you mean?" she asked, as she looked down at the letter once more.

"Climbing, handling those daggers for another thing," he pointed at the daggers in her belt. "I think I can still feel where ye nearly got me earlier this evening." He gestured to his neck.

"Sorry about that," she apologised as she turned the parchment over. There was a basic wax seal, with no imprint on it whatsoever, showing that the letter was clearly trying to maintain some anonymity.

"So? Where did ye learn such things?"

"I was taught," she said, passing the letter to him as she stood up. "Look at that." She pointed at the blank wax seal before crossing to the side of the room to find some ale. She placed two cups on the mantelpiece of the fireplace and filled them with ale before she spoke again. "Walsingham made sure I had the best training. Either from him, or other intelligencers."

"When did ye meet?" Iomhar stared at the seal as he picked up one of the cups with his other hand.

"Twenty years ago," she said, watching Iomhar's face for a reaction. He paused mid gulp, his eyes shooting to hers over the rim of the cup.

"Ye were a child?"

"He thinks I was about four years old," she explained.

"He *thinks*?" Iomhar repeated. "What does that mean?"

Kit turned away and picked up her own cup, thankful for the distraction as she tried to prepare her words. None of this was a great secret, a fair few people knew about her past and how she'd ended up with Walsingham, some who worked for him and his family too, but that didn't make talking of it any easier. It all felt so odd to talk about. Sort of like talking about an empty space, for that was how it felt when she couldn't recall the memories herself.

"He found me on the street, begging for food," she said as she returned to her seat, holding the cup with her two hands. "Apparently, I pulled on his cloak and asked him for help."

"Ye cannot remember?" Iomhar asked, gulping again from his cup.

"No," she shook her head, "I was too young." She looked down at the yellow-tinged ale in front of her and wracked her brains just as she always did. She could picture something, looking up to Walsingham in a street, but she was certain it was an image created from her imagination. The memory of that day itself never came to her, no matter how many times she tried to think of it. "The first memories I have are of Walsingham's house."

"He took ye in and raised ye?" Iomhar sounded baffled, turning the letter over to read the address.

"Sort of," Kit explained, chewing her lip in thought. Some days when she was a child it had felt as though Walsingham were a parent or some kind of relation, watching over her. Other times, he felt more like what she imagined a schoolmaster to be like, demanding and full of instruction. It certainly helped her to understand why she felt this constant need to please him. She wanted once just to hear his admiration for something she had done, rather than the censure of doing something that wasn't up to scratch.

"Wait a minute," Iomhar said, downing what was left in his cup and returning it to the mantelpiece before he turned to face her. "Are ye saying that Walsingham started teaching ye these things when he took ye in?"

"He taught me to read and write first," she clarified slowly. "After that came codebreaking, and these." She gestured down at the daggers in her belt.

"In the name of the wee man," he muttered, shaking his head as he moved to a chair to sit opposite her near the fire.

"What does that mean?" she asked, tempted to laugh at the sudden strength in his Scottish accent.

"The wee man," he gestured to the sky. "Our Lord above."

"I've never heard him called that before." She smiled at the idea. "Something tells me that our God wouldn't be so pleased about being referred to as 'wee'."

"It's a Scottish expression," he explained. "And it merits my amazement."

"Why?" she asked.

"Ye were a child, and Walsingham gave ye *those*," he pointed at the daggers.

"He said it was necessary to stay alive," she shrugged. "It makes perfect sense to me."

"Other children may disagree."

"Well, I wouldn't know about that, would I?" she asked, gesturing for him to hand over the letter.

"Hmm," he hesitated before doing so. "Look at who they've addressed it to."

She took the letter back, turning her gaze down to it. *Number Twenty-One.*

"House number?" Iomhar offered.

"No," Kit said strongly. She could remember clearly deciphering a code once with Walsingham watching over her shoulder in the attic room of his house on Seething Lane. She had deciphered it all except for one crucial thing. It was at the very top of the letter, where someone's name would usually reside, and it was a number. She had been ready to give up on trying to decode it when Walsingham had given her the answer.

"*It is a code for someone's name, Kit.*"

"It's a codename," she realised, uttering the words quickly aloud. "Extremely difficult to decipher. The numbers can have no link at all to who they are assigned to," she explained, analysing the way in which the number had been underlined. There wasn't a doubt in her mind, the number belonged to a person.

"I'm curious," Iomhar said, leaning forward in his chair.

Kit looked up, seeing him moving toward her. "About?" she prompted.

"Is this why ye say ye trust Walsingham and nay other? Because he raised ye?" he asked with a kind of sincerity in his tone.

"That question is a little personal, do you not think?" She sipped from her ale in the effort to deflect the question. She had no intention of answering it. She'd told him the facts of her life, and that's all this man before her needed to know, nothing more.

"Nay," he said with a smirk. "If I was being personal, I would say something along the lines of ye should not try too much to please the man."

"Whoever said I was?" Kit spluttered, nearly choking on the ale.

"Aye, your response certainly convinces me of your denial," he added with sarcasm as she shook her head madly at him. "When we left Walsingham, it was clear his disapproval of ye stung."

"You really are one of the most annoying people I have ever met," she snapped and drank the last of her ale. "You have pried enough into my life for one night. I see no need to discuss it anymore."

"I was hardly prying." He sat back in his chair, though he was smirking still, apparently pleased to have gotten under her skin.

"Stop smirking like that," she warned, earning just a bigger smile from him in return. "That's it. I'm ignoring you now." She placed down her cup and turned both hands to the letter. "I'm going to read this instead."

"What are the chances of it being in code?" he asked, standing up to pour more ale into his cup.

"I'd say it's almost certain," she said and broke the wax seal, pulling the envelope open wide. "What do you know, I was right."

The encrypted letter stretched out in front of Kit, ready to be deciphered. At the top where there should have been a name was the same number as before, *Twenty-One*, and there were no details of an address from the sender. The ink used was thick and black, making the cursive lettering messy and difficult to read in places.

"Can ye decode it?" Iomhar asked, leaning forward in his seat.

Kit didn't answer straight away. She was busy looking across the series of symbols that had been used. It was confusing, with pictorial symbols used for some words and letters used for others. It would not be easy to decipher.

"We should give it to Walsingham. He'll give it to Phelippes or Somers."

"That will not be necessary," Kit dismissed the idea as she stood to her feet and moved towards the candle on the mantelpiece, the better to read the letter in detail.

"They are the best codebreakers he has," Iomhar said, watching her closely. Kit pretended not to notice as she turned her back on him a little.

"They're not the only ones," she muttered so quietly that she hoped Iomhar wouldn't be able to hear her.

"Go on then," Iomhar declared dramatically, "decode it. Impress me."

"You can't just look at a letter like this and know what it says," she turned sharply back to him with a hand on her hip in disapproval. "Give me the night to analyse it. Come back in the morning and I'll have something for you."

"Or we take it to Phelippes and Somers," Iomhar mentioned the codebreakers' names again.

"In the morning, if I cannot do it," Kit assured him with some reluctance. She was determined to prove her worth and decode it herself. "Now, drink up and leave my lodgings."

He followed her order. He downed what was left of the ale in his cup before standing to his feet and walking past her. "Aye, good luck with the letter." He nodded his head toward the letter in her grasp as he reached for the door. "There's nay harm in admitting ye cannot do it, ye know."

"I can do it," she insisted, levelling her gaze at him as he hovered in the doorway.

"We shall see." He spoke with evident restraint as he reached for the handle and opened the door. "Sleep well," he said and bowed his head in a goodbye before he left.

Kit didn't wait to listen for his retreating footsteps on the stairs before she locked the door tightly. Walking back away from the door, she muttered curses against Iomhar's name, all because Walsingham had insisted that she worked with someone else on this commission.

With the curses still falling from her lips, she placed the letter down on the table in the centre of her attic room and brought the one lonely candle across to sit beside it. She took off her weapon's belt and her doublet, leaving her torso in a linen shirt. With fresh ink and a new quill, she sat on a stool beside the table and began to decode the letter.

"Arrogant Scottish intelligencer," she mumbled, louder this time. "I'm more capable than he gives me credit for." She made scribbling notes across the surface of a clean piece of parchment, determined to prove her words were right.

CHAPTER 9

The catcalls of market sellers beyond the windows woke Kit in the early hours of the morning. She snatched her head up off the table, sat bolt straight, only to find a piece of parchment stuck to her cheek. She plucked it from her cheek, feeling the ink that had dried against her skin peel away before blinking a few times to clear her vision.

Sunlight was streaming through the narrow-angled windows, making the candle that had burned all the way down to its brass holder obsolete. She blew out the flame, watching as the smoke trail curled in the air. On the surface of the table was the coded letter, stretched out flat, and in her hand were the notes she had made to decipher the message.

She yawned and stretched her muscles, reading her notes. It had taken a long time to decrypt the letter, forcing her to stay awake into the early hours of the morning. She hadn't even made it to bed in the end and her nap on her notes had smudged some of the ink. With fervour, she picked up the quill to edit her scribbles and make the words more legible.

Beside the letter and perched on the very edge of the table was a bound book of parchment leaves that Walsingham had lent her many years ago. Written by John Somers, it had most of the known codes copied out for ease of use. Fortunately for Kit, the writer of the coded letter in her possession did not have the ingenuity to come up with their own code. Instead, they had used two of Somers' known codes and spliced the two together.

The only thing in the letter that still remained a mystery was the name of the recipient: *Twenty-One*. She supposed she would never know now who they were. If only she had waited and followed Fraser to see where he had delivered the letter to before she had taken it, then she would have had an answer to her question.

"So God mend me," she mumbled. "The Scot was right." She should not have taken the letter when she did.

"Aye, I'm pleased to hear that." The Scottish accent made Kit jump to her feet and nearly send the table flying. She whipped round, reaching for her weapons belt and her daggers to find Iomhar standing in the doorway with the door wide open. "Care to tell me what I was right about?"

"You broke in again," Kit accused him, releasing her hold on the dagger as she marched toward him. She was tempted to push him straight back out. Instead, she grabbed the handle of the door, looking at the lock for a sign of weakness.

"Ye need a new lock," Iomhar explained, walking past her. "All ye need to do is lift the door in its frame and it pops out the lock."

"Or you could just not break in," she said sharply before kicking the door back into its frame, letting the wood ricochet to emphasise her point. Iomhar didn't even flinch at the sound, he merely continued to smirk and walked across to the table where the decoded letter sat.

"Did ye stay up all night?" he asked, bending down to read it.

"Not quite." She tried to hide her yawn as she followed him across the room.

"Looks like ye did it," he said, turning his focus to the letter.

"That I did," Kit smiled with the words and walked around him, pulling the letter to the edge of the table so that she could read it. "It was a simple code, using two different systems. Commonly used words are represented by pictures. For instance, this picture here of the ram's head, refers to Queen

Elizabeth. This one," she paused and pointed down at the inked image of a lily flower, "means death."

"Joyful," Iomhar laughed, reading over her shoulder.

"The other letters are then just a simple replacement. Each letter has been shifted three places up the alphabet to what it should have been before. So, all the 'a's are 'd's, all the 'e's are 'h's, and so on." Kit spoke excitedly. "Though we do not know who the recipient was intended to be, we do know who the sender is. They signed their name using the same alphabet code. It's a Lord Egbert Ruskin."

Iomhar snatched the parchment up from the table, lifting it to his eyes with so much vigour that he nearly tore the paper.

"Careful," Kit warned, trying to take it back, but he didn't seem to be listening. He held the parchment out of her reach, with his eyes tarrying on the name signed at the bottom. "Is something wrong?" Kit asked when she noticed Iomhar's jaw had tightened, with a twitch in his cheek.

Still, he said nothing, he just continued to stare at the letter for some time.

"Iomhar?" she called his name, and when there was still no answer, she elbowed him in the rib instead.

"Och, ye have a sharp elbow," he said, rubbing the rib where she had jabbed him.

"I do not take kindly to being ignored."

"I am not ignoring ye. I am thinking," Iomhar explained as he dropped the parchment back down to the table. "I know the name."

"Lord Egbert Ruskin?" Kit repeated the name as she passed a finger under the decoded words. "Where from?"

"That does not matter." He walked away from her, turning in a circle as he crossed the room.

"Are you keeping secrets?" Kit asked warily.

"So what if I am?"

"We are supposed to be working together." Her sharp tone made Iomhar snap his head back toward her. "Who is he?" She pointed down at the parchment. "Where do you know him from?"

"That I cannot tell you," he said, looking away from her.

"Iomhar!" she barked the word, only to receive a shake of his head in reply. "How do you expect me to trust you when you clearly don't trust me?"

"It's not about trust," he matched her tone both in volume and anger. "It's about something else entirely." He walked back toward the table, stopping on the opposite side to her. "What I can tell ye is that Lord Ruskin is loyal to Mary Stuart. He would quite happily visit the gates of hell and come back again to see her put back on the Scottish throne and take England's as well. Even if he came back up to this earth with the devil clinging onto his shoulders."

His words were met with stony silence as Kit frowned at him.

"How do you know that?" she asked.

He lowered his gaze back down to the letter, evidently refusing to answer her. "If this letter was sent by Ruskin, then ye can be assured they intend to follow through with their plot to kill the queen. It is not idle gossip or just drunken talk. They mean to do it."

"You can tell that from the rest of the letter," Kit said.

"What else does it say?"

"Take a look." She pushed it forward for him to read.

Once Kit had cracked the alphabet code around one in the morning with a clock tower beyond the window striking a single solitary chime, the middle part of the letter abruptly became easy to read. With a trembling hand, she'd read of

Lord Ruskin's plan that had already prepared an army that was currently waiting on the Scottish border.

Unbeknownst to King James VI of Scotland and his regency, defectors in their court were raising arms, and now waited at the border between the two countries. When Ruskin issued the order, the army would march into England and all the way to Sheffield, to retrieve Mary Stuart from her house arrest. It was evident from the wording alone in the letter that Ruskin didn't care how many men would die in the process. They intended to free Mary Stuart from Sheffield Castle come what may.

"Can this be true?" Iomhar asked, gesturing down to a certain part of the letter.

"'Elizabeth dies in two weeks' time,'" Kit repeated from the letter, having already memorised the words. "'She'll die at the hands of *Eighty-Two* and her men.'"

"Eighty-Two … is that another person?"

"It has to be," Kit nodded in agreement, "but who that could be, I have no idea. Each number assigned is arbitrary to the person. Just like the recipient, number Twenty-One."

"*Her*," he emphasised the word, lifting his gaze. "Eighty-Two is a woman."

"That's all we know for now," Kit said, reaching for her doublet and pulling it over her shoulders. "We need to show Walsingham what we have found."

"Agreed," Iomhar folded up the letter and slipped it into a pocket in his own doublet.

"No, I took it from Fraser, I'll be the one to deliver it." Kit stopped in front of Iomhar and beckoned for him to hand over the letter.

"What happened to working together?" he asked, folding his arms and making no move to return the letter.

"I took the letter. I decoded it." She smiled triumphantly at him. "Other than breaking in here twice, what else have you done?"

"Ye mean other than getting ye away from Fraser before he could take his letter back and probably kill ye in the process?" At his words, Kit flinched, dropping her beckoning hand. "Aye, ye're right. I've been nay use at all," he said with sarcasm before walking past her, heading straight toward the door.

Kit let out a frustrated sigh as she tied the laces of her doublet. She pulled on her red leather gloves and fastened the weapons belt around her waist before she followed him. She locked the door behind her, wondering if there was any real point in locking it at all anymore.

Two steps into the street and it was plain to see why the catcalls from the market had woken Kit. The cobbled road was full of stalls set up for market day. The fish stall was particularly pungent making everyone passing by cover their noses with cupped hands, including Kit and Iomhar. Beyond this stall, there were comfits stalls and cheese stands too, with great wheels of cheese wrapped in muslin cloths and set on wooden sticks.

It was busy, with people bumping shoulders in their efforts to get past one another and reach the stall they needed first. Walking amongst them, Kit found herself being cajoled into a narrow footpath, away from the busiest stalls. Ahead of her, Iomhar was being pushed in much the same direction, trying to step out of the way of ladies wearing huge dresses with farthingales that threatened to trip up passers-by. He seemed to barely notice when people bumped into him, giving Kit an idea.

She hurried up to walk alongside him, waiting for the ideal opportunity. When two women walked past, wearing such large farthingales that they appeared swamped by their garments, Kit made a point of bumping purposefully into Iomhar to get out of their way.

"Oomph," he made a noise in complaint as he rubbed his ribs again. "Ye have a habit of doing that."

"At least this time it was an accident," she shrugged, lying to him as she slipped a hand into the pocket of his doublet and pulled out the letter. He didn't even notice, he just carried on walking down the street, clearly believing her lie. She tried to hide her smile as she slipped the parchment between her glove lining and her palm, hiding it discreetly away.

The market began to thin out the more they walked across London. They passed by the walls to the Tower of London with Kit pausing just long enough at the side of the cobbled road to look up to the keep that was barely visible above the outer battlements. The Tower these days was kept as a prison, and more than once had she accompanied Walsingham through its corridors on a commission. As a guard from the top of the battlements caught her watching, she flicked her head away and hurried after Iomhar, catching him up in the street.

They turned a few more corners together before they reached the narrow lane that led to the courtyard in Seething Lane. In the alleyway, Kit pulled on Iomhar's sleeve, trying to get his attention.

"Why do you work for Walsingham?" Kit asked. He turned and frowned in response. "Well, you do not seem especially approving of the man."

"I am loyal to his cause, suffice it to say," he said before turning away and heading under the archway that led into the courtyard. "I may not know what to think of the man, and I definitely do not trust him as ye do," he gestured to her, as she stiffened her spine, "but we are aligned in our aims for now. Mary Stuart will not be queen again."

"Why are you so adamant?"

"Wait…" Iomhar held out a hand in front of her, bringing the two of them to a sharp halt. "Do ye smell something?"

Kit sniffed the air, lifting up her chin and turning her head round to smell better. "Something is burning," she answered, just as they reached the far side of the courtyard and looked up at Walsingham's house.

Before either of them could say any more, beyond one of the windows, Kit could see the source of the burning stench. There were flames lapping at the insides of the rooms and clawing at the glass panes.

"It's on fire!"

CHAPTER 10

Kit forgot their discussion, her mind was on only one thing, the sight of the flames dancing beyond the windows. She ran for the house with Iomhar firmly on her tail. She struck against the hidden door, but with so many locks in place, it wouldn't move.

"Doris? Doris!" Kit screeched the housekeeper's name and moved along the building, banging against the glass of the kitchen window. When nothing moved beyond it and Doris did not answer the door, Iomhar moved her to the side.

"We're breaking it," he said and picked up a rock from the courtyard ground. With one hard strike against the glass, it fragmented into smithereens, casting glass shards into the kitchen. "I cannot fit through that."

"I can," Kit assured him, walking back to the window.

"In ye go, then open the door for me." He offered a hand to help her up. She took the hand and heaved herself through the windowpane, into the body of the house.

The kitchen was hot, the heat in the air so palpable it was cloying against her skin. She rushed through the kitchen, pausing only long enough to search the room for Doris before she reached for the front door. Doris had left the main keys on a small hook set against a timber beam. Kit slid all the bolts back and unlocked the main handle before swinging the door open, finding Iomhar waiting on the other side.

"We have minutes until the building is destroyed," Iomhar's voice was firm as he strode past her and into the corridor.

"Along with everyone in it," she muttered, trying to keep a hold on the fear that was burning in her body, making her hands tremble. "Doris!" This time when she screeched the housekeeper's name, there was a response, a murmuring cry.

Kit ran in the direction of it, finding Doris at the bottom of the stairs. The woman's dress was blackened from ash, and she was bent double, struggling to breathe, but she was alive.

"Doris, quick, head to the door." Kit pushed her forward. The woman nodded, following her instructions, just as Kit and Iomhar hurried up the stairs, heading toward Walsingham's study.

The door opened to reveal a room blackened with smoke, though the flames hadn't yet found it. Three men were stumbling into it from a door placed on the other side. Kit recognised them as Walsingham's three principal secretaries. At the back, Robert Beale seemed the most injured, coughing more than the others. He kicked the door in place behind them as they stumbled through the study.

"The flames are spreading this way," he warned. He stumbled on his feet, appearing minutes away from passing out from the smoke. Kit reached for him, grabbing his arms and holding him up before he could fall to the floor. She steered the older man toward the staircase and out of the room, just as Iomhar did the same for the other two secretaries.

It was hard work with Kit having to strain her muscles to keep the large man standing. As they reached the bottom of the stairs, he nearly tripped, his muscles weakened.

"You have to keep going, Beale," she pleaded with him, labouring to hold him up as his knees wobbled beneath him.

"I can't breathe," he muttered, coughing.

She reached for the ruff and partlet that sat around his bulging neck and snatched them away, creating an awful ripping sound. With the lacey material cast to the floor, it did little to help as Beale still coughed, but he seemed to be trying to breathe deeper because of it. She wrapped an arm around his shoulders and steered him toward the doorway of the house, pushing him out into the courtyard.

There was a kerfuffle of bodies in the square as they all struggled to stand clear of the house. The two other secretaries were frozen in shock with Iomhar at their sides, urging them to breathe. Doris stood at the back of the courtyard, inching away from the sight of the flames with her eyes wide and her bottom lip trembling. Her hands were buried in the woollen skirt of her dress, fidgeting with it incessantly.

One glance back to the house showed Kit that the fire was growing worse. The flames were licking the sides of the glass panes and the outside of the building was beginning to sink and sag. The wattle and daub that held the building together was contorting, until the building was barely recognisable, simply a deformed version of the structure it used to be.

Beale was coughing, heaving so badly that spittle was forming around the edges of his mouth. Kit turned him round, clapping him on the back in the attempt to help him clear his lungs. After a few slaps, he reached behind him, grabbing Kit's wrist and jerking her back in front of him.

"Wal…" he faded as he wheezed, struggling to breathe.

Kit grabbed his arms, helping the man to stand as he staggered on his feet in the courtyard, his heeled shoes wobbling on each rounded cobble. His spherical cheeks were blackened and the hair across his forehead was burnt, now a pale copper colour instead of its natural brown. "What?" she urged him to speak again, shaking his arms.

His body capitulated beneath him, down to the ground, and he landed loudly on his knees. Kit crouched down with him, nearly pulled over from how tightly he was holding onto her elbows.

"Beale, breathe through your nose," Kit pleaded with him. His bulbous face tightened as he closed his mouth and attempted to follow her instruction. He managed just a couple of breaths before he spluttered again. This time, he released Kit entirely and placed his hands on the courtyard beneath him, coughing against the cobbles.

Kit turned her gaze from the man to Iomhar nearby who was walking around the other secretaries. Laurence Tomson was the youngest of the three men and appeared the most shaken. He stood by Iomhar's side, his whole body trembling, while his narrow face darted around, unable to settle his gaze on just one thing. The older man beside him, Nicholas Faunt, was coughing too, though not quite as much as Beale. Out of the three men, Beale had to have been the one closest to the flames, evidenced by the blackened cheeks and burnt hair. In his current bent position, Kit could see the back of his doublet was scorched in places too.

"K-Kit," Beale said, his voice croaky as he reared up and grabbed her arm yet again. "He's in there. He's still in there." He managed to whisper the words, but it was so quiet that with the fire roaring behind them and the cracking of timber beams falling due to the heat, Kit wasn't convinced she'd heard him right.

"He's in there?" she asked, repeating his words. Beale nodded as he collapsed into coughing. She didn't need telling who. She released Beale and stood to her feet. From behind her, Doris's bony hand reached out and grabbed her arm.

"You cannot go in there, Kitty," Doris pleaded with her.

"Walsingham is still in there," Kit answered with strength in her voice. There was no chance she was going to stay outside and leave Walsingham to die in that fire. Doris opened her mouth to argue further with her, but before any sound could come there was a clatter of wood from the house.

"Get back!" Iomhar ordered, pushing Faunt and Tomson firmly in their backs and sending them hurrying across the courtyard. "Fetch the Constable. Get help, now," he took hold of the small ruff around Faunt's neck and used it to catapult him out of the courtyard. "The watchmen may have fire hooks and buckets." Faunt nodded though he still seemed unable to find his voice before he hurried under the archway, back onto the main road.

The courtyard was now filling with people from the other houses nearby. It was only a matter of time before the flames spread between the houses and destroyed them all.

Walsingham's house was beginning to collapse. The latest crack of timber had made one of the front windows buckle and the glass that had been in the window frame was warping, melting in the extreme heat.

Kit took a step toward the house, just as a hand took hold of her elbow. She expected it to be Doris again, but as she swung round, she was face-to-face with Iomhar.

"Do not even think about it," he warned, his voice was loud in order to be heard above the fire and his cheeks were reddened with the effort.

"I cannot let him die in there," Kit said, trying to shake him off her arm.

"Ye think I am going to let ye go in there and kill yourself? Forget it!" Iomhar snapped the words.

As Kit managed to brush him off her arm, she took a leap forward, ready to run for the door, but she found an arm around her waist, not only dragging her backwards but lifting her high in the air, so that she couldn't get any purchase on the ground with which to run and make an escape.

"Release me, Iomhar," she called to him, trying to pull his arm off her waist, but he merely clenched it tighter around her.

"Ye're not going in there."

"Let go of me," Kit ordered again, scratching at his arm to be released. When he refused to move and simply backed up carrying her, she changed tack. "A little forward, don't you think?" She looked back to him over her shoulder and gestured down at his arm around her.

"The situation warrants it," he said sharply.

There was a cry from within the house. A man's voice. Kit's eyes darted to the building just as the panicked chatter of the others around them faded. Everyone watched the building, searching the windows for any sign of Walsingham.

"He will die if you do not let me go," Kit pleaded with Iomhar.

"Ye will die if I let ye go in there."

"It's worth the risk," she insisted quietly.

With one swift movement, she brought up one of her legs that had been kicking wildly in the air and aimed between Iomhar's legs. He saw it coming as he tried to move away from her, but in his effort to do so, he released his arm around her. She landed back on the ground and ran away from him, heading straight for the house.

"Kit!" Iomhar bellowed her name, but she didn't look back. She just continued forward, running straight into the house.

The corridor had already changed since the last time she had been in. Though the fire hadn't yet reached this level, she could see above that the timber beams were warping and bending. The material between the beams was melting too and forming large globules of hot plaster.

She sprinted across the corridor, aiming for the same staircase she had taken before. With each step she took upstairs, the heat grew worse. It clawed at her skin, forming instant sweat bubbles along her forehead and down the centre of her back. As she opened the door into Walsingham's study, she was met with a wall of black smoke.

She bent forward, trying to find some clean air beneath the hovering smoke as she ran through the room.

Walsingham was not there, though it was increasingly difficult to see and be certain from the thick smoke. Out of the two doors set in the far side of the room, she headed for the one out of which Beale and the other secretaries had not appeared earlier.

One touch to the handle made her snatch her hand away from the metal, it was so hot it nearly scalded her skin through her leather glove. She lifted her hand to see the leather glove was burnt with the material gathering together at an awkward puckered angle.

She looked around, desperate for a way to open the door when a figure appeared beside her. Cloaked with a wet blanket over his head, she turned to see Iomhar's face peering out at her from beneath the blanket.

"What are you doing here?" she asked as he pulled her into his side and threw the blanket over her head as well. She knew the wet cover would help to keep off the flames for a little while, even if not for very long.

"Ye might as well have company when ye die," he explained mockingly as he used the damp blanket to take hold of the handle and turn it. One kick to the wood made it spring open and reveal the room beyond.

These were the back rooms of Seething Lane. Walsingham didn't usually let many people see this part of the house as it was his home, but Kit knew it well and she had a few ideas of where to find him. She led Iomhar forward, just as they met the worst part of the fire.

In the main sitting room, the once grand settle chair with the panelled back was alight with fire, each flame so tall that it practically licked the ceiling above it. The blaze had spread to circle the room, with not only the drapes alight, but wooden tables, chairs, and even a wolfskin rug too. With the fur burning fast, all that was left of the rug were the long white teeth set in the head of the wolf's jaw.

"He's not here," Iomhar called in her ear above the roar of the flames.

"His chamber is that way," Kit pointed out from the wet blanket toward a door that hadn't yet been consumed.

They hurried toward it, both bent down in the effort to not breathe in some of the black smoke. It felt a futile effort as each breath Kit took practically burnt her lungs. A deep breath was now impossible to take, and her chest stung with the pain of attempting to do it.

When they reached the doorway, Iomhar had to use the blanket to turn the door handle. When the wood swung open, they found Walsingham's chamber was doused in flames. It appeared to be where the centre of the fire was, for each wall was consumed in the orange blaze, with even his four-poster bed alight.

"Where is he?" Kit called, panicking as she flicked her head back and forth. She was struggling to breathe at all now and it wouldn't be long before she passed out.

"There," Iomhar pointed ahead.

Beneath a covering of black smoke that hung in the air, and between the blaze that had engulfed the bed and a wardrobe beyond, there was a figure on the floor, unconscious.

They hurried toward him with Kit darting her gaze around at the extent of destruction. The wardrobe that was inlaid with mother-of-pearl detailing, designed to mimic sailors on the high sea, was distorted beyond recognition. The mother-of-pearl stones were melting in white liquid beads that dripped to the wooden floor beneath their feet.

"Walsingham?" Iomhar called to the man as he grabbed his shoulder and rolled him over on the floor. His face was revealed, pale and as gaunt as Kit could remember it, only now the eyes were closed.

Kit reached for his neck with a scrambling hand as she rushed to find a pulse. "He's alive."

"Quick, get him over my shoulder," Iomhar ordered. They lifted the blanket off them and heaved Walsingham's unconscious body to his feet before trailing him over Iomhar's shoulder. Once in his grasp, Iomhar wrapped an arm around Walsingham's knees, holding him in place. "Ye take the blanket."

Kit wrapped the blanket back over her head as she followed Iomhar out of the chamber. The flames were growing worse. As they passed back through the sitting room, she had to dance around chairs that were ablaze, reaching the other door as fast as possible. The wet blanket was unable to keep out the heat or the smoke, but it stopped her own clothes from catching fire when she walked a little too close to one of the armchairs.

Back in Walsingham's study, the flames had died down. She kicked the door shut behind them before they ran to the staircase. Within minutes, they were back in the corridor on the lower floor and by the open door.

As they stepped out into the open courtyard, Kit coughed a few times, clearing her lungs of the black smoke as she threw off the wet blanket. Around her, constables and volunteers had arrived. In their droves, they were tossing fire hooks at the roof of the house, pulling off roof tiles and trying to break timbers to stop the blaze from spreading. Leather buckets of water were carried forward too, being passed back and forth between chains of people, before they were thrown at the flames that could be seen through the windows.

Iomhar laid Walsingham down in the centre of the courtyard as others gathered around him. Kit pushed to the front of the throng, elbowing Beale and Tomson to the side so she could bend down and see Walsingham's face. He wasn't moving, his closed eyes didn't even flicker, and his chest barely swelled up and down with his breath.

"He cannot die," Kit said, reaching out toward him and shaking his arm.

Iomhar looked at her once, but what his expression meant, she could not read. He pressed Walsingham firmly in the chest, over his heart.

At once, Walsingham's eyes shot open. He breathed in deeper, gasping with a sharp breath.

CHAPTER 11

Walsingham's breathing was shuddery as Kit bent her head forward, scarcely able to believe he had survived the flames.

"He's alive," Tomson said from beside Kit, turning his eyes to the heavens. "Thank God!" He placed his hands together in the prayer position.

"God had little to do with it," Beale's voice was heavy with relief from Kit's other side. "I think it had more to do with these two."

"God sent them," Tomson muttered sharply, earning Walsingham's gaze who turned his head on the cobbled ground. Kit knew very well how devout a man Walsingham was. Had he been able to breathe deeply enough to speak clearly, he probably would have agreed with Tomson.

"P … papers." He stammered out the word, lifting a hand and pointing back at the house.

"Your life is more important than them," Iomhar said, pushing his hand back down to the cobbles. "Rest now."

"No," Walsingham's word was muted as he coughed another time before he reached out, grasping straight for Kit. She was tussled forward as he grabbed the collar of her doublet and pulled her sharply down toward him, whispering in her ear, "Arsonist."

Her eyes widened as she flicked her head up, looking around the courtyard. Everyone that had gathered was joining the effort to save the building and put out the fire. There were different chains of people passing leather buckets of water between them, as the constables used fire hooks to expose the roof beams and pull down the joins between the buildings.

"Who?" she asked, waiting for Walsingham to answer.

"In my chamber," he wheezed with the effort to speak. "Found him." The sentences were short and breathy, all that he could manage. "Lad. Brown hair. Blue jerkin. Pheasant feather."

Kit sat straight, forcing Walsingham to release her as she looked around the people. From her low point on the ground, she couldn't see everyone's faces. "Iomhar, stand up," she urged, waving a hand at him.

"What?"

"Do it!" she begged, standing to her feet and hurrying around Walsingham. As Iomhar stood, his tall height set him above most of the others' heads. "Can you see a young man with brown hair, a blue jerkin, and a pheasant feather in his hat?" she whispered to him.

He jerked his head back and forth, scanning the courtyard. He did a double take, looking back towards the archway. "There." He pointed to the arch.

Kit followed his gesture, finding the lad that Walsingham had described. He was standing at the side of the archway, plainly not helping the chain of people who were passing buckets of water. He was watching the scene intently with his arms crossed in front of him.

"Who is he?" Iomhar asked.

"Take care of Walsingham," Kit said, choosing not to answer him as she pushed through the people and started heading straight toward the arsonist. It was difficult with the courtyard so busy that she had to knock shoulders, forcing people to let her through.

The closer she moved to the arsonist, the more she could trace the outline of his face. He was very young, barely out of his teen years, still with chubby cheeks and eyes that danced around the scene unfolding before him. There was a small smile on his lips.

He was pleased with what he had done.

The knowledge of it made Kit reach for one of the daggers in her belt and place her fingers firmly over the hilt. When all that separated her and the lad was one of the lines of people passing the buckets back and forth, he flicked his eyes toward her, widening when he realised he had been found.

"Do not run," Kit ordered him.

Despite the words, he did. He turned and ran back through the archway, pushing the people in the chain out of the way so that some collided with the stonework either side of them and others clung to each other, trying their best not to fall over.

Kit followed him. "My apologies!" she called to those he had pushed over as she sprinted after him.

Once back in the main road, it was not so crowded, giving the arsonist the freedom to run. He was faster than Kit, and though she chased him, pushing round carriages that lined the streets and groups of people gathered at the side of the road, she was beginning to lose ground on him. Her only chance of catching up was to take a chance on where he was heading and make a guess at a shortcut.

From their position in London, they were a short distance from the Thames and if he wished to make his escape from her then a boat was his best bet. To reach the Thames, he would have to pass by the Tower of London first. Kit had played in these back streets as a child when she tried to escape Walsingham's lessons; she knew every nook and tight corner there was to be found.

She turned sharply to the left, just as a narrow passageway appeared between two timber buildings, barely wide enough to fit a grown person, and certainly not wide enough for a horse or a cart to slip through. She ran through the gap, appearing out the far side of the street, before she took a sharp turn to the right, through a road that was supposedly a dead end. When she reached the far end that was bricked up, she took a path she used to take as a child, running through the streets when one of the intelligencers chased her, trying to get her to come back to her lessons.

Beside the wall that was flat and difficult to climb, there was a tall timber post with nails placed periodically up the side, set against the side of a building. She jumped at it, reaching for the ledge of the eaves of the floor above and latching her feet onto the nails to heave her body upward. Once she had hold of the upper floor, she placed her boots on the window frame and inched along until she reached the wall, stretching out and climbing on top of it.

"Who's that?" a voice called from behind her.

"What's he doing?" another cried.

She ignored all the cries and jumped down the other side of the wall, landing firmly on her feet in a crouched position. She stood straight and sprinted down the road, heading straight for Lower Thames Street that came out beside the Tower of London.

Ahead of her, between the thatched and tiled roofs of the timber buildings, the Tower emerged. The white stone turrets of the keep dominated the skyline for miles around, and in front of it, the tall battlement walls stood imposingly, looking down on all the people that scurried past.

As Kit exited her lane, she landed against the white Tower wall, using both hands against the surface to halt her fast speed and help her to turn, heading down the road. Up ahead, she could see where Lower Thames Street appeared, and where she had to pray the arsonist would show himself at any moment.

Horse-drawn carts passed through the road, following each other in a neat line, all aiming towards Sugar Quay, the small dockyard beyond the Tower that would take them out into the Thames. Kit's eyes darted between the carts, searching every face that walked past, until a lad appeared, sporting a pheasant feather in his hat, with a bright blue jerkin.

She had found him.

He was walking, apparently confident he had escaped. She ran toward him, using the element of surprise to tackle him to the floor. When she collided with him, shouts went up from nearby.

"Get the constable!" an elderly lady screeched.

"It's just a fight, who's your money on?" a middle-aged man laughed as he walked past.

Kit pinned the lad down to the ground with her knees against his chest, refusing to let him move. She'd knocked his hat off that was soon trodden on by passing horses. He looked up at her, breathing heavily with the fear evident in the frantic movement of his eyes and the way that his hands scrambled to be free. Kit took hold of his wrists and forced them together, down at his side.

"You set the house on fire," she seethed, feeling the anger and venom so strong in her voice that her body shook with the words. "Why?"

"Get off me!" the lad cried, desperately trying to wriggle out of her grasp.

"Tell me why you set the place on fire, and I will let you go," she said, not truly having any intention of doing so.

"Why isn't someone getting a constable?" the elderly lady nearby screamed again, before shouting for help.

"What a good idea," Kit acknowledged, looking back down at the lad. "We will tell the constable you set the fire.

Attempted murder with men and a woman inside. They could hang you for that."

"I'll tell you why, just get off me," the lad pleaded, his face and neck reddening as he struggled to be free.

"Did someone tell you to do it?" she asked, pushing against his wrists harder.

"Yes."

"Who?" she demanded an answer.

Before any more could be said, he heaved his body upward. Kit had been unprepared for it and felt her body roll away from him across the muddy ground. She scrambled to her knees, just as the lad jumped to his feet and took off in a run, back across the road toward the Tower.

Kit wasn't far behind him this time, able to run without falling back as his pace was inhibited by the sheer number of people and carts heading toward Sugar Quay. Her legs burned with the effort of running for so long once more, but she ignored the burn. This lad had followed someone's orders in the effort to kill Walsingham. Someone had to pay for that crime.

As the two of them rounded the white stone walls of the tower, the arsonist's pace was becoming increasingly slowed, until he could go no further, finding himself faced with a line of carts, all waiting in a queue to reach the quayside. He turned back, his eyes widening when he found Kit so close behind him.

He darted to the side, trying to circle her and travel back along the wall of the Tower, but she saw the movement and followed, tackling him this time so he fell flat against the white wall.

"Do not move," she warned. She placed her forearm across his chest and shoulders, fixing him firmly in place. With the other hand she pulled the dagger free of her belt and placed the tip against his chest, using her body to mask the dagger from view of anyone looking their way.

The lad instantly stilled, tipping his head back and closing his eyes in fear of it being used.

"Tell me who gave you the order," she insisted, "and I will let you go." She was already planning to take him to the nearest constable and have him charged for his crime, but it worked well as a bargaining tool. "Tell me!" she urged again, pressing forward threateningly with the dagger.

"She said the house would be empty," the lad's words sputtered. "I-I swear I didn't know there would be someone in there."

"You must have seen there were people in there," Kit hissed with a seething whisper, not remotely willing to forgive the arsonist. He had nearly caused the death of two people that were dear to her, Walsingham and Doris. "Yet you set the fire anyway."

"By that point, it was already done; I couldn't put it out!" he cried, and dived, trying to get away from her.

Kit moved the dagger and laid it against his arm, threatening to cut if he moved again. "Tell me who gave you the order. Who is this 'she'?"

"L … Lady Ruskin," he said with a stammer.

Kit's body stilled. She had just stolen a letter written from a Lord Egbert Ruskin and now a Lady Ruskin had ordered an attack on Walsingham. Was it possible that Lady Ruskin was this number Eighty-Two? In her frozen state, she was not ready for when the lad struck back again.

He lashed out at her wrist, forcing her to drop the dagger. She snatched it up from the floor, but by the time she had done it, he had wriggled free of her grasp and was running away down the street.

Slowly, she placed the dagger back in her belt, catching her breath as she stared after his retreating figure. There was little point in chasing after him anymore as she had the information she needed.

"Lady Ruskin," she murmured to herself.

When Kit reached Seething Lane, the fire had been mostly put out. Though the flames had spread to the two houses either side, none of the houses were destroyed completely and a constable confirmed that only the living quarters in Walsingham's house had been truly affected. His study had fortunately escaped most of the damage, though part of the roof and the outer walls had been destroyed in the effort to stop the spread.

"Let me go back in," Walsingham said from where he was sat up on the courtyard ground, still breathing heavily.

"Ye're in nay fit state," Iomhar dismissed the idea with folded arms where he stood over him. Kit was by his side, chewing her lip in thought. "We need to get ye a physician."

"I'll be fine." Walsingham made an attempt to stand before he gave up and fell back down on the cobbles. He lifted his hands that were scalded in burn marks, creating little blackened bubbles across his palms.

Kit looked away, unable to bear the sight of the man's pain.

"You cannot go in yet until we can assure the building is safe," the constable warned. "For now, you must wait here." He walked away, heading toward the volunteers that were slowly wandering away from the courtyard.

"I'll arrange a physician," Faunt said, before he too walked back in the direction of the archway.

On the other side of Walsingham and a little distance away, the two other secretaries were sat down. Beale was wheezing, but Tomson merely stared at his feet, his body still and his lips permanently parted in a state of shock.

"Did you find him?" Walsingham asked, cracking his back as he turned to face Kit. She nodded, just once. "And?"

"He gave a name," she whispered, so only Walsingham and Iomhar could hear her.

"Who was he?" Iomhar asked, turning to give her his attention. "The boy ye chased?"

"He started the fire," Kit explained, before crouching down at Walsingham's side to make it easier for him to hear her.

Iomhar bent down too, mirroring her stance.

"He did not deny it?" Walsingham asked, his eyebrows lifting in alarm. Well, what was left of them. The once greying eyebrows were now singed and mostly missing, resembling rat's fur more than human hair.

"No, he didn't," Kit said, thinking on what the lad had revealed in his desperation to be free of her. "He just ran."

"I saw him," Walsingham explained, coughing. Iomhar lifted a hand to clap his back, helping to clear his lungs. In response, Walsingham recoiled away. "My back is too old to bear that kind of strength, my friend." Iomhar winced by way of an apology, as Walsingham breathed clearly through his nose. "I heard noises in my chamber and went to investigate. He'd used a tinder box to set the bed on fire. I dived for him, but my body is not what it once was. He only hit me once and it sent me down to the floor."

"We thought you cried out?" Kit watched his face closely. The gaunt face that usually held an impassive expression was far from impassive now.

He stared down at his crumpled body and the feet that were crossed and bent beneath him. "That was later. I tried to get out of the room," he explained, not meeting her gaze. "I tripped on something, then all I remember is … black."

Kit tried to hide her shudder at the words, but she could feel Iomhar watching her all the same.

"Everyone is all right?" Walsingham asked, looking to where Doris and the other secretaries were sat.

"Aye," Iomhar confirmed, moving to his knees. "We'll need to find ye somewhere to stay."

"We need to find somewhere to move the papers."

"The papers are not worth your life."

"That is where you are wrong," Walsingham said with surprising strength for a man who had been so close to death. He turned his almost black eyes on Iomhar, glowering. "Some of those papers *are* worth my life. They are papers of state. They pertain to the queen herself, and they relate to every commission I have ever ordered. There are some papers in there that are more valuable than any other life in this city. They must be moved. They have to be protected."

Kit felt the flicker of a smile before it vanished. Walsingham's dedication to putting the good of the country before his own life was something she had witnessed repeatedly. Only today, he had very nearly lost his life in the cause. "Then we will move the papers too," Kit spoke with feeling.

Walsingham nodded and rested his weight back on his hands, before he remembered the burns and lifted them sharply away. He stared at the burn marks, his fingers trembling. "What did he say to you, Kit? When you caught up with the lad, what did he say?" he asked, not looking up from his hands.

"He said he was ordered to do it by a woman," she revealed, before turning her eyes to Iomhar, watching for his reaction. "A Lady Ruskin."

CHAPTER 12

After they had moved Walsingham to temporary lodgings in Fenchurch Street and a physician went to attend him, Kit was given the responsibility of packing up his papers. Though Beale was also permitted to look over them, when anyone else had offered to help, Walsingham had staunchly refused. Even Iomhar was only allowed to carry the chests of paperwork, but he was not authorised to be anywhere near the papers themselves. Faunt and Tomson were particularly irked that their master didn't seem to trust them.

"Why ye?" Iomhar asked from where he sat by the open window in the study. All the windows had been flung open to let the smell of smoke pass, yet it still hung in the air, cloying at Kit's lungs.

She looked up from the scrolls she had gathered to see Iomhar sat in the window frame with his arms folded. Beside her, Beale was packing up the papers too, though he kept pausing to cough, showing he had not yet recovered from his ordeal in the fire.

"He trusts me," Kit said with a smile, before dropping the scrolls into a chest. "I work for him, after all."

"I work for him too," Iomhar reminded her. "Your argument does not stretch very far."

"He trusts me not to *look* at the files." Kit didn't glance back to him this time. She pulled out a chair and clambered to stand on the seat, reaching for the shelves right at the very top of the bookcase and pulling out flattened papers.

"Why?" Iomhar asked.

Kit didn't answer straight away as her hands closed around the papers. She was thinking of the last time she had been so close to Walsingham's work.

She had been just a child, about ten years old or so, as close as they could guess her age, anyway. In her desperation to avoid some of her lessons, for she had grown weary from the long hours of working from eight in the morning to eight in the evening, she had crept out of the study room placed in the attic and gone hunting in search of Walsingham.

Her teacher at the time was a very old intelligencer who had fallen asleep in his chair, his snoring so loud that he hadn't heard her open the door.

When she had found Walsingham's study, empty and without Walsingham, she had climbed into his chair to find the desk covered in paperwork. With her legs bundled underneath her, she had begun to read the parchments. The next thing she could remember was Walsingham appearing in the room, shouting at her so loudly that her eardrums shook with each word.

"You are never to read my papers. Is that understood?"

When he tipped her out of the chair, she apologised repeatedly. She had also made a promise, never to look at his papers again, for the rest of her life.

"Kit?" Iomhar's voice brought her back to the moment.

"He just knows I wouldn't look at them. That's all," she said, happy to keep the memory to herself.

She collected the papers as quickly as she could, gathering them together then dropped them into one of the chests that were held open nearby. No more was said as she went about her work, and Beale merely continued to cough every few seconds. When Kit lifted her eyes from her work, she frequently found Iomhar watching her across the room, still bearing a frown that suggested some suspicion. She chose to ignore him and not comment on it.

"Everything is ready," she said, once two chests had been filled with paperwork.

"Am I allowed within a yard of ye now?" Iomhar asked with clear cynicism.

"I didn't give the order, Walsingham did." She fastened the lock on one of the chests, turning the key in the brass lock with precision before pocketing it. As Iomhar walked toward her and heaved the chest up into his arms, she hurried out of the room, leading the way, determined to get back to Walsingham as quickly as she could.

"He will be well, Kit," Iomhar assured her as she stepped through the door of Walsingham's lodgings. She stopped in the doorway of the timber-frame building, scuffing her boots on the stone floor. "Ye do not need to worry."

"I'm not worried," she brushed it off, tartly, glancing back at him over her shoulder. He had just jumped down off the cart that had pulled up in the narrow street and was staring at her. He raised his eyebrows at her before he fixed his attention to the cart and lifted the chests into the house.

Kit turned in the entrance hall, hurrying forward through a corridor and toward a set of stairs in the centre of the building. Built of mahogany wood with the balustrades carved into oak leaves, it towered above her. After one floor, the steps split into two different staircases, leading to different wings of the house.

"Kitty, there you are!" Doris's voice appeared from the top of the staircase. Kit craned her neck to look up from the bottom step, finding Doris arching her head over the banister to look down at her. "What a to-do this is."

"What did the physician say?" Kit asked as she hurried up the stairs, taking them two at a time.

"He is still with him," Doris explained, shaking her head with evident worry. "He's been in there so long. My heart is beating faster with the fear of what he will say." She tapped her palm to her chest repeatedly to illustrate her words as Kit reached the landing she was on.

"He has said nothing yet?" Kit asked in disbelief as her eyes flitted around the closed doors beside them, wondering which one Walsingham was behind.

"Nothing," Doris reiterated, lowering her voice as she grabbed hold of Kit's arm. "But the master keeps mumbling something."

"Mumbling what?"

"I do not know," Doris hissed, before glancing over her shoulder, apparently fearful of being overheard. "It is as though he is speaking in tongues. A man who is partly there and partly not. I am not sure what he said, but I heard your name more than once."

Kit felt her body freeze beneath Doris's clutch. "Why would he say my name?" she asked.

"I do not know, Kitty," Doris said, shaking her head.

"Where is he?" Kit gestured to the closed doors, each one was made of darkened oak and etched with different patterns, some with Celtic knots, others with the Tudor rose.

Before Doris could answer, the door at the far end of the corridor opened and the physician stepped out.

The elderly man was holding a handkerchief to his forehead, dabbing away some sweat.

"Mr Thibault?" Kit called to him, crossing the corridor as quickly as she could with Doris still on her tail. The man lifted his chin to see them clearly, peering at them through squinted eyes and above a bushy white moustache. "I take it you have finished your examination of Walsingham?"

"I have," he nodded. "Oh, it is grave, grave indeed," he muttered before closing the door behind him. "Have his family been sent for?"

"They have," Doris answered. "They are at his family estate. I wouldn't expect them to arrive until tomorrow morning."

"Well, at least they are on their way," the physician murmured.

"What are your thoughts?" Kit asked.

"Once he was brought here, he collapsed from the pain and the coughing," Mr Thibault said, looking between the two of them. "I have administered laudanum which has helped, but his words are muddled. It is as though his mind is struggling to calm itself."

Kit glanced at Doris, remembering what she had said about Walsingham mumbling her name. "He will recover though, will he not?" she asked, remembering how unwell Walsingham had looked when he was sat in the courtyard.

"I should think so," the physician spoke with a kind of wariness in his tone. "The burns on his hands are the worst and he keeps coughing up black ash. Should he live through the night, I'd say he'll live for many years yet."

"Thank our Lord," Doris said, casting her eyes to heaven, as Kit turned her attention to the closed door.

"I must visit other patients, but I would recommend he is nursed through the night and watched."

"We'll do that," Kit declared without hesitation.

"Are you sure?" Doris asked, turning her head to Kit. "Are you not needed elsewhere?"

"I'll stay," Kit affirmed with conviction. "I'm not going anywhere."

The night was a difficult one. The heat beyond the windows was clamouring, reminding Kit of being in the fire. Even by throwing open the windows to let in some air, there was hardly any breeze at all. In the end, Doris tried to bring some coolness to Walsingham by waving blank pieces of parchment in front of him, as Kit wet a damp cloth and pressed it to his forehead.

Their only company for the night was a single lonely tallow candle placed by Walsingham's bed. It sat within its iron frame mounting, sinking further and further down as the flame burnt through the hours. The feeble light it offered in the room did little, except casting Walsingham's gaunt face into an apricot hue. His pale pallor was warmed by the effect, as his lips moved, sometimes soundlessly, sometimes muttering words.

"Why does he talk so?" Kit asked as Doris moved to sit in a chair in the far corner of the room.

"Mr Thibault said it was the effect of the laudanum," Doris sighed as she shifted, trying to get comfortable in the settle chair. "He will not have control of his mind for some time."

Kit nodded as Doris rested her head back, letting her eyes close. Where Doris could find sleep, Kit found the mere idea impossible. She sat by Walsingham's bed with her eyes darting between the hollowed cheeks and the bandaged hands. She would not find peace until he woke properly and cast off this strange muttering.

As the candle beside the bed continued to burn down and Doris's soft snoring filled the room, Kit sat back in her own box chair, her mind drifting to the fire itself and the lad that had ran from her.

Lady Ruskin.

The memory of the woman's name burned strongly in her mind. It was too much of a coincidence for the name Ruskin to appear twice in the space of a day. She leaned toward a sideboard where she had placed her leather gloves and slipped out the parchment she had hidden within the lining. It was the decoded letter from Lord Egbert Ruskin. She re-read the note, trying at length to see if there was anything she had missed when Walsingham's muttering grew louder.

"Cannot know. Can never know..." he mumbled, then thrashed his head from side to side on the flat wool pillow. The abrupt animation made Kit replace the note in her glove and lean toward Walsingham. "She can never know," he said again as his bandaged hands pulled at the blanket around him.

"Walsingham?" Kit whispered.

His head flicked toward her, though his eyes remained firmly closed. "She cannot know. You cannot tell her."

"Who cannot know what?" she asked, watching his face as the cheeks above the scraggy beard twitched in his mad sleep.

"She will find out. She will know the truth."

"What truth?" Kit whispered, but still she had no reply.

Walsingham just continued to mutter the same things over and over again, with his head turned toward her. She was about to reason that he was simply having some kind of nightmare when her name fell from his lips.

"Kit..." he muttered.

"Am I the woman you are talking of?" she asked, glancing to Doris to check she wasn't listening before pulling on the bed sheet around Walsingham. "Am I the one you're speaking of?"

He didn't answer her question. His lips fell still, and the muttering stopped completely. As he lapsed into a peaceful sleep, she sat back in her chair once more, unsure what to make of his ramblings.

CHAPTER 13

"How is he?"

A voice woke Kit. She started in her seat, whipping her head round to the doorway to find Iomhar leaning on the doorframe.

"Did you break into this house too?" she asked, bleary-eyed as she yawned.

"I did not need to, Doris let me in," he explained, turning his gaze back to the bed. "How is he?"

"He woke once, about an hour ago," Kit said, cracking her back as she stood to her feet. "He seemed quite coherent then. If what the physician said about him making it through the night is true, then he should be fine from now on." She glanced toward the windows, seeing the sunlight streaming through. The sight of it made her sigh with relief, for Walsingham was to live.

"We need to talk," Iomhar beckoned her forward. Kit moved to the doorway just as he stepped beyond it. Once in the corridor, he glanced up and down before lowering his voice. "If ye are right in that the arsonist was told to do it by a Lady Ruskin, then this is more organised than I thought."

"I presume this Lady Ruskin is related to Lord Egbert Ruskin?" Kit asked, watching Iomhar's face for a reaction.

"He is married," he spoke slowly. "If I were to place a wager on it, I'd say the Lady Ruskin your arsonist spoke of is his wife."

"You know he is married?" she asked, knitting her eyebrows together.

"I have made it me business to know much of Lord Ruskin."

"Why?" Her word was a little sharp as Iomhar turned his gaze away from her, his face set rigid.

"The reason why is not important. What is important is that the Ruskins are involved in this plot," he spoke quietly. "I know Lord Ruskin will do anything for Mary Stuart. I would expect his wife is nay less capable, especially if she ordered the fire."

"Why order the fire?" Kit asked. "It does not make sense. An attack on Walsingham is an attack on our queen's privy council. The crime would be a death sentence, why would she risk that?"

"Maybe she was not so bothered about seeing Walsingham dead, but more bothered about destroying those papers he values so much," Iomhar said, leaning on the wall. "After all, Lord Ruskin's letter was stolen, was it not? Where would they presume someone to take a letter like that?"

"Ah…" Kit realised, hanging her head. "They thought we would take the letter straight to Walsingham's door, so they sought to destroy it within his walls."

"It's as good a guess as any," Iomhar shrugged with the words.

"What letter?" a third voice joined them. The sound of it made Kit dart her head round in the doorway to see Walsingham was sat up in his bed, leaning awkwardly on his hands and the pillows. "Kit…" his voice was weak. "What letter are you speaking of?"

"Two nights ago, we intercepted a letter from the plotters at the alehouse in Blackfriars," she explained, walking back to the bed with Iomhar close behind her. "It was being carried by a man called Graham Fraser."

"Loyal to Mary Stuart," Iomhar added.

"Yes, I have heard the name," Walsingham said weakly as he tried to rest back against the bed head. With each breath he took, his shoulders lifted and fell, suggesting the breaths took a lot of effort.

"Kit decoded the letter." Iomhar went to the pocket where he had placed the letter, but when he found it empty, his eyes widened.

"You do not need to panic," Kit said as she rounded the bed, reaching for the sideboard where she had placed her gloves and hidden the letter. She retracted it and held it high in the air to be seen.

"Ye stole it?" Iomhar's eyebrows raised.

"Stole is not accurate," she began slowly as she passed it over to Walsingham to read. "I merely … retrieved it."

"Without me knowing," Iomhar pointed out, tilting his head to the side. "Sounds like stealing to me."

"Stop bickering," Walsingham uttered weakly as he flattened the letter, trying to read it. "Lord Egbert Ruskin." He repeated the name from the bottom of the code. "Well, that is hardly going to be a coincidence."

"Last night, I did some asking around," Iomhar said, pulling out one of the high-backed box chairs and positioning it to sit beside Walsingham's bed. "Lady Ruskin has taken a house in London for the year, in Temple Bar. Her husband is not with her."

"Then *she* brought this letter to London?" Walsingham asked.

"Aye, it would seem so," Iomhar agreed with a slow nod. "I watched the house into the early hours of this morning. She had many visitors."

"Was Graham Fraser amongst them?" Kit asked as she took the letter back from Walsingham.

"Nay," Iomhar answered, "I did not recognise any of them, but those that did visit her came at night because they did not want to be seen there during the day."

"Always a good sign," Walsingham said, before a violent cough wracked his body. He tipped forward, retching into his hand. Kit snatched up one of the linen cloths Doris had deposited on a table nearby and thrust it forward. Walsingham coughed into the rag for a few minutes before he sat back and let the cloth fall down to the bed.

Kit picked up the corner of the cloth between her fingers, staring open mouthed at the black marks that were left smattered across the white linen. One glance at Iomhar showed he bore the same look of worry. She tossed the cloth onto the side.

"We need to know what it is they are meeting about," Walsingham's voice was hoarse and croaky.

"She was delivered a letter this morning. I may have opened it before she had a chance to," Iomhar leaned forward in his seat. "She has been invited to an evening dinner at a house in Cheapside, owned by Sir Horace Jacobs."

"Jacobs?" Walsingham sneered, his body tipping forward jerkily. With the sudden animation, he began to cough again. Kit offered another clean rag, but he waved her away. "Stop fussing."

"Who is Jacobs?" Iomhar asked.

"He is a pretender," Walsingham said with disgust. "I am sure of it, though I have never found evidence of it. At court, he is friendly to our queen, but I have always suspected he sympathises with Mary Stuart. If Lady Ruskin is going to a dinner at his house, I'd warrant the topic of conversation would be very interesting indeed."

"I could get an invitation?" Iomhar offered, sitting straight in his seat. "By listening into their discussions, it may give us something."

"That is too much of a risk," Walsingham said, leaning back on the headboard. "If anyone at that party has seen you before, then they'll know you would not be loyal to Mary Stuart's cause."

"How would they know that?" Kit asked, looking between the two men.

"Iomhar has something of a reputation back in the Scottish court," Walsingham spoke quickly.

"What did you do?" Kit turned her attention to Iomhar.

"Now is not the time for that story." He turned his eyes away from her.

"What we need is someone they would not recognise," Walsingham said, shifting his gaze to Kit. "Someone who can fake a Scottish accent and with the right false identity, could be taken in as one of their own."

"Kit's accent is not quite convincing enough," Iomhar refuted boldly as he stood to his feet.

"I convinced you, did I not?" She folded her arms as she stared at him across the bed.

"Barely," he remarked before turning back to Walsingham. "Sending Kit in would be too dangerous."

"What else would you have us do, hmm?" Walsingham's voice was surprisingly sharp as he sounded more like his usual self. "Do nothing and our queen could be dead within a fortnight. Kit." He turned his eyes to her. "We will give you a false identity and organise an invitation to the party. You are to watch and listen only, then report what you have heard. Agreed?"

"Why only watch and listen? I could do more —"

"That is an order, Kit," Walsingham interrupted.

"Very well," she shifted between her feet. "I will watch and listen only."

"Good," Walsingham said and relaxed back onto the pillows.

"Sir, your family are here to see you," Doris's voice came from the doorway.

As Iomhar left the room, Kit reluctantly followed behind him, though she kept glancing back at Walsingham's dilapidated figure in the bed.

His wife and daughter had arrived with panicked cries as they ran into the room. As the daughter pushed passed Kit, she was shoved to the side and the door was closed firmly in her face.

"Are ye all right?" Iomhar asked, standing further back in the corridor.

"I am fine." She tried to feign a smile as she walked past him. "He has his real family with him now," she muttered under her breath so that Iomhar couldn't hear her.

"Can I come in yet?" Iomhar asked impatiently, later that afternoon.

"Definitely not," Kit called back to the closed door in her attic room. "You are an impatient man."

"In the name of the wee man and all his followers. I have never known anyone to take so long to get dressed. Aye, it's a wonder ye can get dressed at all in the morning," Iomhar's amused voice came through the closed door.

"In case it has escaped your notice, men's clothes are significantly easier to put on than women's. So, until the day you have to put on a dress, you can keep your opinions on how long it takes to yourself," Kit said, turning away from the door and looking to the mirror closest to her.

"Do ye need a hand?" Iomhar called with a note of intrigue in his voice.

She ignored the teasing and held the corset closed tighter around her body. "Break through my lock again and you'll find me waiting for you with that dagger in my hand," she said, flicking her gaze back to the closed door.

Iomhar's laugh was his only reply.

Kit returned her focus to the mirror, struggling with the clothes. She so infrequently wore women's clothes that the effort to put them on was a great task, especially without the aid of a maid to help her. She had a standard linen smock as an underdress, followed by stockings that were held up high around her thighs and a corset that laced at the front.

"It's too hot," she murmured, fanning her cheeks to try and calm the reddening that was spreading across her skin. Moving to the window, she flung it open before breathing in the cool air. Deciding against the stockings for they only increased her temperature, she rolled them back down and tossed them to the side. Next came the hooped skirt with the farthingale.

"Ye done now?" Iomhar called.

"You have no patience at all, do you?" she remarked as she loosened the laces to hold the skirt around her waist and stepped into the skirt. The hoops hung about her ankles, bobbing up and down with the weight attached to the fabric.

"It is limited when the queen could be facing death at any moment."

"Then you go and dress up as a woman. Maybe you will be faster than me."

"I think ye will be more convincing as a woman."

"I am a woman!" she pointed out. She turned round in the room so quickly that her large skirt sent the chair closest to her flying.

"I noticed," Iomhar chuckled. "What was that noise?"

"It was me suffering with this ridiculous skirt," she huffed, ignoring the fallen chair as she reached for the petticoat and kirtle she had pulled out of her wardrobe. "It is like walking round with a permanent shield attached to my body."

"I would have thought ye liked that."

"Hmm, true," she acknowledged, before reaching for the gown. She was already struggling to move from the sheer weight of material draped across her body, but the dress added to the problem. Heavy and made of soft silks, it was not the most refined dress that could be found in court or in the upper class, but it was well-made and of recent fashion, suggesting its wearer had some affluence. It was a gift from Walsingham a while ago. He had bestowed it on her for if such an event as this took place where it might be needed.

She pulled the gold silk up over the farthingale and the petticoat before slipping her arms through the short sleeves. Once she had tied the dress in place, she attached the frilled collar that fitted to the dress, opting for the high ruff-like collar that left the front of her neck exposed, rather than choosing the full ruff.

"Are ye nearly there?" Iomhar called again from the closed door. "I think my beard is greying waiting for ye to change."

"I'm just about there," she said, turning her gaze to the mirror. Before her eyes, she had transformed herself into a womanly figure. The corset and frilled golden silk of the dress flattered her, being cinched at the waist before flowing down to the ground. The white collar contrasted her auburn hair too, making her stand out all the more. "I do not look like me anymore."

"Let's see then," Iomhar called to her.

She turned, ready to walk to the door and open it when the door moved. Just as before, Iomhar lifted the door slightly within its frame, popping it out of its lock and swinging it open. He stood in the doorway, falling still as his eyes landed on her.

"I do not think you know the meaning of being polite," she huffed. "You should wait for me to answer the door."

"Ye were taking too long," he said, though his eyes were no longer on her face. He was looking at the dress instead, his eyes darting back and forth across her figure.

"You do not need to stare so intently, you know." She looked away from him and turned back to the mirror. "Is something wrong with the gown?" she asked, twirling back and forth in an effort to see the back of the dress in the mirror.

"Nay … nothing wrong at all." Iomhar's voice had turned deeper, and she looked back to him, seeing him still rather dumbstruck in the doorway.

"Is something wrong with you?" she asked.

"Nay." He seemed to shake himself out of his bewilderment as he walked into the room. "I just have not seen ye dress so before. Ye look quite…"

"Quite what?" She narrowed her eyes at him.

He opened his mouth to answer then closed it again with a smirk. "Never mind," he said. "For one thing though, ye look warm."

"I'm on fire," she answered, waving her hands at her face again.

"Aye, your cheeks are nearly as red as your hair."

"You're lucky I do not yet have my daggers on me," she said, as she walked past him, heading to pick up some shoes from the bottom of the wardrobe. She slipped her feet into small, heeled court shoes, black in colour and rimmed with gold thread before turning to face Iomhar. "There. Will I be convincing as a proper lady do you think?"

"I would say aye," he smiled, folding his arms. "If ye did not look so uncomfortable wearing those clothes."

"They really are insufferable," she sighed and grabbed the skirt before moving back to the mirror and pinning her hair into place.

"If ye are to be convincing, ye still need to work on your accent."

"What do ye mean? I think my Scottish accent is really rather good," she said, adapting her accent and eyeing him in the reflection of the mirror as he appeared behind her.

"It's not bad, but your choice of words is poor. 'Really rather good'?" he repeated her words, making her pause as she fussed with her hair. "That is as English as it gets. Choose more Scottish phrases."

"Aye, such as in the name of the wee man," she declared with a smile, remembering the silly phrase he had used before.

"Aye, that's a good one," he agreed. "Do not speak unless ye are spoken to, just in case. I think that is the best bet. Ye are to watch and listen only, that is Walsingham's instruction."

Kit didn't comment on the order for she already thought it a foolish one. Surely by merely being there as an observer she was unlikely to discover very much?

"Kit." Iomhar's voice was surprisingly sharp.

"Yes?" she said, lapsing back into her English accent.

"Promise me that is all ye are going to do." His gaze was unblinking as he stared at her in the mirror. She looked away from him and focused on pinning her short hair up a little. "Kit?"

"That is the order I was given," she confirmed.

"That is not a promise." His voice was tart and full of warning, but she merely ignored him.

"There? How is that?" she asked, releasing her hair. "Will I be convincing now?" She turned back to face him, startled to find his face deadly serious. "What is wrong?"

"I do not like this," he spoke emphatically.

"You do not like what? Me in a dress or using a Scottish accent?"

"Neither of those things," he said, his voice loud. He breathed deeply, clearly making the effort to control his temper. "I do not like ye going into this dinner without anyone else. Ye are going alone into a room where we already know one person is sympathetic to an assassination of Queen Elizabeth. What if ye are walking into an entire room full of such people? It is too dangerous."

"And you think I am not capable enough to handle it?" she asked, feeling the burn of his words.

"I did not say that, what I said was —"

"I know what you said." She moved past him, heading to the side of the room where her daggers were resting on a table with a leather garter. "I am more capable than you give me credit."

"It is not about that."

"Then what is it about?" she asked, turning round as she placed one of the daggers into the garter. She found Iomhar staring back at her, his arms still folded, and his brow furrowed.

"If Lady Ruskin did order that fire, then she has already risked many lives for the sake of destroying a letter. What do ye think she will do to ye if she suspects ye for a single moment?"

"She will not suspect me."

"Ye cannot be certain of that."

"Trust me." Kit tried to summon a smile to ward off the sudden worry his words had caused.

"Trust *me*," Iomhar said, matching her tone. "If Lady Ruskin is anything like her husband, then she is not to be trusted."

"How do you know Lord Ruskin?" Kit asked for what she felt had to be the third time that day. Iomhar still didn't answer her, he just stayed quiet. "Right, I see you still will not tell me. Now, turn away."

"Turn away?" Iomhar asked.

"I am hardly going to lift my skirt and tie this to my leg with you watching, am I?" Kit said tartly, holding the leather garter high in the air for him to see. To her surprise, a smile broke through Iomhar's countenance, before turning round. "Stop smiling like that," she warned him. Once his back was turned, she lifted her skirt to attach the garter to her thigh, listening to Iomhar's laughter, though her mind was much more on what he had said about Lady Ruskin.

There was a chance she was about to walk into a building she might not walk out of again if she put a foot wrong.

CHAPTER 14

"Ye ready for this?" Iomhar asked as he took Kit's hand and helped her down from the carriage. In the darkness that had fallen, outside of Sir Horace Jacobs house there were torches of flames fixed to the walls, casting orange and red hues around them. The light fell on only half of Iomhar's face as the other half was covered in the shadow from the hat that he had pulled low, to disguise himself as her servant.

"Stop worrying," she whispered to him as her feet touched the cobbled ground. "All will be well." Yet in the torchlight, she could see he was not convinced.

"Ah, ye must be Mrs Katherine Allaway?" a Scottish accent called to her from the doorway.

Kit tried to release Iomhar's hand when she found he didn't let go straight away. His fingers clamped around hers instead, holding her in place.

"Welcome to my home!" the voice boomed from the doorway just as a middle-aged man appeared, dressed in such finery that he resembled a peacock more than a human being. His ruff was so large, it was almost as wide as his rounded belly that was covered in a bright blue doublet and laced with white embroidery and pearls.

Kit didn't have time to tell Iomhar to let go of her. Instead, she slyly stepped on his foot with her heel and pressed down. He muttered a curse under his breath as he released her hand and stepped back.

"Good evening," Kit said, hurrying forward and offering a curtsy. She adopted her Scottish accent and was careful to add inflections Iomhar had been teaching her as they travelled from her lodgings to the dinner. "Ye must be Sir Horace Jacobs."

"That I am." The man took her hand and kissed the back. "I must say it was a pleasure to receive your husband's letter to hear of your arrival in London. I was only too happy to extend the invitation for tonight when I received it."

Kit was pleased to hear their ruse had worked well. To get her into the dinner, Iomhar had written a letter to Sir Horace, posing as a Highland soldier who was well-known for his support of Mary Stuart, his name was Captain Fergus Allaway. He had spoken of his new wife's recent arrival in London and a wish for her to make friends amongst like-minded people in the city, hopeful that Sir Horace could help. A day later, the invitation for Kit to join the dinner had arrived.

"Ye are very kind." She smiled just as Sir Horace looped her arm with his. "I am afraid I am new to the city, and I know very few people."

"Then allow me to escort ye to the dinner and introduce ye to my friends, who nay doubt will soon by yours too," Sir Horace said warmly, before turning his attention to the doorway and steering her through.

Kit had just enough time to glance over her shoulder to see Iomhar watching her from under the brim of his hat before the doors were closed, blocking him from view.

"This evening is an intimate dinner with my closest friends," Sir Jacob said, patting her hand on his arm. "So I am certain ye will find them good company." A servant opened a door leading into a large chamber.

The room that opened before Kit had been decorated grandly for the evening. The hall was draped in tapestries on one side that bore a tale of a hunt for a white hart in a forest, and on the other side the space was full of standing candelabras of candles, each draped with summer flowers. In the middle of the room were at least fifteen different guests, all speaking attentively to one another.

Kit swallowed at the sight, feeling her nerves grow worse and prompting her fingers to tremble. When Sir Horace had mentioned an intimate dinner, she had presumed there would only be a few guests. Clearly, Sir Horace considered many people his closest friends.

"Here, let me introduce ye to my friends." He drew her toward the nearest group where she fixed a smile in place, determined to prove that she could handle the deception. Iomhar's note of worry before the carriage ride had put her nerves on edge. Now, she had to breathe deeply, to ensure her trembling stopped before her host noticed it through the hold he had on her arm.

As he led her around the group, he slowly began to introduce her to everyone present. She hung on his every word, anxious to hear Lady Ruskin's name, but it never came. She smiled sweetly and practiced her Scottish accent, pleased she seemed to convince her new acquaintances that she was the young Scottish bride of a Highland soldier, yet her nerves would not be settled, for Lady Ruskin was still missing.

"Are these all your guests for the evening?" she said, attempting a nonchalant tone as Sir Horace returned to her side.

"All but one," he spoke quickly, then leaned toward her, as though to impart something that was a great secret. "Aye, the last likes to make something of a grand entrance."

"Pray tell, who is it?" she asked.

"It is Lady —" Before Sir Horace could say any more, the doors to the hall opened and a woman walked in.

Dressed head to toe in a red tartan gown with plaid thrown over her shoulder, she was the epitome of a Scottish symbol, and had even gone so far as to wear a thistle in her hair, with the purple feather-like petals standing proudly against her black hair.

"Lady Ruskin," Sir Horace declared, walking forward in greeting with his arms outstretched. "I see ye have come tonight to make a statement with your dress."

"I am glad ye noticed," Lady Ruskin's voice was strangely husky and deep as she lifted her chin high.

As the two lapsed into conversation, Kit watched avidly from afar. Lady Ruskin had clearly not wanted anyone to be in doubt of where her affinities resided when wearing such a gown. Anyone would wonder why she had deigned to visit London when her heart so clearly belonged in Scotland.

Watch and listen only. Walsingham's order echoed in Kit's head, yet it seemed less and less appealing to her. She could abide by the order and watch from afar, but what good would that do?

She saw her opportunity and walked forward, heading straight to Sir Horace with a smile, knowing the gentleman was too polite to refuse an introduction.

"Ah, there ye are Mrs Allaway, here, let me introduce ye to someone of great importance," he said and took Kit's hand, steering her toward the incomer. "May I introduce Lady Lillian Ruskin."

Kit curtsied deeply, then stood straight to find Lady Ruskin's dark eyes stared back at her without a flicker of a smile in her cheeks.

"Ye are a stranger here," Lady Ruskin said, her voice growing deeper than before.

Kit was too startled by the strength in Lady Ruskin's voice to think of an immediate reply. She merely stared open mouthed as Lady Ruskin smiled triumphantly. She was thankful to the kindly host who took up the thread of the conversation.

"Mrs Allaway is new to London. She recently married Captain Fergus Allaway and has come to England for a few months to see the place, before her husband joins her. I have offered to introduce her to a few friends," Sir Horace gestured to himself, standing so straight that his belly stood proud and appeared even more rounded than before.

"Your benevolence is too much, Sir Horace," Lady Ruskin said, looking away from Kit. "I was expecting a quiet evening with friends, and I find a stranger amongst us. How can I enjoy myself now?"

At the insult, Kit knew she had to say something, or she'd find herself without any information and sent away from the dinner. She would have to go back to Walsingham with her tail between her legs, confessing that she had failed. That couldn't happen.

"I realise ye do not know me yet, my Lady, but I promise ye I am not such foul company that I could ruin your evening," Kit declared with confidence, thrilled when Lady Ruskin turned back to her.

The high cheekbones were slightly more hollowed with apparent age, but the white cream she had applied to her skin was working well to hide any wrinkles. The scent of honey and beeswax in the air told Kit exactly what kind of cream Lady Ruskin was using to hide the signs of her age. The curved nose was plastered in this same white cream, but her red lips were painted in vermillion, almost as scarlet in colour as her tartan dress. Her naturally dark eyes were rimmed in more white paint, possibly ceruse, making her dark brown eyes look beady and black. Those same dark eyes narrowed on Kit.

"Well, she speaks with confidence," Lady Ruskin said, though her manner did not soften. "What else can she do?"

"I am quite a bright conversationalist, my Lady, if ye would care to talk with me a little longer."

"Really?" Lady Ruskin spoke with apparent scorn. "I somehow find that difficult to believe. I would infinitely prefer to speak with my friends tonight rather than a stranger, but … I suppose one makes friends by accepting strangers."

"Then I am permitted to stay?" Kit asked, testing the waters further.

"Now, Lady Ruskin would not be so rude as to send away one of my guests." Sir Horace laughed with the words.

Kit only had to glance at Lady Ruskin to see this was not the case, for she did not join in the laughter. Her vermillion lips were flattened together in a small straight line.

"Who are ye exactly?" Lady Ruskin asked, tilting her head to the side as she analysed Kit. "So, ye have married Captain Allaway, quite a well-known name, I warrant ye, but who were ye before that?"

"Merely a merchant's daughter, my Lady," Kit said, remembering the tale she and Iomhar had come up with in case she was ever asked this question. "My father was a quicksilver merchant in Edinburgh. I married a few months ago and have since been with my husband."

"Well, ye have gone up in the world. Though it does surprise me to hear Captain Allaway has married and the news has not yet reached us in London." Lady Ruskin's eyes were still wandering up and down Kit, clearly trying to find fault with her. "Perhaps he has sent ye here to learn a thing or two about higher-class society. If ye are to fit in with London events, I recommend ye find yourself a new dress, Mrs Allaway."

"Would it have been more acceptable if I had coming in wearing plaid? As ye did?" Kit's boldness this time earned laughter from Sir Horace. When the corner of Lady Ruskin's lips turned up, she could see she was beginning to make progress. Evidently Lady Ruskin didn't want Kit to be overly nice to her, she wanted her new acquaintance to have a personality of her own.

"Ye do have a quick tongue." Lady Ruskin's smile grew. "Well, your new guest is acceptable, if not completely welcome. We shall make a judgement on that later this evening. Sir Horace, do take me to a glass of wine. I am dying with thirst." She managed to swiftly retrieve Sir Horace from Kit's arm and draw him away across the room.

The two left with their heads bent toward each other, talking in confidence. Behind her, Lady Ruskin's tartan dress trailed across the floor. From this new angle, Kit could see beneath the lady's ruff the plaid on her shoulder was held in place with a brooch shaped into a thistle.

Kit was left standing alone uncertain whether she had made the correct move or an error. For now, she could at least stay, but Lady Ruskin was not going to lower her guard yet.

Kit had been sat at dinner for some time trying to figure out a way into the conversation. Beside her, Sir Horace sat at the head of the table, and Lady Ruskin sat opposite. Around her, a rather spirited debate was taking place, concerning the queen.

"Mrs Allaway, care to comment?" Sir Horace spoke up, trying to draw Kit into the conversation.

"Mrs Allaway is still young and has spent most of her life in Scotland. What can she know of the queen of England?" Lady Ruskin said with a little scorn.

"I may not know much, but I have an opinion of my own, and I think our opinions are all narrowed by our experiences," Kit turned her attention to Sir Horace with the words, though she watched Lady Ruskin out of the corner of her eye. Most present were upset that Sir Horace still had a more favourable opinion of the queen than others at the table. "Nay doubt ye think higher of the queen because ye have seen her at court frequently whilst ye stay in London."

"And what do ye think of her?" Sir Horace asked, leaning forward with interest.

"I think that Scotland has suffered a lot in these last few decades. Perhaps I should leave my opinion at that."

"Mrs Allaway, what an interesting thing to say. Allow me to pour ye another drink," Lady Ruskin said with a smile, lifting a jug of mulled wine and pouring some more into Kit's glass.

"Thank ye," Kit picked up the goblet once more. "To what do I owe the kindness?"

"An appreciation of your view," Lady Ruskin affirmed, sitting back in her chair and lifting her chin higher. "We may not all agree on the particulars of our current debate, but ye have said what is probably the smartest argument here. Believe me, that is an achievement indeed. Ye are quite right, our opinions are all formed by what we have seen and some of us have seen the suffering more than others." Kit smiled, warmed by Lady Ruskin's words. "In fact, Sir Horace, this is not nearly enough wine. Please, send for some more, I wish to interrogate your new guest on her other views."

Kit was careful with her goblet. Just as Lady Ruskin turned her head away, she poured what was in the cup into a trencher of pheasant cooked in red wine in front of her, determined not to lose her focus.

Once dinner had finished, Lady Ruskin led the women of the party through to an adjoining sitting room. Rather than a fire being lit, windows were flung open, trying to urge a little fresh breeze into the room. Kit went to take a seat beside another lady in a large settle wooden bench, but before she could sit, she found Lady Ruskin's hand on her wrist.

"Not there, come sit with me," Lady Ruskin pulled Kit closer to the windows and urged her to take a seat by a bench in front of the leaden-framed glass. "Do not look so frightened as to why I have separated ye from the others, Mrs Allaway. I am curious on your views."

"In what sense?" Kit asked, careful to mirror Lady Ruskin's stance in sitting perfectly in the chair. Though Walsingham had sent a governess to her for a year or two during her training to teach her how to act a lady, it was never the focus of her instruction. She was being very careful to maintain the illusion that she belonged in this crowd.

"Ye alluded to possible objections to our queen, could ye be more open in your opinion of her?" Lady Ruskin paused with her glass in the air, clearly transfixed to what Kit's answer would be.

Kit's hand tapped around the goblet in her own grasp, thinking carefully on how to proceed without speaking openly of supposed treason. "Who can be open on their own opinions, my Lady?" she asked, watching as Lady Ruskin's smile grew.

"Ye have me even more intrigued than before," Lady Ruskin said with a whisper, her voice turning even deeper. "If I were to ask your opinion of our Scottish monarch, how Mary Stuart was deposed to make way for her infant son, would ye be any more forthcoming in your opinion on it?"

Kit bought herself some time by sipping a little of her wine, enjoying the mulled spices of cinnamon and star anise. "Officially, I will always pledge my loyalty to our crowned monarch."

"And unofficially?" Lady Ruskin asked in a whisper.

"This is a very serious conversation for a party, my Lady," Kit said with a smile, watching as Lady Ruskin laughed under her breath. She knew if she was open in condemnation, Lady Ruskin would not believe her to be honest. Any true objector to Queen Elizabeth would be wary of announcing their views so openly.

"I see ye are as artful as ye are cagey," Lady Ruskin remarked, sitting back in her seat. "Here, drink up. I will fetch us some more wine." She downed what was in her glass before standing to her feet and walking across the space. Kit could see she was a little unsteady on her feet and growing increasingly merry on the wine.

With Lady Ruskin's back turned, Kit looked down at the full cup, determined not to drink it and lose her concentration. She looked around and, finding the window open behind her, she turned and made an appearance of pushing it further open, as though trying to get some cool breeze on her face, but she actually used the opportunity to tip the wine out of the goblet and into the street below.

A quiet yelp of surprise followed, urging her to turn back into the room. Fortunately, one glance round showed no other guest had heard, they were too absorbed in their own conversations.

Lady Ruskin was walking back toward her with a goblet in her hand, catching her eye. "Here we are," she said, tottering on her feet as she topped up Kit's goblet.

"Oh me," Kit feigned a merry tone. "Any more of this and I will struggle in and out of my carriage."

"Well, ye'll be in good company then," Lady Ruskin laughed and took the seat beside her, balancing the goblet of wine on the windowsill. "I have to say…" she paused and leaned in toward Kit, "I am always on the lookout for like-minded people. Perhaps your arrival here tonight was a much pleasanter incident than I expected."

"I feel I should thank ye, my Lady, but I am still not certain if that was a compliment." Kit's laughter drew another chuckle from Lady Ruskin.

"I should like to see ye again," Lady Ruskin said, sitting straight in her chair though her eyes were glazed slightly from the wine. "Pray, give me your address before ye leave tonight."

"I will." Kit hid her smile as she lifted the goblet to her lips.

Lady Ruskin drank half of what was in her goblet in one gulp before looking down at the cup in dismay of it being gone so quickly. She reached behind her, her arm flailing in the attempt to grasp the small handle on the wine jug. Yet she knocked the jug over entirely.

Kit winced, watching as the window was knocked further open, and wine fell out of the jug, down onto the street below. There was another yelp of surprise, this time louder than the last.

"Oh dear," Lady Ruskin said, her smile showing her humour, "I seem to have caught someone with that."

Kit laughed with her.

Kit was about to take her leave for the evening, hovering by the exit to Sir Horace's house when Lady Ruskin waved at her across the space, clearly still intent on finding out Kit's address. Kit held up a finger showing Lady Ruskin she was coming before she poked her head out of the door.

At a distance, standing by the street and the carriage that awaited her was Iomhar. She beckoned him to come forward. As he moved forward, his silhouette filled out from the candlelight that bled through the doorway. The hat upon his head was dampened and his face was splattered with dark red droplets.

"What happened to you?" she asked, dropping her Scottish accent.

"The fact ye're smiling suggests ye ken exactly what happened. Did ye throw the wine out of the window?"

"It depends which time you are referring to," she said, trying to hide her smile. "Why didn't you move after the first time?"

"I hardly thought it was going to happen again."

"I need an address."

"An address? What for?" he asked.

"Lady Ruskin wishes to know it." She watched as Iomhar's face stiffened.

"Tell me ye are jesting."

"I'll explain everything in a minute," she waved her hand at him. "Just give me an address. I can hardly tell her my own address, can I?"

"Tell her Two Charterhouse Street, Smithfield," he whispered quickly, before stepping out of the door again and pulling his sodden hat low over his head.

Kit turned back into the entrance hall, finding Lady Ruskin approaching her.

"Well, it was certainly interesting to meet ye tonight, Mrs Allaway, ooh!" She tottered to the side, so dizzy on her feet that Kit gently took hold of her arm, keeping her straight. "Thank ye, I might have ended up on my face then."

"Here, let me help ye to your carriage," Kit said, adopting the Scottish accent once more. "Ye asked for my address. It is Two Charterhouse Street, Smithfield."

"Wonderful. Keep an eye out for a letter from me." Lady Ruskin paused just as Kit helped her toward the carriage that awaited her. She turned back, dropping her voice to a whisper. As she leaned toward Kit, the stench of alcohol followed, and Kit had to try not to jerk her head away. "I hope once we are in private, we may discuss your views on the monarchy without fear of being overheard."

"I look forward to it." Kit forced a smile into her cheeks then helped Lady Ruskin into the carriage. Once the door was closed, Kit turned and walked toward the carriage that awaited her. Iomhar stood beside the door with his face still hidden and his hand outstretched to help her in. "I do not need your help to get into a carriage," Kit whispered to him.

"Aye, I know that, but it is customary, and your host is still watching ye, so ye best take it."

Kit took his hand to step up into the carriage, looking back to the doorway to see Sir Horace was indeed watching her. She waved once in a goodbye before she turned and stepped inside the carriage, sitting back on the seat with a sigh of relief.

Iomhar followed her in before closing the door with a heavy thud, so loud that it made Kit jump in her seat.

"Is something wrong?" Kit asked. "I mean beside from the wine on your head."

"Did ye throw it out the window?" He snatched the sodden hat off his head.

"Only the first glass," she said. "I couldn't allow myself to be inebriated, so I sought to get rid of the alcohol every time Lady Ruskin topped up my goblet, and believe me, she did it a lot."

Iomhar's face darkened again. He said nothing for a minute, only leaning forward and resting his elbows on his knees. The brightness in the carriage faded into shadows, broken every now and then by the moonlight shining through the windows as they moved through the streets of London. The momentary glimpses of silvery light showed Kit the set of Iomhar's expression. His jaw was tightened, and his eyes were fixed on the floor.

"Ye were supposed to watch and listen only," he said firmly. "Clearly, ye did not do that."

"No, I did not," Kit acknowledged. "I spoke to Lady Ruskin, for a lot of the evening, and have made a friend of her. She wishes to write to me which is why I needed the address."

"Ye disobeyed Walsingham's order!" Iomhar suddenly snapped the words.

"So what if I did? Iomhar, there is no need to be upset just because Walsingham sent me in there and not you."

"Ye think I care if Walsingham favours ye? Oh, God's blood, ye have nay idea how wrong ye are." Iomhar leaned forward, closing the distance between them a little. "Ye think I care for his good opinion of me? I may agree with Walsingham's aim for the time being, but I trust the man about as far as he can walk right now, holed up in that bed of his."

"What do you mean by that?" Kit gripped the seat of the carriage firmly beneath her. "Why would you mistrust him so?"

"That is my own business, and if ye had any sense, ye would mistrust him too." He raised a finger to her. "Ye should have followed his order tonight, Kit. Why did ye not do it?"

"Because it would have made the night useless," she said tiredly. "I would have been all trussed up and at this party, practicing this silly accent —"

"Oi!"

"Do not take offence at that," she said with a wave of her hand. "My point is that it would have all been for nothing. Lady Ruskin was hardly going to discuss anything of importance to their plot when she knew there was a stranger in the room. This way, she begins to trust me. It means in the future she could tell me more."

"Tell ye more?" he repeated, sitting bolt straight in his seat. "This is suicide, Kit. Ye are making friends with a woman who could well be helping to plot to kill the queen."

"Then I need her to be my friend to trust me."

"We make plans for a reason. If ye are going to throw the plan out of the window every time, then how exactly can I trust ye and work with ye?"

"What are you saying? That just because I have changed the plan you do not wish to work with me anymore?" Kit asked, startled by how much she shifted in her seat at this news.

"Aye, if I could back out of this partnership now, believe me, I would." His words silenced her.

Words died between them as they stared at one another. Kit could feel herself shifting in her seat as she watched Iomhar breathing deeply. Before she could think of what to say, the carriage came to a stop. She reached for the door first, about to jump down when the farthingale of her skirt got caught in the doorway.

"Do ye need some help?" Iomhar asked.

"No," she said decisively, tired of him thinking her not capable. She twisted the hoop of the skirt sideways, allowing her to jump down from the carriage into the cobbled street below.

Iomhar followed her down, closing the door behind them. He tipped the coach driver who pulled on the reins of the horses, taking the coach away, and leaving them alone in the moonlit road. "Kit, listen —"

"If you do not like working with me so much, then go to Walsingham and tell him tomorrow." Kit turned to the doorway leading to her lodgings. Before she could unlock the door, Iomhar stretched an arm out across it, placing his hand on the opposite frame and preventing her from entering.

"He would never have it," he said quietly. "I could argue until I am blue in the face and still he would say nay."

"Then you will have to put up with me." She pulled on the sleeve of his doublet, trying to get him to move out of the way, but he wouldn't move an inch. "Let me pass."

"I do not think your instinct is wrong, Kit, it just does not work to always follow it," he spoke clearly, earning her gaze.

"I spoke to a woman at a dinner party tonight. Oh yes, what a dangerous thing to do indeed!" she declared, throwing her hands to her chest dramatically.

"Ye spoke to a woman who could be plotting murder," he hissed in a whisper, prompting Kit to fall still. "Ye have brought yourself to her attention and placed yourself in danger. That did not need to happen."

"For the sake of the queen, is it not worth that risk?" she asked.

He lifted his other hand, pinching the bridge of his nose in apparent stress. "Are ye really willing to die for all this?"

"Are you not?" This time her question earned his gaze.

"I am willing to die for this cause because I have my own reasons." He kept his voice quiet. "What are yours? And please do not tell me it is for Walsingham."

"I…" Kit faltered for a minute, searching her mind for an answer. "I am willing to risk my life for the queen. That is all."

"Not because Walsingham asked ye to risk it, then?"

"No," she said strongly, hoping she believed her own words. Iomhar did not appear convinced. "Now, release the door." She gestured to it. "I need to get out of these ridiculous clothes."

"One last thing," Iomhar muttered, still not releasing the doorframe.

She persisted regardless, trying to get her key in the lock and open the door. "What is that?"

"Walsingham may be happy to be cavalier in risking your safety, but I am not the same." His words made her abandon her attempt to open the door. "Life is not so expendable to me. If we are to continue to work together, I will not let ye risk your life so easily."

"Iomhar, I just spoke to a woman."

"Let us hope that was all it was and not a thing more," he said deeply before releasing his hold on the doorframe. "Goodnight, Kit." With his words, he turned and began to walk away down the street.

"Goodnight?" she repeated in amazement, stepping away from the door too. "You have nothing else to say?" she asked as he walked on down the cobbled road.

"There is one other thing."

"Which is?"

"I like the dress," he called back to her as his figure began to fade down the road.

She glanced down at the dress, bundling the skirt in her hands in frustration.

CHAPTER 15

Kit was no longer in her bed. She was beneath the water surface, trying to swim through it, though her arms were smaller than they should have been, as were her legs, and no matter how many times she kicked them, she didn't move anywhere. All her maddening strikes produced were bubbles in the water, marring her sight.

Through the bubbles and the murkiness, she could see someone standing over her above the water. A woman, perhaps, from the outline of the dress and the French hooded-style hat upon her head, though Kit could not be certain.

She stretched out a hand, trying to break the surface, attempting to reach out toward this figure, yet she couldn't do it. Her small and pudgy fingers couldn't stretch very far. As she let her hand drop down in the water, the figure above moved.

She began to sink further and further down with the murkiness and the bubbles clouding her vision even more. Then the figure walked away.

Kit sat upright in bed, breathing heavily and gasping for air. She blinked frantically, looking around the attic room.

Her room was just as she had left it, with the golden silk dress tossed across the settle chair and her shoes kicked at odd angles on the floor. Around the headpost of her bed was the garter with the dagger inside. She placed her hand close to the dagger, needing the comfort of having it nearby, even though it couldn't do anything to calm her erratic heartbeat now.

She moved to the edge of the bed and bent forward, placing her other hand to her chest as she breathed deeply. For a few minutes, she had truly thought she was back in the water, unable to breathe. It was hardly the first time she had suffered the dream. It was a memory, from so long ago that she couldn't recall when it had actually occurred. She couldn't even remember what happened around the incident, beyond being in the water, yet it was the reason she still avoided large bodies of water —lakes, rivers, the sea — even to this day.

Slowly, her heartbeat began to settle down to normal and she sat up in the bed, gazing around the space that was beginning to lighten with the sun of the new dawn peering through the windows. As she calmed herself, she recalled something about the dream, something she had never dreamt before.

The figure watching her had walked away.

She leaned forward, resting her face in her hands as she searched the memory, trying to decide whether this new information was part of the original memory or if she had merely created it from her imagination. She spent many minutes wracking her brains, trying to find out something, but she couldn't. In the end, she had to accept that she couldn't answer her own question.

Kit was hurrying up the stairs of Walsingham's new lodgings, rushing to his chamber after hearing the good news from Doris. He was up and about at last, his coughing up ash had ceased and the burns on his palms were beginning to heal.

As she reached the landing, she crossed the corridor quickly, heading toward the door. She placed her hand on the door handle, yet it moved beneath her grasp without her having to turn it. She stepped back, just as the door swung open and a face was revealed.

"Ah, it's you," a familiar voice said. The lady stepped out from the room and closed the door behind her, blocking off Kit's access to the chamber.

"Lady Sidney." Kit curtsied quickly. Walsingham's daughter bore the same dark eyes her father had, though it was set within a much prettier face. Younger than Kit, at only seventeen years old, she had a lot of confidence for her age.

"I see you are still avoiding dresses," she said with a smirk that was not kind as she nodded her head at Kit's outfit.

"No, they are far too cumbersome." Kit had worn her usual attire with the doublet, hose and gamache boots.

"What an interesting objection," Lady Sidney spoke quietly though she said no more.

"If you would excuse me, Lady Sidney," Kit motioned toward the doorway, showing she intended to go through.

"Now is not the time for business." She dismissively waved a hand at Kit, urging her to move away down the corridor.

"I was just coming to see how Walsingham was doing?" Kit spoke tightly, hearing the dismissal and choosing to ignore it regardless.

"That is mine and my mother's matter, not yours," she said, looking away from her. "I am simply waiting for Doris to bring him some fresh water and food."

"I could wait with him whilst you check on her," Kit suggested as she reached a hand toward the door, trying to step around Lady Sidney.

"That will not be necessary," she smiled with the words, despite the firm push she gave to Kit's wrist, pushing her out of the way. "*You* can check on Doris for me and I will keep watch over my father."

Kit tried to think of another argument, but she found Lady Sidney staring back at her, unblinkingly, clearly intending not to move away.

"May I not speak with him for a few minutes?" Kit asked.

"Not today," Lady Sidney gestured down the corridor another time. "You may go."

This time, Kit knew she couldn't refuse the dismissal. She turned and walked away, fidgeting uncomfortably with her sleeves when she found Iomhar standing at the top of the staircase, clearly having witnessed the exchange.

"If you wish to also see my father, that can wait too," Lady Sidney called, gesturing for Iomhar to descend the staircase again.

"Who is that?" Iomhar whispered to Kit as she reached his side.

"Walsingham's daughter, married to Sir Philip Sidney," Kit explained as she took hold of the banister and walked down the stairs.

"And why are we not allowed to see Walsingham?"

"Because she said so."

"I see. And there is more to this than meets the eye, is there not?" he asked, bringing Kit up short. The two of them came to a stop in the corner of the staircase just as the split stairs formed one set that led down to the ground floor. "Why would she not let ye see Walsingham?"

"She sees me as staff," Kit explained, surprising even herself by being willing to tell Iomhar such a thing. "She has never liked me very much."

"Why not?"

"I think it has something to do with her father allotting money to raise a vagrant girl he found in the street," Kit gestured to herself.

"What a weird reason not to like someone," Iomhar said, shaking his head as he turned and descended the last of the steps with Kit following behind him. "There is a difference though between not liking someone and refusing to let them see a sick man."

"Well, I would agree with you there," Kit paused as she craned her neck up to see the top landing. Lady Sidney was there, watching the two of them, apparently trying to listen in on their conversation. Kit caught up to Iomhar's side and dropped her voice to a whisper. "Walsingham usually keeps the two of us far apart from each other."

"He knows she does not like ye?"

"Well, she has hardly made a secret of it," Kit explained as she urged him to follow her. She crossed through the finer rooms, heading to the servant quarters in the poorer section of the house. "Once when I was little, he took me to their country home in Barn Elms in Surrey. When he introduced me to Lady Sidney, or Franny, as she was known back then, she was so upset she began to cry, saying a demon girl had been brought into the house."

"I beg your pardon?" Iomhar said, his voice rising a notch as he hesitated in his walk. "Why in the name of the wee man would she do that?"

"I told you. She doesn't like me," Kit shrugged as though it were no big deal. In truth, she had at first not minded Lady Sidney's dislike, but when it stopped her from seeing Walsingham, she minded very much. "She set my hair on fire once."

"What? She set your hair on fire?" he asked, clearly bewildered.

"She dropped a candle on me," Kit explained, remembering the last day that she had been welcome at Barn Elms. "That's when they cropped my hair short. I was not welcome at Barn Elms after that."

"She's ruthless." Iomhar released her arm. "Rather like her father."

"There is a difference between the two," she murmured, walking away from him and into the kitchen.

"Is there?" Iomhar muttered, just as Doris appeared before them on the far side of the kitchen.

"Ah, Kitty, there you are," Doris said, rushing around the kitchen with pots in the effort to hurry and make some food for Walsingham. "Did you see the master?"

"No, I did not," Kit tried to keep the disappointment out of her voice.

"Lady Sidney has prevented us both from seeing him." Iomhar did not bother to keep the resentment out of his own voice.

"She can be like that," Doris chuckled. "She is a sweet girl really. Just like her father."

"Sweet?" Iomhar repeated in disbelief.

"Doris likes to see the good in people, no matter how difficult or hard that might be," Kit explained as Iomhar laughed softly. "Doris, I am afraid Lady Sidney is asking after Walsingham's food."

"I am on my way now," Doris said, placing the last plate down onto a tray before she walked past them, heading to the door. Iomhar watched her go, shaking his head to himself.

"Is something wrong?" Kit asked, watching his confused expression.

"I was just wondering how Walsingham is a man who can inspire such devotion in people."

"I suggest that you do not know the man very well."

"Perhaps not," he admitted, though he still did not appear certain. "Now, to business. I am glad I found ye. This turned up at my door addressed to ye this morning." He reached into

153

his doublet and pulled out a closed letter with a red wax seal. "And *that* —" he gestured to the seal, "is the mark of the Ruskin family."

Kit snatched the letter out of Iomhar's hand and pulled apart the wax seal to read the letter. The parchment that unfolded before her was covered in extremely cursive lettering that was difficult to read, making the paper appear as though it were covered in spider's legs rather than ink.

Kit felt Iomhar move to her shoulder, ready to read the letter. She held the letter to her chest to stop him from reading it.

"Do ye not trust me?" he asked, frowning.

"It is addressed to me," she hurried to say, by way of an explanation.

"Well, it's addressed to a Mrs Allaway," he corrected her. "I brought it to ye, did not I? Ye're going to have to learn to trust me one of these days." He stared at her, without the trace of a smile in his face. She knew he was right but knowing it and persuading herself to do it were two different things. Nevertheless, she lowered the parchment again so they could both read it, even though she did the movement very slowly.

Dear Mrs Katherine Allaway,

What a delight it was to meet you last night! As I said, I'm always eager to meet like-minded people, and I believe from hints you dropped last night that we may be more aligned in our thoughts than you may think.

Pray, come and see me tomorrow. When the clock strikes midday, I'll be waiting for you. We have much to discuss.

Yours etcetera,

Lady Lillian Ruskin

"Well, ye did make a good impression, did not ye?" He took the parchment out of her hands to read it again.

"Tomorrow. She wishes to see me tomorrow," Kit said as she paced up and down the kitchen. "There is not long left before they make their attempt on Elizabeth's life."

"Just one week," Iomhar confirmed.

"Tomorrow will have to do then," Kit sighed, as Iomhar's head darted up.

"Ye are not going."

"I beg your pardon?" Kit stopped in her pacing and turned back to face him. "Why am I not going?"

"Because ye cannot."

"Because you say so?" Kit laughed at the idea. "I will not do anything just because you tell me to do it, Iomhar."

He rolled his eyes at her words and placed the letter flat on the kitchen table, leaning over it so that the table was the only thing separating them.

"Do ye not remember our conversation last night about how dangerous Lady Ruskin could be?"

"I remember it very well," she agreed.

"Then ye understand why ye cannot take this any further. Ye could be walking into a trap."

"A trap?" Kit leaned across the table too and snatched the parchment from under his hand. "Read the letter again. If I am not mistaken, she likes me very much indeed and is clearly trying to scout out what my opinion is on the monarchy. If I can make her trust me, she could tell me of her plot."

"*If…*" Iomhar stressed the word, leaning on the table with both of his hands. "I told ye last night, I will not be so cavalier with your life as Walsingham is." The words made Kit flinch in surprise. "*This* is being cavalier. I will not let ye go."

"I neither seek your permission, nor your blessing. If I want to go, then that is my decision," she declared, matching his stance as she leaned on the table too, with her hands down on the surface and the letter discarded between them. "You cannot change my mind."

Iomhar was breathing deeply, his cheeks above his beard reddening with the extent of his anger. Kit merely smiled back at him, knowing he couldn't argue with her any further.

"Am I interrupting something, Kitty?" Doris's voice from the doorway disturbed her.

Kit stood straight from the table, turning to face the housekeeper. "Not at all, Doris. Iomhar and I were just having a difference of opinion," Kit said, still smiling.

"I hear from the master you two have a lot of those," Doris chuckled as she walked into the room. "Mr Blackwood, the master wants to see you as you are here."

Kit froze and looked back to Doris.

"Lady Sidney is allowing it?" she asked.

"It was her father's order, she cannot disobey it," Doris explained with a shrug.

As Iomhar moved toward the doorway, Kit went to follow, but Doris placed a hand on her arm. "He just wished to see Mr Blackwood, Kitty."

Kit pressed her lips together, tempted to argue though she knew it would do little good. She turned and watched Iomhar as he left the kitchen, his face just as sombre and disquieted as it had been in their argument.

CHAPTER 16

"Stop fidgeting," Iomhar whispered in Kit's ear. She tried to stand perfectly still, but a second later she began again, this time wringing her hands together. "Can ye not stand still for just a few minutes?"

"How can you be so calm?" she asked in a harried murmur. "Considering who we are about to meet, I would have thought you as nervous as I am."

"Nay," Iomhar sighed. "She is only a woman after all."

These words prompted Walsingham, who was standing in front of the pair of them, to turn and stare at Iomhar.

"She is not *just* a woman. Never refer to her as such again, you fool," he muttered quietly before turning back round.

Iomhar turned his head to Kit and raised his eyebrows, clearly trying to communicate silently with her that Walsingham was a little sensitive on the subject. She chose not to respond and looked forward, surveying the room around them.

The day before when Iomhar had been called in to see Walsingham alone, Kit had first thought it must be a more personal matter they were discussing. When Iomhar returned to reveal that Walsingham wanted them both to accompany him the day after to see the queen, to talk of the planned assassination and warn Her Majesty, Kit had been stunned, wondering why she had not been welcome at the meeting with Iomhar and Walsingham.

Still irritated at the isolation, she elbowed Iomhar once Walsingham had looked away, determined to have his attention.

"Did you truly discuss nothing else with Walsingham?"

"Yesterday?" Iomhar whispered, with risen eyebrows. "We may have spoken of something else."

"What?" Kit asked impatiently, but had no answer, as Iomhar looked away from her. "Is it something to do with our task?" She began warily, looking toward Walsingham to see if he was listening in, but he was concerned so much with his own thoughts, he seemed unaware of their conversation. "The assassination attempt, perhaps? Or why you know the name Lord Ruskin?" Her words at last had a reaction, and Iomhar snapped his gaze toward her. "Ah, so you had a meeting to discuss Lord Ruskin's involvement?"

"Nay. Not exactly."

"How do you know this man?"

"Another time, Kit," Iomhar insisted, as Walsingham turned to look at the two of them again. He said nothing, but eyed them, clearly perturbed by their harried whispers. It prompted them both to fall quiet and Kit turned her gaze on the room.

The Hampton Court Palace throne room was perhaps not the biggest of chambers in the building, but it was grand, enough to leave Kit's mouth a little dry and feel extremely out of place in her man's hose and doublet. The walls were panelled in dark oak and draped in wide tapestries that told tales from the bible. Looking across the embroidered faces, Kit could see the birth of Jesus, along with the killing of Judas and the tale of the good Samaritan. Each picture was inlaid with bold colours, the reds as vibrant as the red canopy that hung above the throne on the far side of the room, opposite where Kit stood.

Beneath the canopy, the throne was surprisingly small, though the panels on the seat and back were as bold and ornate as the walls of tapestries. By the foot of the throne was a small stool, for the sitter to place their feet. It was this seat that kept drawing their gaze in the room, whilst they waited for the arrival of the person they had come to see. On the far side by a double door entrance stood one footman to the castle, dressed in a doublet and a tiny ruff, with his chin tucked high, as though he looked down on the three of them standing in the room.

"Did we really have to come for this?" Iomhar asked, sighing with the words.

"It was imperative," Walsingham said over his shoulder. "The queen is not one to run when I warn her of danger, but if she hears it from another's lips, perhaps from you two, who have seen this threat with your own eyes, maybe then it could make a difference. She may take more precautions. Besides, I needed to be escorted here somehow, and I do not want any other intelligencers to know what you two know yet."

"Why?" Iomhar asked. The sharpness of the word made Kit flick her head toward the two of them, yet Walsingham didn't answer.

"Shh," he urged, just as the doors opened and a train of elderly men walked in.

"Who are they?" Kit murmured quietly, her eyes darting between the men. They could have all been brothers for they were so alike, all aging, with white beards and greying hair, dressed in long black smocks, or dark doublets, incredibly refined.

"The privy council," Walsingham nodded his head forward. "There is Lord Burghley."

"Oh," Kit gasped in amazement. For all that she had heard about the man, she had expected someone of quite a grand presence, or at least someone tall and intimidating in stature. He was really rather short, with his clothes swamping him and the thin black cap on his head most likely hiding a balding spot.

"Who's Lord Burghley?" Iomhar asked, earning both Kit's and Walsingham's dark gaze.

"William Cecil," Kit prompted. "Lord Treasurer. Chief Advisor to the queen. Does none of this sound familiar?"

"Aye, I remember now," Iomhar nodded.

"Maybe it is best you stay quiet after all," Walsingham said, shaking his head as he turned back to face the front of the throne room.

The privy council gathered around the room, all lining up so that they formed the three sides of a square, leaving just the throne itself unmanned. The door opened another time, and on this occasion no man walked through it, but a woman, followed by two others.

"Bow, now," Walsingham ordered the two of them.

As the privy council all bent their heads, Kit and Iomhar did the same, bowing and curtsying with their heads turned down. Kit snatched the hat off her head too, trying to show due deference, but to also give her a chance to raise her eyes a little, to keep sight of the woman in the room.

Queen Elizabeth crossed the room, walking through the privy councillors and barely looking at them, as she aimed for the throne under the canopy. As she took her seat, the ladies-in-waiting helped to fan out the skirt that was easily twice as large as any other Kit had ever seen.

It seemed to Kit's mind that where a young woman once must have sat, now sat an aging woman, looking even more ancient beyond her years. Despite the evident creases and lines in the face, there was a heavy thick white paint upon the queen's cheeks, not only nearly masking these lines, but her eyebrows too. Her lips were small and painted a kind of coral orange colour, almost as bright as the wig upon her head. It was the eyes though that Kit found most captivating. Dark, nearly black from the depth of the brown, they were piercing as she gazed around the room. One bony and pale hand was shaken in the air, urging the privy council and her guests to stand straight.

"Who has called this meeting?" she spoke at last. Her accent was excessively refined, and the voice was strong, ricocheting back at her visitors off the wood-panelled walls. "You have disturbed my rest for the day, I hope you had good cause for it."

"I called it, Your Majesty, and I assure you I had good reason." Walsingham stepped forward and bowed another time.

"Walsingham." Queen Elizabeth rested an elbow on the arm of her chair and lifted the hand high in his direction, motioning toward him. "I should have guessed. If you're not interrupting my respite with follies and trivial matters, then it is some nonsense of a threat. Why is it you disturb me today?"

"A threat, Your Majesty," Walsingham said, just as loudly as she had done.

There was a ripple of whispers amongst the privy council, yet the queen did not move. Instead, she stayed perfectly still, and fixed her dark gaze on her councillor.

"You say there are threats every week, what makes this one so different that we must call an emergency meeting?" Lord Burghley asked from his position closest to the queen.

Kit turned her eyes to the Lord Treasurer, startled his voice had been as high-pitched as it had been.

"This one is not idle. It is not just tongues wagging, it has intent behind it, funding, and it is imminent." Walsingham took a step forward, using the thin cane that had been provided to him by the physician due to his injuries. "I have brought two intelligencers with me, who can testify to the fact. Burghley, if you wish to doubt my tongue, I hope you will not doubt theirs. They have been working to protect our queen and they are the ones who have discovered the plot." He lifted the cane and pointed it at Kit and Iomhar.

Kit began fidgeting yet again as the eyes in the room turned on them, but a quick glance and darkening glare from Iomhar made her fidgeting stop, knowing what he was trying to say to her.

"Is that a lady or a boy?" Queen Elizabeth asked.

Kit stood a little straighter, lifting her chin to be seen clearer as she stared back at the queen. Those dark eyes had narrowed on her, and Kit felt strangely burrowed into by that gaze.

"A lady, Your Majesty," Walsingham answered, nodding his head toward Kit. "This is Miss Katherine Scarlett, and Mr Iomhar Blackwood. If you wish to hear proof of the plot against you, you need only ask them."

"Send the woman dressed as the boy forward," Queen Elizabeth ordered, waving her hand at Walsingham.

Kit didn't move at first. Her legs seemed frozen to the spot out of surprise. Even Walsingham's ordering gaze couldn't make her move, yet Iomhar's firm shove to the back did. She stepped forward, reaching the same place as Walsingham in the room.

"How intriguing," Queen Elizabeth said, leaning forward, the better to look at Kit. "You have never brought a lady intelligencer to me before, Walsingham." The smile upon her face rather changed the angular features. It softened the hooked nose and made those dark eyes lighten a little.

"Kit is my only one," Walsingham admitted.

Kit glanced his way briefly, startled by the words. She had long suspected she was the only one, but she had never known for certain.

"Well, woman to woman, then, even if you are dressed like a boy." Queen Elizabeth seemed to be holding back laughter at the idea, which only made Kit fidget with the hat in her hand even more. "Tell me what you have discovered? Though be brief."

Kit glanced once to Walsingham, as though looking for confirmation before she spoke up. He nodded, urging her on. "There is a Scottish plan afoot, Your Majesty. It begins with your assassination and an army that will march on Sheffield Castle to free Mary Stuart."

The privy council erupted in whispers once more, this time of horror at Mary Stuart's name being mentioned at all.

Kit kept her gaze on the queen, watching as those small coral-coloured lips pursed together. "We only have one week left, Your Majesty."

"One week!" Lord Burghley's voice was outraged at the side of the room. It was followed by equal exclamations of horror and dread. They were only stopped when the queen held a hand sharply up in the air. At once, the reactions of her councillors were halted.

"When and how is this to occur?" Queen Elizabeth asked, still addressing Kit.

Kit's mouth went dry as she tightened her hands around the hat in her grasp. "We do not yet know, Your Majesty. Only that it will be within a week."

Kit's statement was met by even more outrage. This time, there were such cries and exclamations of panic that even the queen's raised hand could not stop them. In the end, she had to stand to her feet. The abrupt movement made the councillors all grow quiet and hang their heads.

"Tell me you have a plan, Walsingham." The queen turned away from Kit, apparently dissatisfied with her answer and having no wish to speak to her any further. "Tell me you have something to counteract this."

"Without knowing when they are going to strike, I advise you stay in the palace for the next two weeks, Your Majesty," he said with a gentle tone, one Kit had rarely heard him use.

"You wish to make me a prisoner in my own house?" Queen Elizabeth's voice echoed off the wood-panelled walls, making clear her indignation.

"That is not what I said —"

"Yet it is what you meant." The queen stepped away from her throne and began to walk around the small square of privy councillors, circling Kit and Walsingham within it. "Do you wish me to stay indoors forever more? You bring threats against my name almost weekly. I will not be a prisoner, Walsingham."

"No, Your Majesty, I merely meant —"

"I will hear no more!" Her order was met by silence. The only sound in the room was that of footsteps of people walking the corridors outside of the chamber. "I cannot stay indoors forever. I have duties to attend, the people to see. I will not be cowed now by a threat against me, nor will I ever be. Have I made myself clear, Walsingham?"

"Abundantly," he sighed with the word, holding her gaze as she came to a stop at the side of him. "Yet you are putting yourself in unnecessary danger. If you were harmed, without an heir the country could be plunged into civil war, uncertainty. What then —"

"I am not interested in hearing any more of your opinions."
The queen turned away and faced Lord Burghley. "I have
made my decision. Lord Burghley, what do you think?"

"I think your courage does you great service, Your Majesty,"
he said as he bowed his head to her.

"Then that is settled. I will not go into hiding, and I will not
be a prisoner of my own house. Everyone is dismissed." She
walked back to the throne. "Walsingham, you may stay, along
with your intelligencers, the tall one and the one with
interesting choices in clothing."

The moment the door was closed on the other privy
councillors, Kit retreated to stand beside Iomhar, leaving
Walsingham in the centre of the room. The strength that the
queen had shown a minute before seemed to have vanished, as
if the courage demonstrated had been snuffed out like a flame
on a candle. Instead, there was a woman pacing up and down,
with her hands placed on the waistline of her corset as she
looked at her feet. Her movements were frantic, nervy too.

"Tell me you have some other plan, Walsingham." Her voice
shook slightly.

The woman before them was such a transformation
compared to who they had seen a minute before that Kit and
Iomhar exchanged glances.

"We are working on it," Walsingham said softly, stepping
toward her and using his cane to clack against the floor. "Kit
and Iomhar have made contact with who they believe is behind
the plot. We have set up a watch on them. With a little time,
they will discover the plot."

The queen lifted her head at last, as her eyes flitted between
Iomhar and Kit. She looked shaky as she bit her coral-coloured

lip. "You place a lot of faith in your intelligencers." She turned back to Walsingham.

"With good cause. I promise you that," he said with feeling.

The queen took a step forward, bringing herself closer to Walsingham before she turned her back on Kit and Iomhar, lowering her voice. Kit rather imagined she hoped they wouldn't be able to hear her, but they could, all too clearly.

"You will not let me die, Walsingham. Will you?" Queen Elizabeth asked, her voice taking on a pleading tone.

Walsingham held out a hand to the queen and she took it, grasping it so tightly, that the skin on their aging fingers crinkled. "I have vowed to never let any harm come to you, and I will uphold it. Until the day I die," he promised, and lifted her hand to his lips, kissing the back.

Kit couldn't help the slackening of her jaw in wonder as she looked at Iomhar. He seemed to hold the same look of shock and awe. The woman who had appeared so strong and unmoved a minute ago, was transformed by fear into something akin to a child, pleading for help. It shook something within Kit, a desperation to protect the woman that was so scared.

As Walsingham released her hand, the queen turned back to face Kit and Iomhar.

"God be with you two," she said, affecting her stronger countenance once again. "Let us pray He is with you in your endeavour."

Walsingham waved behind her back, urging them both to bow. As they did so, the queen turned and left the room, quickly, with her two ladies-in-waiting hurrying behind her.

As the door closed after her, Walsingham sighed and wiped his brow with his fingers. "Well, that could have been worse," he spoke cautiously.

"Worse?" Iomhar asked. "Aye, I think we heard different things. She refused to hide in the palace."

"She will not be a prisoner of her fear, Iomhar," Kit found her voice.

Iomhar snapped his head toward her, looking at her with an expression she could not decipher. "Ye sound as if ye admire her for it. Or at least, understand it."

"I do understand it," Kit agreed with a nod.

"This is absurd," Iomhar muttered, ruffling his hair with his hand. "Now our task has become a lot harder."

"That may be the case, but I am not giving up yet," Kit said. "I will not let anything happen to our queen."

"Are ye willing to lay down your life for her?" His voice was quiet and yet irate. "Because it may come to that."

"Then so be it. I'll happily take the risk."

CHAPTER 17

"Ye are going to have to stop fidgeting," Iomhar said as he walked Kit toward the door of Lady Ruskin's house. He was dressed in his usual attire of dark green jerkin, but with the black cloak over his shoulders and belted around his waist, it hid the affluence of the clothes. The hat he had pulled low over his face masked his features too, making him appear as her servant to the casual onlooker.

"Easier said than done. This corset is too tight," Kit complained, trying to adjust the corset beneath her dress.

"Kit, stop," Iomhar warned.

She released her dress with a huff. "I am starting to wish we could trade places. Then you could go and suffer wearing this absurd outfit in the name of our queen."

"Do I need to remind ye of the declaration ye made last night?" Iomhar asked as she reached the bottom of the porch steps that led to the house.

"No." She sighed. "I remember it very well, thank you."

She had already been determined in this commission, for Walsingham's sake, but last night had changed things. Now, the danger facing their queen's life felt even more real to her than before. With less than a week to go and an uncertainty of the exact date the assassination attempt would take place, it made her fear grow worse. It was as though she could see a storm coming, somewhere on the horizon. She knew lightning was to strike and was anticipating it, but she didn't know when or where.

"Aye, ye'll have to put up with wearing a corset for now," Iomhar said as he leaned on a wall at the bottom of the porch steps. "I'll wait for ye here."

"You do not need to keep watch," she whispered to him as she paused on the bottom step.

"A servant would wait for his mistress," he pointed out.

"Ah, it has nothing to do with you looking out for my safety then?" she teased, watching as he glanced back at her beneath the brim of his hat.

"It has everything to do with that." The depth of his words made her humour vanish. "Now, go. And for the wee man's sake, be careful."

"When am I not?" she asked, watching as Iomhar's eyebrows furrowed in response. "Do not answer that."

Kit turned and headed toward the front door. A soft knock to the oak door was answered within seconds. It swung open to reveal a steward wearing not only the formal black attire often found in his station, but a tartan cap too, pinned to his hair with a clan brooch.

Kit bit her cheek to stop herself from laughing. It seemed Lady Ruskin even demanded physical displays of loyalty from her staff in the way that they dressed. "My name is Mrs Katherine Allaway. I believe Lady Ruskin is expecting me," she said, adopting her Scottish accent.

"Aye, this way." He bowed his head and beckoned her inside to follow him. She glanced back once to see Iomhar staring after her, before she closed the door behind her.

Lady Ruskin's house was just as much a display of her loyalty as her clothes had been two nights before at Sir Horace's dinner party. The black and white tiled entrance hall was flanked with tall portraits either side, each one either a Scottish monarch or a member of the nobility. Amongst the paintings,

Kit could see the familiar faces of James IV and James V, as she had seen etchings of such paintings at Walsingham's house in one of her lessons when she was young. As she followed the steward all the way to the end of the hall, her feet slowed beneath her and fell to a stop as the last painting came into view.

Placed in the grandest golden frame in the entire room was a painting of a woman, the only one in the hall. She was young in the painting, with her hairline high, revealing a bold pale forehead and a long narrow nose, with the cheeks flushed almost as red as the hair that was drawn back under a tight coronet and hood lined with pearls. There was a delicacy to the woman's features, one that suggested the painter had found the subject rather fascinating. Yet the thing that drew Kit most into gazing at the painting was the eyes. They were light brown in colour though they had piercing strength and stared boldly out from the canvas, staring at anyone who passed by the frame.

There was a similarity in the features to the lady she had met the night before.

"I see ye have found our queen already."

Lady Ruskin's voice made Kit jump. She spun round in the hallway to see the steward had vanished and, in the doorway where he had disappeared, now stood Lady Ruskin.

Unlike at the party, she was not dressed so formally. The gown she was wearing was relatively open and loose with a blue shroud around her shoulders. Balanced precariously at the tips of her fingers was a long thin white smoking pipe, made of ivory. She gently drew on the end of the pipe before blowing a perfect smoke ring into the air.

"Ye look surprised," Lady Ruskin said with a smile.

"I have not seen many people smoke before," Kit rushed to explain.

"Then it seems I have something to introduce ye too." Lady Ruskin's smile grew even greater as she stepped away from the doorway and came to Kit's side, turning her attention to the painting. "What do ye make of her?"

"The woman or the painting?" Kit asked.

"Very astute," Lady Ruskin laughed. "Our old queen of Scots does not look quite like this anymore, but those eyes…" She paused as she took another drag from the ivory pipe. "Aye, they are just the same."

Kit glanced at the painting of Mary Stuart, knowing now why she looked so like Queen Elizabeth. It was the family resemblance of being cousins. "Ye have met her?" Kit said, trying to subtly lean away from the pipe. It stank. She had seen a few affluent people in the streets smoking on occasion, but it was a rarity. Now she was up close to it, she was startled by the power of the stench.

"I have." Lady Ruskin turned her gaze on Kit.

"When?" Kit asked, knowing she could be finally getting some usable information. Lady Ruskin was helping to plot the assassination of Queen Elizabeth, that was evident in the letter signed by her husband and her ordering of the fire, but they had no link that Mary Stuart was involved in the plot herself, nothing that suggested she was the mastermind of it. If Kit could find evidence of such a thing, she knew Walsingham would be overjoyed.

It would be the final evidence he needed to convict Mary Stuart of treason and do away with the threat she posed for good.

"Oh, some time ago," Lady Ruskin beckoned Kit to follow. "Now, come with me."

Kit tried to hide her disappointment at not finding out more. As she followed Lady Ruskin through the open doorway, she glanced back at the painting just once, where those light-brown eyes still followed her.

Stepping through the doorway, Kit clenched her hands into the skirt of her dress at the scene before her. Lady Ruskin was not alone. Around the grand room that unfolded in front of her was a myriad of people, some of upper class, some of lower class, but all wearing some kind of plaid or brooch to declare where their loyalty resided. Above their heads and hanging in the room was a layer of thick smoke, trapped inside by the closed windows.

"Welcome to my secret boudoir," Lady Ruskin whispered to her with a giggle before presenting her arm dramatically to the people before her.

Kit had to work hard not to shift nervously between her feet. Not one person seemed alert or fully conscious, for they were all prostrate on settle chairs or on rugs, leaning against each other. "What is wrong with them?" Kit asked.

"Wrong? Nay, nothing at all," Lady Ruskin beckoned Kit to follow her further into the room. "They are merely suspending reality for a while, that is all."

Kit's gaze shifted from the faces to the tables. There were many more pipes on the surface such as the one Lady Ruskin carried in her fingers, and there were other things too, with tiny, dried leaves laid out on handkerchiefs. "What is that?"

"Oh dear, ye are unwise to the ways of the world. I suppose that is what happens when one is so young. Sit here awhile." Lady Ruskin turned to Kit and pushed her firmly in the shoulder. Kit fell back into a Savonarola chair, not having any choice in the matter, just as Lady Ruskin sat in the chair beside her. "Every man and woman ye see before ye thinks like me."

Kit looked around at the faces, trying to discern what she meant. "What is it they are smoking?" she asked, watching as some of them lifted the pipes to their lips, inhaling deeply.

"Some smoke tobacco, for others it is something called a cocoa leaf."

"Why do they do it?" Kit tried to hide her disgust as she clamped her hands around the arms of the chair.

"They are imagining a better life," Lady Ruskin said with gravity as she tipped her head back and relaxed in her chair, managing to look somehow regal, despite her slumped form. "Tell me, Mrs Allaway, what do ye imagine a better life to be?"

Kit flicked her eyes to Lady Ruskin, finding how closely she was being watched. "As I said the other night, we are not all permitted to be so open in our opinions. Ears may hear us that never should." She knew she had to maintain her resistance and not capitulate right away to condemning Queen Elizabeth and supporting Mary Stuart. Lady Ruskin had to believe she had worked hard to persuade the information out of her.

"Nay mouth here would tattle on ye." Lady Ruskin pointed around the room with the end of her pipe. "As I said, everyone here thinks as I do. They think of the queen the way I do."

"Which queen?" Kit asked with a small smile.

Lady Ruskin laughed deeply, the suddenness of it nearly made Kit jump. She shifted in her seat, trying to cover up the moment. "Quite so." Lady Ruskin gestured to her with the pipe. "Ye play a good game, Mrs Allaway, but I think I see a fellow mind in ye. Wait here a moment." She stood to her feet and crossed the room, moving into the centre of the dazed group staring at the smoke cloud above them in wonder.

With Lady Ruskin's back turned, Kit fidgeted all the more. She was uncomfortable, incredibly so, and desperate to be free of the place. For the first time, she understood what Iomhar meant. She'd had no idea what happened behind Lady Ruskin's walls, and she was beginning to understand the threat. She glanced back at the window, wondering how close Iomhar was and if he still waited for her by the porch steps.

"Here we are," Lady Ruskin said. "Try this."

Kit was presented with a shorter pipe than the one Lady Ruskin was using. Made of equally fine ivory and carved into swirls, it appeared more like an ornament than something that could be used. In the bowl cavity, small black leaves were pressed down, emitting a thin vapour trail.

"I am sure it will help ye to relax." Lady Ruskin pressed the pipe into Kit's hand before retaking the chair beside her. Kit was tempted to throw the pipe on the ground and run from the house, then the image of the night before flashed in her mind's eye.

She could not let anything happen to her queen, and if that meant trying the pipe, then she had to do it. Slowly, she lifted the stem to her mouth and inhaled. The smoke that filled her mouth was so sudden and choking that she coughed violently, bringing tears to her eyes. By the time she calmed down, breathing deeply, Lady Ruskin was laughing softly.

"Everyone does that their first time. Ye will get used to it. Try again." She ushered the pipe back to Kit's mouth.

A few minutes passed in silence as Kit tried the pipe a few times, looking around the room at others nearby, then her focus began to slip. Where faces had been fixed before, the world almost appeared sideways. She blinked madly, trying to hold onto it, but she couldn't. She realised she was slipping into the same dazed state the others were in.

"There we are," Lady Ruskin said, clearly delighted. "Now ye are as happy and relaxed as the rest of us."

"This certainly is powerful!" Kit remarked loudly, sitting back in the chair until she was slumped, just like Lady Ruskin. Her hold on reality was becoming weaker as she looked around the room, marvelling at the change. It abruptly seemed so absurd to her that she was here at all. Someone who worked for Walsingham and was staunchly loyal to the queen was now keeping company with those that plotted to overthrow her.

"Now, tell me, Mrs Allaway," Lady Ruskin nudged her knee, earning her attention. "Tell me what ye could not tell me the other night, and what ye could not tell me when ye looked at my painting of Mary Stuart. Who do ye think deserves to sit on our throne?"

Kit was so comfortable in her chair, so relaxed, that she could feel the temptation to tell the truth. It was on the tip of her tongue, ready to come out: *Queen Elizabeth*.

She leaned forward, ready to say the words when Lady Ruskin did too. The movement Lady Ruskin made nudged the ruff around her neck down a little. It revealed something black and inky across her neck. It was a tiny mark and could easily be mistaken for a blemish if it weren't for the darkness of the emblem. It was a tattoo, stained on Lady Ruskin's skin to recreate an animal at the bottom of her neck. It was a unicorn, a distinct symbol associated with Scottish royalty.

"Mrs Allaway?" Lady Ruskin prompted Kit on.

Kit snapped her gaze away from the tattoo and back to Lady Ruskin's face. Though she couldn't quite focus on it completely, the sight of the Scottish symbol had brought some of her sense back to her, and the lie fell from her lips instead of the truth.

"Mary Stuart should be sitting on our throne, my Lady," Kit said with a dazed smile. "If only wishes could become reality."

"Sometimes, they can," Lady Ruskin began slowly. "Allow me to let ye in on a little secret."

Kit couldn't stop the smile from spreading across her features, amazed her ruse had worked, as Lady Ruskin placed an arm around her shoulders and pulled her in closer, whispering in her ear.

"I have many friends in this world. At this moment in time, they are hard at work, trying to make your wish a reality." Her deep voice tickled Kit's ear.

"They are?" Kit asked, placing her free hand to her chest in an attempt to appear shocked at this news.

"That they are." Lady Ruskin smiled as she took another drag on her pipe, apparently delighting in Kit's shock. This time, she tipped her head back as she blew out the smoke, enveloping them both in a cloud. Kit's nose wrinkled at the stench, fortunately Lady Ruskin's head was tipped so far back, she didn't notice. "If we wish to see our rightful queen back in her place and usurp the bastard queen —" the insult and reference to claims that Elizabeth was illegitimate made Kit tighten her hand around her pipe, "— then the bastard must be nay more."

"Nay more?" Kit prompted her on, leaning all the more toward her. Here was the full confession from Lady Ruskin's own lips, she just had to urge the words to come freely. "Ye intend to imprison her?"

Lady Ruskin released her hold on Kit's shoulder and leaned back, laughing heartily. "Aye, how sweet. Ye think that would work? Talk of the wee ones and all their mad ideas." She continued to laugh, shaking her head. Her eyes had become so glazed from what she was smoking that she was madly blinking, almost as many times as Kit was. "Listen to this. Ye imprison your enemies, Mrs Allaway, and people will always rise up to try and free them. Nay, pay my words great heed. Ye wish to do away with a threat, there is only one thing for it. Ye must see them dead."

Hearing the words spoken so plainly made Kit sit far back in her chair, leaning as far away as possible from Lady Ruskin. She could feel her palms had grown clammy and the insufferable heat of the summer's day had become worse, increasing the sweat beading at the back of her neck.

"Ye wish to kill her?" Kit asked, aiming to be perfectly clear on the matter.

"I will not be the one to do the deed, naturally," Lady Ruskin spoke as though the words were obvious, "but such deeds must be done. What say ye to that?"

Kit could see she was being watched closely, her reaction evidently analysed. "With Elizabeth gone, more would rally to Mary Stuart's cause." Kit brought a false smile to her face, though her cheeks ached with the effort.

"Precisely," Lady Ruskin said and pointed her pipe at Kit in agreement with her.

"When is it to happen?" Kit asked, trying to find out more information, but Lady Ruskin merely laughed.

"Ye think I will tell ye that? Pah! I may like ye, Mrs Allaway, but I cannot tell ye such a thing when I barely know ye."

"Aye, of course," Kit held up her hand in an apology as she drew on her pipe. The world grew even more out of focus than before. As she tipped her head sideways, trying desperately to make the world stand straight, she had an idea. It was a bold chance to take, but she had come so far already, it seemed it was worth the risk. "Well, though ye cannot tell me the details,

I would be interested to help if I could. If there is anything ye need of me, I hope that in time ye will tell me, my Lady."

"How strange ye should say that," Lady Ruskin said, sitting straight in her chair and earning Kit's gaze once more.

"Strange? Why?"

"For there is something I need help with." Lady Ruskin lowered her pipe to a small table nearby and leaned toward Kit, taking her hand and pulling it forward, so that Kit was forced to veer forward, almost out of her seat. "This help is the very reason I invited ye here. Ye are married to Captain Allaway, aye?"

"Aye," Kit forced the lie to reach her lips.

"He is well-known for being sympathetic to our cause," Lady Ruskin spoke quickly, her words so fast and quiet that Kit had to strain to hear her. "He is a military man and will surely have access to gunpowder."

"Aye, of course," Kit nodded. "What of it?"

"Gunpowder has a particularly useful purpose in this world," Lady Ruskin said, squeezing Kit's hand harder. She lifted her free hand and flung the fingers wide open, making a sound effect with the movement. "*Boom.*"

Kit felt her stomach knot, understanding Lady Ruskin's meaning perfectly. She wished to create an explosion.

"We need more gunpowder. There is a problem with our planned supply. Surely ye could speak to your husband and persuade him to help us?" Lady Ruskin leaned toward Kit even more. "What do ye say?"

Kit bought some time by lifting the pipe back to her lips and taking another small breath. Still, she hated the taste, but it gave her a minute to think of an answer, seeing Lady Ruskin looking at her with so much hope that her vermillion lips were pressed firmly together, and her ceruse-coloured cheeks quivered.

"Aye, I can certainly ask him. Leave it with me, Lady Ruskin. I'll see what I can do."

CHAPTER 18

As Kit stepped out through the doorway, the fresh air made the world slip further sideways. She reached for the stone wall that bordered the porch steps, yet it disappeared beneath her hand. She tipped forward, stumbling down the steps at a rate so fast that her feet couldn't keep up with her.

"God's blood," a familiar voice said with panic, just as a pair of hands grabbed hold of her waist and held her up.

Kit had to blink a few times to realise what had happened. Her feet were not straight on the porch steps with one ankle bent under her, but she was being held up by Iomhar, with his hands on her waist and the face beneath his cap betraying his worry.

"Are ye all right?" he asked, as he set her on her feet and released her.

"Aye, I have not been better," she declared happily, holding onto her Scottish accent. She turned back to the doorway to find Lady Ruskin still standing there, offering a wave. Kit waved back before jumping down the last step, noticing out of the corner of her eye how Iomhar pulled his hat down a little more, as though to ensure Lady Ruskin did not see his face.

Once Kit was a few steps away from the house, she felt Iomhar take her elbow.

"What is wrong?"

"Nothing," she said, lapsing back into her normal accent now they were away from the house and the watchful eyes of Lady Ruskin. "What an *interesting* house that was." Her pitch was unusual, bouncing all over the place.

"Ye do not sound like ye." Iomhar used her elbow to steer her through the crowd of people wandering the streets. Secretly, she was thankful for it, for putting one foot in front of the other didn't feel as easy as it normally did. "What happened in there?"

"They had this thing…" She waved a hand in the air, gesturing toward her mouth.

"What did she give ye, Kit?" he insisted on knowing, his voice deeper than before.

"It was a pipe of something," she explained with a shrug.

"A pipe?" He came to a sharp halt, tugging so much on her elbow that she fell back into him. He adjusted his hold completely and caught her around the waist, holding her up. "God's blood!" he exclaimed, catching her just in time before she fell to the earth beneath them. "Kit, ye're not yourself."

"As much as I prefer to argue with you than agree with you, I think you're right on this occasion." She placed a hand over her eyes, hoping the darkness would stop the world from swaying back and forth, yet it only seemed to make the dizzying worse, so she opened her eyes again. She was still leaning against Iomhar, unable to get properly back on her feet.

"What did she make ye smoke?" Iomhar whispered in her ear.

"I do not know," she answered honestly.

"Then why did ye take it?"

"Iomhar!" she snapped, looking over her shoulder up at him. "Can we argue about this later?"

"Aye, fine," he said sharply, "because do not think I am going to let this go."

"You have already made it clear how poorly you think of my decisions. I do not need to hear it another time."

181

"True," he agreed, then tried to heave her back to her feet. She balanced momentarily on her feet, but as she took another step forward, her legs seemed to vanish beneath her, numb and without feeling, they couldn't hold her up. As she began to fall to the floor yet again, Iomhar was there, holding her up. "Right, that's it."

"That's what?" Kit asked, looking up at him in surprise.

"Put your arms around my neck."

"Well, that's the first time I have heard a line like that," she teased, smiling.

"Ye are out of your head," he said darkly, though a small smile still broke through. "I'm going to carry ye."

"You cannot do that!" she objected, about to step away from him yet finding the task an impossible one. Instead, he easily took hold of her waist and held her up in the air, just as she rested one hand on his shoulder. "For one thing, the farthingale makes it impossible." He clearly paused, seeing she was right when his arm couldn't reach under her knees. "Secondly, I think we'll draw attention to ourselves in the street if you start carrying me." He still held her in the air with just one arm around her waist, pulling her against his side.

"Ye were drawing attention to yourself well enough without me."

"I was not," she complained.

"Shall we have this argument later?"

"Very well," she agreed with a nod, then stilled her head with one of her hands, trying to stop the dizziness. "We need to get to Walsingham. There's something he should know."

"Later," Iomhar said, gesturing to an open-top cart full of hay nearby.

"Now, Iomhar. It's important."

"And what do ye think Walsingham will say to ye if ye turn up in this state?" Iomhar's question stopped her dead. "Aye, I thought ye may not like that. We'll get ye straight, then we'll go and see him."

"How long will this last?" she asked as Iomhar dropped a coin into the hand of the driver of the open-top cart.

"It depends on what ye took," he warned before heaving her up to sit on the back of the cart.

"That any better?" Iomhar's voice called from the other side of the room, muffled by the water.

Kit lifted her face out of the bucket of cold water, breathing deeply as the rivulets streamed down her forehead and cheeks with her eyes firmly closed. It had been some hours since she had left Lady Ruskin's house and come back to her lodgings. In that time she had changed into her men's clothes, eaten something and drank too, but the last ounce of dizziness was lingering.

"A little," she remarked slowly, splashing the water over her face and down her neck. Her hand halted on her neck, remembering what she had seen on Lady Ruskin's skin, the tattoo.

"It was reckless, Kit," Iomhar said softly from across the room. This time, his voice didn't hold its usual admonishment, just worry instead.

"I know," she accepted. "But after last night, can you blame me for being willing to take the risk?" She turned away from the bucket and looked back to Iomhar. He said nothing, but he nodded just once, as though in agreement with her. "Walsingham needs to hear what I found out."

"Are ye in any fit state to walk now?" he asked.

"I will be fine," she assured, gesturing to the door and urging him to be ready to leave. As he turned his back, she stood, ensuring she was steady on her feet before she followed him across the attic room toward the door. The staircase was easier than when she had arrived, for Iomhar had practically shoved her up the stairs with his hand firmly on her back to prevent her from falling. This time, she was able to take the stairs by herself.

As they walked through the street, she was not oblivious to the way Iomhar hovered by her side more than usual.

"I am not made of glass," she remarked, just as they rounded a corner and he pulled her out of the way of a horse rider. "I will be fine."

"Hmm, I'm tempted to give ye an argument on your last statement."

"You are always tempted to give me an argument on everything," she said as they walked on toward Walsingham's lodgings.

"Well, I cannot argue with that." He smiled, drawing one from her too. Still, he hovered, watching her closely the entire time they walked across London.

By the time they reached Walsingham's new lodgings, Kit was irritated with him. He was even opening doors for her and helping to steer her through, assistance that she did not need.

"If you continue like this, you will regret it," she warned with a whisper.

"Fine. Then the next time ye fall over, I will not catch ye. Ye can pick yourself up off the ground." At his words, she sent him a dark look, but she could say no more as Doris appeared.

"Ah, the master has been asking after the both of you," Doris waved them toward the stairs. "Come quickly."

"Is Lady Sidney here?" Kit asked warily, taking hold of the banister to help her walk up the steps.

"No, she left earlier today. The master is quite alone."

"Worried she'd send ye away again?" Iomhar whispered at Kit's side.

"Something like that," she admitted, as they reached the landing at the top of the stairs. A quick knock at the door was answered by Walsingham.

"Enter," he called, his voice more like its usual self.

Kit opened the door to see Walsingham was up and about. He was standing by a desk that had been brought into the room and placed by the window. Beside the desk was one of the chests full of papers that they had brought from Seething Lane. As they entered, he closed the lid of the chest quickly. "Where have you two been?"

"That is quite a story," Iomhar said as he hovered in the doorway. "Kit, would ye like to tell it?"

Kit shot a look his way before turning to Walsingham, seeing the way his dark eyes widened, waiting with expectation of her answer. "I have been at Lady Ruskin's house."

"Tell me you are not serious," Walsingham barked, waving his hands in front of him. "God have mercy, Kit! What were you thinking?"

"Allow me to explain," she pleaded, stepping toward him. "At the dinner, I spoke to Lady Ruskin. It was clear she was not going to let anything slip when she thought me a stranger, so I tried to make friends with her."

"She did that rather too well," Iomhar added, still moving no further into the room as he leaned on the doorframe. "She was invited to Lady Ruskin's house today."

"You defied my order, Kit." Walsingham's manner was strangely calm despite the obvious anger in his voice.

"With good reason," Kit said, pleading with him to believe her. "After today, she trusts me. She confirmed that there was a plot against Queen Elizabeth. I heard it from her own lips that she is helping to orchestrate the plot, though she doesn't intend to do the deed herself."

Walsingham reeled from the information. He tottered between his feet for a moment before he pulled out the chair at the desk and sat down, placing his hands on his knees. "What else did she say?"

"Gunpowder," Kit uttered the word slowly, watching as both Iomhar and Walsingham stiffened. "She believes me to be the wife of a Scottish soldier loyal to Mary Stuart, so she asked for my help to persuade this fake husband into providing them with gunpowder."

"This cannot be happening," Walsingham said, shaking his head in disbelief as he sat back in the chair.

"Are ye saying that they are planning to use an explosion to kill the queen?" Iomhar asked, earning her gaze from across the room.

"She didn't say that in so many words, but it certainly sounds like it," Kit explained quickly. "She wants me to help organise gunpowder for her. She will then send the men who work for her to collect it."

"Then we can set up a trap." Walsingham's previous anger at her seemed to be forgotten. He was animated, leaning forward and motioning between the two of them. "We can set up some gunpowder in a store in London, lure them there. When they arrive, you two can be watching and we will trap the men. With them arrested, we can interrogate them for more names in the plot, then arrest them all, before the attempt is even made on our queen's life."

"It could work," Kit agreed.

"We need more men for such a plan to work," Iomhar's voice was sudden and strong.

"More men? Why?" Walsingham asked, frowning.

"There are only two of us," Iomhar said, pointing between himself and Kit. "Who knows how many will turn up to collect the gunpowder? Ye want them caught, we need more intelligencers."

"I am not sure I can give you that."

"What?" Iomhar's sharp voice was met by a stony stare from Walsingham. Slowly, the older man stood to his feet. Despite his age and the way he clung to the back of the chair for support, there was strength and bitterness in his countenance.

"You heard me, Iomhar. This is your commission. The two of you can handle it."

"Set up this trap with us two alone and ye are risking both of our lives, unnecessarily."

"Everyone else is busy," Walsingham explained quickly. "This is not the only commission I have at the moment; it is not the only threat facing this country. You have your commission, you have your order, I have given it to you. It is your choice, Iomhar. Take it or go back to Scotland. Which is it?"

Kit watched Iomhar's face as the silence stretched out between the two men. After a minute, Iomhar returned Kit's gaze for just a second before he turned back to Walsingham.

"I'll do it, but if we end up dead, it will be because ye did not give us the men when I asked for it."

"You will live," Walsingham said, sinking back down into his chair.

Iomhar's grave expression showed he clearly didn't agree with Walsingham.

CHAPTER 19

Kit waited patiently for the door to Lady Ruskin's house to open. Behind her, Iomhar was waiting in the same spot he had occupied before at the bottom of the steps, with his final words still ringing in her eyes: *Do not take anything she gives ye this time.*

She had no intention of doing so. This was to be a quick meeting only, to inform Lady Ruskin of where she could find the gunpowder and to set the trap. It had been two days since she had last seen Lady Ruskin, giving the illusion of enough time to set up such a provision of gunpowder, whilst still giving them time to lay the trap for Lady Ruskin's men.

As the door opened, the steward appeared. "Mrs Allaway, Lady Ruskin is not expecting ye today."

"Nay, it is something of a surprise visit, but one I am sure she will be pleased by," Kit said, urging the steward to let her in.

He bowed at once and beckoned her to follow him. Just as before, he led her toward the drawing room, where today the only person sat prostrate on the chairs was Lady Ruskin herself.

"Mrs Allaway?" she exclaimed with surprise, sitting straight in her seat. "To what do I owe this visit?"

"I have come with good news," Kit affected an excited manner and rushed toward her across the room. She did not miss the way Lady Ruskin picked up some letters from her side and hid them beneath her skirt, though she pretended not to notice. "I have done as ye asked and wrote to my husband."

"From your manners I am guessing his answer was a good one," Lady Ruskin shrewdly observed. "Well, we must celebrate. Hawkins?" she called the attention of the steward who hovered in the doorway. "Bring us some wine."

He bowed and left at once. Kit was already recalling Iomhar's words about not taking anything Lady Ruskin gave her this time.

"I cannot stay long," Kit spoke hurriedly, trying to evade the promise of wine. "I have simply come to deliver my message."

"Very well. What is it?"

"My husband's message was very short," Kit whispered, "but he has already set his plans in motion. Tomorrow night, ye will find what ye need." As she spoke, she reached into a hidden pocket in her dress and pulled out a folded piece of parchment. "Send your workers to this address. It is a storehouse on the south side of the river."

The smile that spread across Lady Ruskin's face was one of elation as she snatched the parchment away and unfolded it quickly, reading the address as fast as she could.

"I do not know what to say," she said after a moment, hurrying to fold the parchment up again before she took Kit's hands in her own and squeezed them tightly. "Ye may have saved our objective, Mrs Allaway. Thanks to ye, we can go ahead as planned. How fortunate the world is!" She laughed as she spoke, with tears in her eyes. "It seems God is smiling on us at last. It is His will after all."

Kit worked hard to fix her smile in place, marvelling at the extent of Lady Ruskin's belief in her goal. "My husband mentioned Lord Ruskin in his last letter," Kit raised the matter of Lady Ruskin's husband. She was struck by the lack of mention of him at all and Iomhar's interest in the name had left her curious. "He suggested a wish to meet him."

"I am certain that could be arranged, now that we know we are alike in our wishes," Lady Ruskin said. "My husband is in Scotland at the moment, so I will write to tell him." She laughed suddenly, her joy overflowing. "Come, let us look at her." She moved to her feet and dragged Kit with her. Kit didn't have time to ask who she meant, for she had been towed into the hallway where Lady Ruskin brought the two of them to a stop before the portrait of Mary Stuart. "She will be free at last and returned to the place ordained to her by God and removed by man."

Kit couldn't look at the painting. She was too busy looking at Lady Ruskin and the tears she was working hard not to let fall. It struck her how devoted Lady Ruskin was to her last queen, it was almost fanatical as she released one of Kit's hands and used the backs of her wrists to dry a tear that escaped across her cheek.

"We are nearly there, Mrs Allaway," she announced, rather breathlessly, her smile so great that it had to hurt her cheeks. "I can feel it now. This is God's will, and it will not be long before all is as it should be."

Kit said nothing but continued to watch Lady Ruskin. When the older lady turned to her, clearly expecting an answer, Kit hurried to find her voice. "I cannot wait for the day," she spoke with animation, trying to sound hopeful and not fearful at all. She turned her eyes to the painting of Mary Stuart, wondering how merely the idea of the woman could stir so much trouble in the hearts of two countries. Men rallied to her name, though they had never met her, and yet there were those like Lady Ruskin too, who had met her, and despite all the tales of Mary Stuart's greed and murderous intent, they still wanted her on their thrones. "What was she like?" Kit found the question falling from her lips without much thought. "When ye met her?" She nodded her head toward the painting.

"She was…" Lady Ruskin paused, looking at the painting with a smile as she considered her words, "majestic. I am certain there could not be another word for her. She knows better than any other in this world the position that was ordained for her. When she walks, she carries herself with that knowledge, for nay person looks more regal. In conversation, ye would find her to the point and blunt, she does not have time for folly, nor for fools and bampots. Aye, I admire her more than I can say."

Kit couldn't agree. She stared at the painting and the light-brown eyes that glared back at her. The younger version of Mary Stuart had her hand on a table where a map of the British Isles had been laid. Though her palm rested on Scotland, her fingers were trailing over England and Wales too. It was a statement of intent by whoever had created the painting, a statement that made Kit stiffen where she stood.

Mary Stuart would not get her hands on the throne of England and Wales, Kit would make sure of it.

CHAPTER 20

"What do ye think?" Iomhar asked, standing back from the barrels. Kit stepped further into the barn they had selected for their trap, looking around the space. Usually used as a storage barn for straw and other equestrian needs, a stench lingered in the air of horse manure. Not a single window was in the barn, casting the place in shadow, with the only light that leaked through into the space emanating from the double open doorway.

"Do you think it looks too empty?" Kit folded her arms as she looked at the barrels they had brought for the deception. They were filled with stones to give the illusion of weight and heaviness if they were carried, but not a grain of real gunpowder was in sight. After all, they were hardly going to give Lady Ruskin's men what they truly wanted. The few barrels they had brought were clumped close together in the centre of the floor.

"Ye do not need much gunpowder to make an explosion," Iomhar said as he moved one of the barrels further along the room, creating more space. "Have ye not seen any used?"

"Never," she acknowledged.

Iomhar stopped and turned round, staring at her wide eyed. "What about the new matchlock pistols? Have ye not seen them used?"

"No," she confirmed, watching as he shook his head.

"I would have thought Walsingham would want ye to have one." Iomhar walked past her to move one of the other barrels along the floor. "The result of the weapon is devastating."

"Walsingham said they are inaccurate."

"Very," Iomhar agreed. "But they will get better. Weapons always do."

"So, if Lady Ruskin was to get her hands on this many barrels of gunpowder, what kind of explosion could that cause?" Kit asked, watching as Iomhar finished with the barrels.

"Just one would be enough to blow up a boat and sink it, or an entire wing of a house," he said, tapping the lid of one of the barrels.

"Oh," Kit gasped in amazement.

"Aye, think of what could happen if they wanted to get this many barrels near the queen? Actually, it does not bear thinking about," he shook his head. "What time are her men due?"

"This evening."

"Then we best hide." He gestured to the door for her to leave.

She hurried outside, waiting for him to step through too before she closed the door behind them. The strong sunlight of the day was beginning to wane, making the heat soften a little. In the distance, over the tops of the thatched and tiled rooftops she could see the sun sinking down, casting orange and purple streaks across the sky.

Iomhar turned away from the sunset and moved to the other side of the road, with Kit following close behind. They'd chosen the barn especially as it was far away from the city walls of London on the quiet streets of the city, though not too far from the River Thames meaning they could get their new prisoners back to the Tower of London relatively easily. A few coins in the owner of the barn's purse solved the problem of using it for one evening.

In the quiet road, the street wasn't even lined with cobbles, but with mud and dirt instead. Opposite the barn was a stable with horses that were snorting as they wandered around their small stable block. Kit and Iomhar took up their positions behind one of the stable doors, peering out into the wide set road.

Every now and then horse riders wandered up and down as did open-top carts, with a few pedestrians milling between them, but the longer they watched, the quieter the street grew, until darkness threatened to fall. As the sun slipped down below the rooftops, light did not completely leave them, but a greyish dusk fell on the street, making it increasingly difficult to see.

"They are not coming," Iomhar said, sighing at the light change.

"You are impatient," Kit warned, leaning opposite him on the other side of the open doorframe. "Wait a little longer, they are hardly going to try and move gunpowder in the day, are they?"

"Maybe not," he agreed with her, "but it still does not look good. Are ye sure Lady Ruskin believed ye?"

"I am positive," she explained, her voice firm as she held his gaze. "She was on the verge of tears."

"Tears? Why?"

"Tears of happiness. We were standing by a painting of Mary Stuart, and she was having to control them. She talked much of God ordaining Mary to be queen and how men had interfered with God's desires. She believes what she is doing is God's wish. In her mind…" Kit paused, thinking through her own words carefully, "I do not think she believes she is doing anything wrong."

"I can believe that. It sounds just like her husband." Iomhar turned his gaze out to the street.

"How do you know her husband?"

"Ye have already asked me that before."

"And I got no more answer that time than I seem to be doing now."

"So ye know it is pointless asking me then," Iomhar pointed out plainly.

"Why is it a secret?" Kit asked, tilting her head to the side to watch him closely.

"It is not a secret, I just do not talk about it."

"Mysterious indeed." Kit turned her attention back out to the road as well. "If you will not tell me how you know her husband, will you at least tell me more about him? What is he like?"

"I have already told ye, he is loyal to Mary Stuart. I rather think it is an obsession of his."

"It is that strong a feeling?" Kit asked.

"Undoubtedly," Iomhar lowered his voice to a whisper as all movement in the street faded into emptiness. "I heard him talk of God's will once too. Mary was born to be queen and coronated when she was just six days old. As far as he is concerned, God was so impatient to see her queen that He would rather have an infant on the throne than her father."

"That is a little maniacal," Kit said, thinking back to the painting she had seen in Lady Ruskin's house.

"Aye, it is," Iomhar agreed firmly. "I heard Lord Ruskin speak of how it was his life's duty to defend Mary Stuart and return her not only to the Scottish throne that was usurped from her and given to her son, but to also place her rightfully on the English throne. He believes nay more in Elizabeth's right to the throne than he would a wild boar's right to the same position."

Kit winced at the very idea. Queen Elizabeth may have been born of Henry VIII's second wife, but at the time the marriage was seen as legal and binding, therefore Elizabeth's legitimacy had not been in question. It was only much later that it had been questioned, around the time that Mary's wish to take the English throne from her cousin had appeared.

Kit turned her gaze from the road back to Iomhar, watching as something twitched in his jaw whilst he talked of Lord Ruskin. "Did he do something to you?" she asked in a whisper. Her words startled Iomhar as he flicked his head toward her.

"It was a long time ago," he said quietly. "It hardly has a bearing on what is happening now."

"Yet you still resent him for it?"

"I will never forgive him for what he did," he spoke with perfect clarity. The words hung in the air for a second as Kit took a step toward Iomhar.

"What did he do?"

"Now is not the time for that discussion," he shook his head. As though to back up his point, there was a sound beyond the door. Iomhar urged Kit to step back behind the frame to hide herself, just as three men appeared in the road. Their figures were basked in shadows with their faces difficult to discern, yet the way they kept glancing over their shoulders, apparently fearful of being seen was plain to observe. "I would say Lady Ruskin's men have arrived."

Peering round the doorframe, Kit watched as the three men approached the barn, slowly and warily. Two of them were dressed in black with scarves around their necks and hats pulled low, the third was not so covered up and dressed much finer. He wore a ruff around his neck, an earring glinting in his ear and a smart doublet, even if it was slightly rough around the edges.

"I do not believe it," Iomhar muttered.

"What?" Kit hissed across the doorframe between them.

"Look again," Iomhar said, pointing at the well-dressed man. Kit arched her head around the doorframe, the better to see him. He turned his head and what light was left out in the dusk of the evening fell on his face, revealing his features. It was Graham Fraser, the man she had stolen the letter from in the alehouse.

"Ready?" Kit asked.

"Not yet," Iomhar warned, shaking his head. "Wait a while." He reached for the weapons around his belt, lifting the crossbow that usually hung beneath his cloak, hidden. "We do not want to give them a chance to run."

Kit turned to look back through the stable door, watching the three men. Fraser gestured to the other two, urging them to move toward the doors of the barn. They went together as Fraser looked up and down the street, constantly looking for anyone watching, though he never noticed the open doorway where they stood, for they were cast too much in shadow.

One of the men opened the doorway of the barn, scraping the oak door across the muddy ground before stepping in and beckoning the others to follow. They left the door open behind them, giving Kit a view of what they were doing. Beside her, Iomhar loaded a bolt into the crossbow, locking it into place.

"Ye have a view of them?" he asked.

"Perfect view."

He moved to her side and lifted the crossbow, aiming through the gap.

"You kill them, and Walsingham will have no one to interrogate," she whispered.

"I'm not intending to kill them," he said, "just to shock them and stop them running away. Though I imagine death may be preferable to *interrogation*."

"What does that mean?" Kit asked, looking up to Iomhar in time to see the crossbow hover.

"Well, ye do not really think he only talks to them, do ye? If ye think that, ye really are naïve."

"Are you capable of a compliment or is everything that comes out of your mouth a condescension?" she snapped, turning back to watch as Fraser and the others counted up the barrels, talking and making a plan between themselves.

"Of course I am," Iomhar returned his focus to the crossbow. "I just do not give compliments out lightly."

"Stretch yourself, see what happens."

"Very well," he said quietly. "Ye did well to convince Lady Ruskin of the trap. Ye convinced her of your loyalty when I doubted it was possible. Impressive." Despite fishing for the compliment, Kit was startled enough by it to look sharply up to Iomhar. "Step back." She followed his wish and moved out of the way.

The crossbow fired. The bolt whistled through the air, crossing the street and heading straight into the barn. It landed firmly in one of the barrels, but not before piercing the loose cloak of one of the men, fastening him to the barrel. Fraser and the other jumped back, yelping in surprise.

"Time to go." Iomhar stepped out of the stable and pulling a rope free from his belt, ready to arrest the men. He passed the rope into Kit's hands as he crossed the street. Kit pulled her hat lower over her face as she followed behind him, stepping through the shadows and running into the barn.

"Do not move," Iomhar ordered, lifting the crossbow with a fresh bolt in the barrel. Fraser stopped first, holding his arms out wide as his body stilled. The man fastened to the barrel was trying to tear himself free as his friend went to help him. "All of ye, stay still." The men froze. "Ye two, wrists together."

Kit walked toward the two men as they followed his instruction. She wrapped the rope around the first man's wrist when a sound behind her revealed that Fraser had taken a step forward.

"I said do not move," Iomhar warned.

"I know ye, I've seen ye before," Fraser murmured, looking between the two of them. "Ye two … the letter."

"He's a quick one," Iomhar said with humour.

"Do not belittle me."

"Ye made it too easy," Iomhar snapped back. "Put your wrists together."

Fraser followed the instruction, just as Kit turned her attention to the man attached to the barrel. As she wrapped the rope around his wrists, she was too busy glancing over her shoulder to notice that he moved his hand to grab hold of the end of her rope.

He tugged hard on the rope, releasing it from her grasp, then lifted his hand and made a strike for her. She saw it just in time, dodging the blow and bending her head out of the way.

"I said do not move!" Iomhar barked the words, turning the crossbow toward them, but it was too late.

Kit felt the man she had already tied up tackle her to the ground. Her head fell back on the cobbles, dazing her for just a second, long enough to allow him to stand. One of the blades she always carried was snatched from her belt and he used it to break through the ties around his wrists.

"Run!" Fraser ordered his friends.

As the two men ran from the store, Kit tried to get to her feet, still a little dazed. She turned round on her knees to see Iomhar was being tackled by Fraser, with the two of them wrestling over the crossbow.

"Kit, get after them," Iomhar ordered, yet she didn't. She stumbled to her feet and lifted the lid off one of the barrels, heading straight for Fraser and knocking him across the head. He stumbled away from Iomhar, clutching his head. "That will do," Iomhar nodded. "Ye tie him up, I'll get the others."

She lifted the rope from the floor and went toward Fraser as Iomhar ran out of the barn. She had the rope around only one of Fraser's hands when he stopped stumbling from the pain to his head. He snatched up something from the ground — it was Kit's blade, the one that had been taken by another of his men and then dropped — before turning it on her, pressing it straight against her throat.

"I do not believe it," he said, his eyes widening as the dagger moved against her throat. "Ye are a woman! Release me. Now," he warned, panting as he tried to catch his breath. "I do not want to hurt a lass, but I will if ye push me to it."

Kit didn't release him at first. She kept as tight a hold on the rope as before, then he pressed the blade firmer against her throat. Feeling the cold metal of her own dagger against her skin, she knew she had no choice. If she wished to live, she had to let go.

She released the rope and stepped back, away from the cold touch of the blade.

"Good lass," Fraser sneered. "Stay there. Do not follow."

"You know I am not going to do that," she said, watching as he backed out of the barn.

"Then I will not be held accountable for what happens to ye." He turned and ran from the barn, sprinting so fast that his boots thumped against the earth loudly. Kit ran after him, trying to keep him in view as he fled down the street.

He dived between narrow houses built of timber, thrusting her dagger into his belt as he ran. She pursued him all the way, keeping good pace. With the street so empty, it was easy to keep him in sight and track exactly where he went. After travelling through a few small lanes, he emerged into a wider street where carts and horses were heading toward the river, ready to cross the bridge over the Thames.

Fraser headed into the road without warning, startling one of the horses so much that it whinnied high into the sky and reared back on its hind legs. Fraser backed away from the horse, diving between another two carts.

Kit couldn't follow straight away. She ran along the side of the road, keeping parallel to Fraser the whole time. They were heading in the same direction, aiming straight for the river that was up ahead. As the road began to camber down, petering away as it neared the entrance to London Bridge, peppered with houses, Fraser kept glancing to his side, apparently looking for something.

Kit was working hard to keep him in view between the carts and horses, seeing he was looking for something, probably a way off the main road. She turned her focus to the road itself, trying to find a way through the horses. It was too busy to get across easily, with the evening movement and deliveries to the docks travelling back and forth.

There was a gap on her side of the road, just as a cart pulled up not far from her on the other side, carrying boxes of bottled small beer. She ran alongside it for a moment before leaping out and grabbing onto the back of the cart, levering herself up onto the back. Once up, she moved to the opposite end of the cart and dropped down, reaching the other side of the road.

Fraser jumped away, finding her close and reaching for the blade in his belt. He turned as she reached out to grab him, missing him by a whisker and nearly colliding with a nearby wall as he dived off the road, taking a path that passed alongside the river. She scrambled to follow him, struggling as the darkness began to fall. Where it was grey before, the shadows had grown thicker and blacker, making tracking Fraser's path even more difficult.

"Fraser, get back!" a voice called from up ahead.

Fraser's pace abruptly slowed, giving Kit a view of what was happening ahead. Fraser and his friends must have agreed a route in advance as they were in front, with Iomhar fighting the two of them. One was on the floor, struggling to get back to his feet as Iomhar tussled with the second. He had his rapier drawn, parrying quickly with his opponent who was using an errant plank of wood he must have found nearby to defend himself.

Fraser's hesitation gave Kit the advantage that she needed. She launched herself toward him, using her body weight to tackle him in the back. He was knocked from his feet, colliding with the floor. She grabbed another rope from her belt and pulled it loose, ready to tie him up, yet the rope was tangled, and the task was not so easy to accomplish. The brief struggle gave Fraser the time to drive his hands down into the ground and push his back upward, dislodging Kit from her hold on him. She rolled away, slipping on the stony earth in the effort to stand straight.

"Kit, look behind ye," Iomhar's roaring voice made her turn round. On the ground amongst the dirt there were stones, either kicked up from the roads nearby or splashed onto the lane by the Thames. She grabbed one of the largest flints she could find and spun round to see Fraser advancing toward her with her dagger in his hand, the blade pointing directly at her chest.

She threw the flint straight at his face. It collided perfectly with his brow, causing a bead of blood as he staggered from the impact. Kit used the brief moment to leap to her feet and reach toward Fraser. She took hold of his ruff to stop him from staggering too far away and then kicked him in the stomach, forcing him forward.

She used her hold on Fraser's ruff to pull him down even further, stopping him from lifting the weapon to her, and kicked the dagger out of his hand. It clattered to the earth, bouncing up and hitting the wall that lined the river momentarily before falling flat. As she struggled with him, pulling the ruff out of place, something dark and inky caught her eye. She pushed the ruff further up his neck, shoving down into his back to keep him bent over as she analysed the mark.

She had seen it before. Except this tattoo wasn't black, but midnight blue, shaped into the Scottish symbol of the unicorn with the horse rearing its head so high the horn between its ears was pointed upward, toward Fraser's head.

She was too startled by the sight of the unicorn to notice that Fraser had found his balance. He kicked out behind him, making contact with Kit's knee. She released her hold on his ruff and lurched back, falling away until she collided with the wall beside the river, placing both hands behind to hold herself up. Her leather gloves scraped against the stone, making an awful scratching sound against the cries of pain around her.

She only glanced to the side long enough to see Iomhar had struck one of the men, who was lying on the ground with a bloodied nose. The other he had within his grasp, who was crying out for help.

Fraser had stood straight and was walking directly towards Kit, his hands outstretched. Kit reached for the other dagger in her belt, snatching it high, ready to strike, yet Fraser was prepared for it. He blocked the blow by driving his forearm into her own. The sheer strength of the blow made the dagger drop from her fingers to the floor, then he brought up his other arm, driving a straight hit into her stomach.

She bent forward, winded, unable to catch her breath, then felt herself lifted from her feet. With horror, she realised what was happening. He was shoving her shoulders, forcing her back over the river wall and towards the water. She fought against him, but it was too late. She tipped backwards over the wall, lifting her chin as she rolled over it to see the green water coming up to her.

She tried to catch one last breath before hitting the water, but it was ill timed and she ended up with a mouth full of water, inhaling that instead. Her body hit the water with a loud smack, her body reverberating from the force against her and falling still before she began to sink through the depths.

She tried to swim, but not knowing how, her arms and legs merely flailed in the water. Bubbles filled her vision, masking the river surface from view in the frantic action.

The past was here again, only this time it wasn't a dream, it was a reality. Just as in the memory where she couldn't reach the surface, she couldn't do so now. In her mind's eye, she could see the figure above her, watching her, before it walked away.

She began to slip further and further down into the murky water.

CHAPTER 21

Kit felt something around her waist and under her arms, a pressure of something driving her upward. She blinked a few times, trying to see through the water, but it was still too murky and filthy, filled with bubbles and brown streaks through the green. Something was kicking behind her and she was being dragged upwards, closer and closer to the surface, until the moon could be seen, with its outline contorted and wobbly through the water.

When her head broke through the surface, she still couldn't breathe straight away. The water was in her lungs and in her mouth, stopping her from taking a single breathe.

"Breathe, Kit!" Iomhar ordered behind her, then a slap came to her back. The water was dislodged from her mouth by the utter force, and she coughed up the blockage. She continued to cough for many seconds, trying to clear her airways from the pain of the water. It took a minute for her to breathe clearly, then she tipped her chin back, looking up to see Iomhar's head slightly above and behind her, to realise what had happened.

His arm was around her waist as he swam toward the edge of the River Thames, dragging them both towards the riverbank.

"Wh-what happened?" she stuttered, before collapsing into coughing once more.

"Let's just get ye to the riverbank first," he said, dragging her away. He had to have dived in to pull her out of the water.

They reached the edge of the river, just as Iomhar pushed her onto the earth that was piled high at the side. She clung to it, pressing her hands and knees into the boggy mud as Iomhar lifted himself up onto the bank too. He slapped her back a few more times, urging her to clear her lungs completely.

Once she was clear, she fell down on the bank with her cheek pressed against the wet soil, breathing deeply. For a minute, she just laid there and said nothing, watching Iomhar's silhouette in the moonlight. He was drenched with the water droplets falling from his dark hair and trickling down his cheeks.

"What happened?" she asked, clearer this time. "They fled?"

"Aye, ye could say that," Iomhar nodded, not looking down at her but back up at the wall high above them, over which she had fallen. "Once ye went in, there was only one option."

Kit's eyes widened as she slowly sat up, using her sleeve to try and clean the mud off her cheek. The soil from the riverbank was damp and stuck to her skin. "You let them run?" she asked in disbelief, as he looked back to her.

"It was either that or let ye drown. It was plain to see ye were struggling in the water. Which would ye rather I have done?"

"Go after them!" she said loudly, moving to her knees and pointing up to the top of the wall. "*They* could be the ones about to try and kill the queen. You should not have let them go."

"Then ye'd be dead," he pointed out calmly. "Is that really preferable?"

"I…" She struggled to answer.

"I've heard ye say before ye're prepared to die for this, but ye do not have to die, and I told ye." He paused as he stood to his feet. "Walsingham may be as cavalier with your life as ye are your own, but I do not treat life so lightly." He shook the water off his hands before offering one to her. "I can barely believe ye are angry at that."

"I am not." She took his hand as he helped to pull her to his feet. "Erm, thank you." She struggled with the words as she glanced down at the river beside them. She felt a tremble to her fingers by merely looking at the water. For an awful minute, she had thought she had met her end, that her memory had come back to reclaim her death, only this time, it would make certain of it.

"Are ye all right?" Iomhar's voice made her snap her head toward him, startled to see she still had her hand in his. She retracted it quickly.

"Yes," she said, a little shakily, avoiding his gaze as she looked at the water. "I cannot swim," she confessed, saying the words aloud at last that she had always refused to tell anyone.

"Surprising." There was no judgement in his voice.

"Why?" she asked, looking to him as he began to walk away up the riverbank with her following.

"I saw ye climb down that rockface in Edinburgh with a rope around your waist. I've seen ye clamber up walls like ye were born to do the task. I have rarely seen anyone with that kind of athleticism. I assumed swimming would be nay trouble to ye either."

"It is." She kept her head low as she followed him. She opened her mouth, for some reason ready to tell him about her memory, then the words died in her throat, and she closed her mouth.

"We need to get ye out of these clothes," Iomhar said as he found a set of steps heading up from the riverbank through the wall and leading to the very top.

"No, we need to find Fraser and the others." Kit struggled to breathe deeply as she climbed the steps. Once she reached the top, she leaned on the wall beside her, trying to catch her breath. She stood straight when she caught Iomhar watching her with a frown.

"Nay, we do not. Ye are in nay state to go chasing after anyone right now." He took a step away, bending down to the ground where he retrieved a blade. As he passed it to her, Kit realised what it was. It was the dagger that Fraser had taken from her. She placed it back in her belt.

"I am well."

"Ye still have water in your lungs. That's why ye cannot breathe deeply. A physician needs to look at ye and ye need rest."

"I cannot."

"Why not?" Iomhar asked, his voice louder than hers as he opened his arms wide.

"We have failed tonight," she said simply, leaning on the wall beside her.

"Failed Walsingham?" He tried to provoke her.

"Failed the queen," she responded tartly. "I cannot give up now."

"Ye can give up for one night," he said, taking her arm and steering her away from the wall. "We will start again tomorrow. For one thing, I did not even see which way Fraser and the others went, I was too busy jumping over the wall to get to ye, so running madly around London in any direction does not sound appealing. Let's just find somewhere to dry up."

"My lodgings are too far from here." Kit stopped walking as she coughed again. She bent forward, practically retching with the need to get the water out of her.

"Keep doing that," Iomhar assured her, tapping her back. "I know it's not nice, but it's what ye need to do."

"Easy for you to say. Not so easy to do," she panted, standing straight.

"Well, next time try not to breathe in when ye go in the water."

"I hardly did it on purpose!" she complained, throwing up her arms when she caught sight of Iomhar's face. He was smirking. "Do not tease me now."

"Very well. Ye need to rest. We'll go to my lodgings instead."

"Where is that?"

"Ye already know," he said, taking her arm and helping to steer her down the street. "It was the address we gave Lady Ruskin to deliver her letter too."

Kit was slowly starting to feel better as they walked towards Iomhar's lodgings. Though she still had to cough every now and then, it was getting more infrequent. When Iomhar took her arm and steered her toward a front door, she barely took notice, as she was too busy trying to squeeze the dregs of water out of her hair. She was drenched and in the chill of the night the cold of the water was clinging to her bones, making her shiver.

"We need to get ye into fresh clothes," Iomhar said as he pushed her through the door.

"I am fine," she murmured quietly.

"That would be more convincing if your teeth were not chattering as ye said it." He pointed to her face as they stepped into the house. She tried to clamp her teeth shut and stiffen her jaw, but it did little use.

Once the door was closed behind them, they were encased in darkness. Kit stood against the door, wrapping her arms around her waist in the attempt to keep warm as she grew aware of Iomhar moving. The sound of a tinderbox ruffled nearby, then a flint was struck against a piece of wood and a candleflame appeared. The soft orb lit Iomhar's face, highlighting his cheekbones and the dark hair on his chin, along with the scar at the top of his right cheek. He passed the flame to two other candles, until there were three prepared. He left one on the windowsill, carried a second and passed the third to her.

"This way," he beckoned her forward.

Lifting the candle high, Kit followed him down the corridor. It only took a few steps to realise that Iomhar did not live in a cheap attic room as she did. It was a townhouse, smaller than Lady Ruskin's, but certainly grander than Kit had been expecting.

Dark wooden floorboards stretched out before them in a long corridor. Beside them, a towering set of wooden stairs dominated the space, leading up to the rafters. On the wall beside the staircase was a tapestry, and on the other side, a painting grew out of the darkness. Kit hovered by it for a minute, aware that Iomhar was continuing on, but she could not.

"Do you come from money?" Kit asked, realising how odd her question was.

Iomhar stopped at the far end of the corridor, turning back to her, with the candle flame setting his narrowed features in an orange orb. "If ye mean do my parents have money, aye, some," he acknowledged.

"It looks a little more than some," Kit pointed out, raising her eyebrows.

He smirked slightly, visible in the candlelight. "Aye, so it is a little more than some."

Kit still didn't move to follow. She returned her gaze to the painting and lifted the candle a little higher, the better to see it. The canvas revealed a portrait of a family together. At the back and in the centre was a tall man, not dissimilar to Iomhar in his features. Beside him had to be the man's wife, then around them were five children of various ages. There was one boy in the painting who looked very familiar. Perhaps the second eldest, not as tall as one of the other boys, but bearing the same dark hair and the green eyes she had seen every day for the past week, the identity was impossible to mistake.

"It's you, is it not?" Kit gestured to the painting.

Slowly, Iomhar walked back through the corridor, stopping at her side. With the light of his candle falling on the painting too, it made it clearer to see. Each figure in the painting was dressed well. There were two girls, apparently the youngest of the brood, then three older boys, of which Iomhar was among them. The wife had the same green eyes Kit had observed in Iomhar's face, though his features were much more like his father's.

"Aye, it's me," he confirmed, holding his candle closer to the part of the painting that resembled himself. "I remember sitting for the painting all too well."

"You make it sound like a normal thing to do," Kit said with a small laugh.

"It was for my family." He shrugged.

"If I wanted a drawing, I had to steal charcoal from Walsingham's desk to draw something myself," Kit explained, watching as Iomhar smiled at the idea.

"Aye, rather different," he acknowledged. "I was told I had to sit for this painting. Ordered to by my mother." He gestured to her in the painting.

"Big family," Kit said with a smile, passing her candle near all the children's faces. "Who are they all?"

"My eldest brother, Duncan." He pointed to the tallest of the children. He had Iomhar's same dark hair, but not the eyes.

"Then there's Niall," he gestured to the last boy. "Then Rhona and Abigail."

Kit turned her gaze on the two girls. They were standing together, hand in hand, both smiling. "They look rather sweet."

"That is just the painter's work," Iomhar said with a shake of his head. "Rhona is more mischievous than ye can imagine, even now, and Abigail will happily give ye an argument on anything, for the sake of it."

Kit looked up at him, turning away from the painting to observe him better.

He lifted the candle to his parents' faces next, tarrying for a while over their features.

"You have your mother's eyes," Kit observed, pointing to his mother.

"Aye," he agreed. "She writes to me often these days, wants to know when I will next be coming home."

"She probably misses you," Kit spoke slowly. "I've heard it's painful for mothers to be away from their children." She had heard such things more than once, even if she had never experienced it herself. Looking at the way the mother in the portrait had her hands on two of her children's shoulders, one of which was Iomhar, Kit couldn't halt a small leap of envy in her chest. She longed to know what an upbringing with a family around her could have been like.

"Aye but look how many other children she has to keep her company," Iomhar gestured to the other children. "Believe me, that house can get so loud sometimes, ye need to come all the way to London, just for some peace."

Kit turned her attention to the father in the painting, the one who bore such similar features to Iomhar. "And your father? What is he like?" she asked.

212

Iomhar did not reply. Instead, his candle was lowered away from the painting, casting a shadow over the father's face.

"Iomhar?" she prompted him, turning to him completely.

"I do not talk about him." He veered away, walking down the corridor.

"Wait, Iomhar?" she called and hurried after him, catching up with him. "Why not?"

"It does not matter," he said tartly.

"Well, I just meant that —"

"Kit," he turned sharply back to her, cutting her off. "I do not talk about him. Understand?"

She held his gaze for a moment, seeing the unblinking strength there. In the end, she nodded, unwilling to push it any further.

"Good, now, let's get ye a physician and some dry clothes to wear."

CHAPTER 22

Kit watched as the cook placed some food down in front of her at the kitchen table. She hadn't realised when she had first entered the house that Iomhar had staff, but the more she saw of the place and the more she understood its size, it made perfect sense.

The cook was humming a happy tune as she slid the pewter trencher towards Kit. "Now, you eat up, pet," the woman said with a strong Northumbrian accent. "You must be frozen after your swim in the water."

"Thank you," Kit reached forward and dug in. "What is it?"

"Arbroath smokie," the cook said with glee. "One of the master's favourites. Call me if you need anything, pet." She smiled before waving and hurrying out of the kitchen with some laundry in her hands.

Kit returned her attention to the plate. It was some kind of smoked fish with greens cooked until they were pale and wilted on the side. She eagerly dug into the fish and brought it to her mouth, but the moment she took a bite, she was tempted to spit it back out.

"Not a fan?" the Scottish accent from the door made her snap her head towards it, to find Iomhar walking in. He had bathed and changed clothes himself, wearing a waistcoat over a white shirt above trews as he sat down at the table where a plate was waiting for him.

"What is this exactly?" Kit asked as she struggled to swallow it.

"Smoked haddock," he explained, almost laughing at her. "Ye look like ye are about to be sick. Try it again, it is not so bad." Kit dutifully tried it another time, but was as repulsed as before, practically gagging on the food. "Aye, Elspeth will be disappointed. She works hard on her food."

"Why would you eat this?" Kit moaned, turning her attention to the greens instead that were not so repulsive.

"It's a Scottish dish," he explained, breaking up his own fish and eating eagerly. "My favourite."

"You can have it," Kit said, pushing her plate toward his.

"Ye have to eat something." He pushed it back to her. "Eat it with the greens." She did as he instructed but persisted in gagging with every bite. "Now, what did the physician say?"

Kit paused with her food and looked down at herself. After they had arrived back, she had been offered a warm bath by one of the few members of staff Iomhar had and was then given some of Iomhar's old clothes to wear. They were far too big and baggy on her, with the doublet hanging loose and the hose held up by a tight belt. A physician had arrived shortly after to check her over.

"He says I will be fine," Kit confirmed. "Though he gave me a lecture on swallowing water, like you did. He said I might be ill in a few days, stomach upset from the water."

"That is not surprising, have ye seen what people throw in the Thames?"

"I do not want to think about it," Kit said, shaking her head and closing her eyes.

"All right let's talk of something else instead," Iomhar said, concentrating on his food.

"I could ask you about this house?" She was much more interested in this new topic. "The chamber you put me in is huge. I have never seen a bath so big."

"I do not wish to talk about that," Iomhar shook his head. "I wish to talk about swimming."

"I do not," Kit insisted firmly, sitting back in the chair. "I have had the lecture from both you and the physician now. I do not need it another time."

"That is not what I am trying to say," he assured, looking at her over the candles on the table. "Would ye like to learn how to swim?"

"What?" she asked, startled by the question.

"Ye said ye cannot swim. I could teach ye," he shrugged as though it were no great deal. "There is a stream in the garden, I could teach ye tomorrow."

"A stream in the garden? You say that as if it is a normal thing to have in one's garden."

"Well, it is for me."

"That was one hell of a boast!"

"Do ye want to learn to swim or not?" he asked, holding back a laugh as he stared at her.

She hesitated in her reply, turning her gaze back down to the fish. "I..." she faltered, trailing off. She was uncertain how to tell him that it wasn't just that she couldn't swim, but that she was afraid of the water.

"Kit?" His voice urged her to look up at him. "One swimming lesson, that's all I ask. If ye do it, then I promise to get the cook to make ye something else other than the fish."

That was a deal she couldn't refuse. She gave up eating the fish and looked up at him with a smile. "Very well, when do we start?"

"Is now really the time?" Kit asked, trying to think of a way to avoid the swimming lesson after all. It was morning, not long after the sun had risen and they were standing in Iomhar's garden, looking over the body of water that stretched across the back of not only this garden, but the adjoining houses too. The stream wasn't too deep, she could see that from the yellow rocks at the bottom, but that knowledge didn't help her. Her hands were still clammy.

"Aye, why not?" Iomhar joined her side at the river.

"We should be thinking of what to do next about Lady Ruskin," Kit said, trying to return to the matter at hand.

"Later," Iomhar pointed at her. "We made a deal. Ye are going to learn how to swim." He stepped toward the water and didn't hesitate from jumping in. Just like the night before, he was dressed in trews and a shirt, but he had shed his waistcoat, the easier to swim, apparently.

Kit was still wearing some of the clothes that had been given to her, with the hose being held up tightly by a belt. She also had a white long-sleeved shirt and a sleeveless jerkin over the top. She fiddled with the sleeves of the shirt, preferring to do anything else other than the task ahead of her.

"Kit, are ye getting in the water or not?" Iomhar asked, then turned back to her. He was standing in the middle of the stream with the water reaching up to his waist.

She said nothing, she merely looked down at the river and moved slightly toward it, until the toes of her boots were against the very edge of the water. The stream was clear of dirt, but staring into it, Kit felt that same fear ripple beneath the surface.

"Ye are as white as a newborn lamb," Iomhar said, abruptly striding back to the edge of the riverbank.

"I am fine."

"Aye, ye look it, ye bampot," he said sarcastically, coming to a stop in front of her in the river.

"What does that mean? Bampot? Lady Ruskin used it too."

"Scottish word for a fool."

"Oi!" She folded her arms.

He laughed but moved on regardless. "Now, are ye going to tell me what is wrong, or do I have to guess?"

She said nothing for a minute. She glanced around him at the water but figuring there was no real way out of this, she began to remove her boots and tossed them onto the riverbank. When she was done, Iomhar offered his hand to help her into the water. Any other time, she would have happily pushed his hand out of the way, refusing his help, but not now. Instead, she took his hand. She could see the equal look of surprise on his face as he helped her into the water.

Once she was in, she didn't release his hand. She stood frozen to the spot, very aware of how high the water rose around her waist, practically up to the middle of her chest. Her breathing was growing fast.

"Ye are afraid of the water," Iomhar summarised quietly, figuring it out without her having to say anything. "Why did ye not say?"

"Why do you think?" she snapped quickly. "Who likes to admit to a thing like that?"

"Kit, enough people have drowned in water to make it an understandable fear."

"I know you think that helps, but it really does not," she said, closing her eyes and trying to ward off the sight of the water before her.

"Let's start again then," he spoke with a softer tone and tugged on her hand, urging her to open her eyes. "Kit, listen to me. This is a small stream. It is not deep, and I am here with ye. Nothing can happen to ye here, aye?"

"Aye," she mimicked his Scottish accent. It brought a brief smile from him.

"First, why do ye not just try walking about the water. Ye will see it is not deep and ye are perfectly safe. I promise ye."

She nodded, realising it was the best idea, yet when he released her hand, she felt the clamminess climbing up the back of her spine and up her neck too. In her mind, she could see herself back in the water as a child, staring up at the silhouette of the woman who had walked away. It was all too easy to relive.

When she grew aware of Iomhar watching her closely, she began to walk forward, aiming for the other side of the riverbank. She started slowly at first, getting a feel for the rocks beneath her feet that kept slipping. Gradually, she grew used to the feeling, and crossed relatively easily. Though it didn't stop her from clinging to the riverbank on the other side as though it were her saviour.

"There ye are," Iomhar said with a smile. "Want to walk back the other way?"

"Want to?" Kit huffed mockingly. "I could think of other words for it." Dreading it, for one thing.

With trepidation, she walked across, aware that he watched her all the way. She did it back and forth a few times, until her body began to relax a little and it was not as stressful. Soon, she was walking with ease, and her grasp on either riverbank was not so tight as it had initially been.

"Ready to swim?" Iomhar asked. His simple words made her grasp on the riverbank tighten. "Nothing will happen, I promise ye."

"I think I find it unsettling how nice you are being," Kit said, looking at him and desiring to change the topic.

"Ye wish me to go back to teasing ye instead?"

"Anything else would be preferable."

"As ye wish." He moved to her side. "Ye're holding onto the reeds like they're a lover."

"Iomhar!" She snapped her hands away.

"Well, it worked to make ye release them," he chuckled as he moved toward her in the water. "Now, time to swim."

This time, Kit fell silent and paid attention to everything he said. He was patient with his instructions as he taught her what to do. It was slow progress, with her eagerly placing her feet down on the stream bed at every opportunity at first, but little by little, she grew more confident. Her arms trembled as she tried to swim back and forth, and initially she refused to put her head under the water at all, finding that an impossible feat to traverse.

"There, how's that?" Iomhar asked as she reached his side.

Her last practice had not been so successful, with her mouth slipping beneath the river surface more than once. When she tried to put her feet down on the ground, her legs were shaking so much that the rocks slipped from beneath her. The ground slid away, and she fell backwards, straight under the water. When she floundered around, frantic to try and reach the surface, she felt an arm under her waist, pulling her up. As she broke through the surface, she came face to face with Iomhar.

"Your feet on the ground yet?"

She planted them firmly down. "The ground fell away," she said angrily.

"Aye, I wish I could say ye handled it well." He smirked.

She struck him around the arm in anger, but it just brought laughter from him. He still hadn't released her and had his arm firmly around her.

"At least this time ye did not swallow any water."

"Are you going to release me now?" she asked, struggling in his grasp.

"Once I am certain ye will not fall another time."

"I will not fall." She became still and stood firmly on the riverbed.

"Good," he said, lifting his arm from her. She took a couple of steps away, startled by the close proximity. "Now, try again."

Reluctantly, she did as he instructed. It took some time and a lot more practice, but soon she was swimming back and forth across the stream with relative ease. Not before long, she didn't need to put her feet down when she swam. As she stopped and the rocks moved beneath her, she was able to reset herself without slipping under the water and without Iomhar's help.

When it came to learning how to swim completely under the water, Iomhar concentrated on teaching her breathing techniques instead. Surprisingly, Kit found this helped the most. Once she had control of her breathing, she could be more confident that she wasn't going to drown in the water. She had to practice across the stream, more and more until she could easily slip beneath the water and come back up.

"What do you think?" Kit asked as she reached the riverbank and popped her head out of the water, wiping the loose droplets from her face.

"Aye, much better," Iomhar approved from the other side of the river, where he was sat on the riverbank, fiddling with some of the reeds between his fingers. "Ye still scared of it?" he asked, gesturing down to the water.

She knew her answer, for it was a firm yes, so she decided not to answer him instead.

"Och, maybe that fear will pass in time," he said, shrugging. "At least you can survive in it now."

She nodded in agreement before she slipped under the water another time and swam back toward him. When she lifted her head out of the water, she clawed at the reeds beside Iomhar, pulling herself up to sit beside him. The weight of the water dragged down the doublet she was wearing, making it heavier than before.

"Feel better about it?"

"A little, then I think about last night and it vanishes," Kit answered honestly as she kicked her feet through the water. "We let them get away, Iomhar."

"Nay, we did not let them get away. Circumstances dictated it, there is a difference."

"That I do not see."

"I certainly see it," he said with strength to his tone as he turned to look at her. "Are ye disappointed because the threat to the queen is still there? Or because ye feel like ye have let Walsingham down?"

Kit wasn't sure why she felt the need to be so honest with him, perhaps she felt she owed him that much, after he had pulled her out of the water the night before and was now taking the time to teach her to swim, regardless, the words came freely on their own. "Can it not be both?"

Iomhar sighed and placed his hands behind him on the riverbank, leaning on them.

"You look like you disapprove."

"Let's just say I do not understand this obsession ye have with pleasing Walsingham."

"It is not an obsession!" she said quickly. "It is loyalty."

"Aye, I am loyal to his cause, but ye go one step further." He motioned toward her.

"We've discussed this before, why do we have to discuss it again?"

"Because not one time have I had a firm answer to my question," his words were calm. She tried to turn away and look across the river, find anything to stare at other than him, but he tapped her arm, urging her to look back to him. "Just answer me why ye are so fixated with pleasing him."

"It's not a fixation," she said wildly, lifting her arm so that his hand fell away from her. "I owe him, that is all."

"Owe him? For what?" he asked, dropping his hand away.

"For … everything." She gestured to herself as though it explained it, but seeing Iomhar frowning, it told her she would need to say more. "I told you how Walsingham found me, begging on the streets."

"Aye, ye said," he nodded.

"According to him, I was starving, as thin as a piece of string. If Walsingham had not taken me in, what do you think would have happened to me?" She turned fully to Iomhar, watching as he averted his eyes down to the river. A muscle seemed to tick in his jaw, as if he were unwilling to think of the idea. "I could have died."

"Ye do not know that for certain."

"It is highly likely, is it not?" she asked. "That or I could have ended up stealing food and been placed in prison for it. I do not like the sound of that life." She waited to see if he would respond, but he merely continued to stare at the river in thought. "Walsingham may not be the perfect man, but he is the reason I am alive today. He gave me a life to live when I had none. He paid for my upbringing, bought me food, lodgings, taught me to read and write. What other girl of the street has that chance? Why wouldn't I want to repay that kindness every day for the rest of my life?"

Iomhar said nothing, but he lifted his eyes at last from the river, turning to face her and return her stare. "Ye owe him," he repeated her earlier words.

"Exactly." She emphasised the word, needing him to understand it. "I will do almost anything that man asks of me."

"Well, I cannot say I like the idea of that, but I can hardly argue against it either," he said, holding her gaze. "I just hope one day ye will not cling so much to trying to repay him."

She had no answer for his words, she was too perplexed by them. She just kept looking at him with a frown on her face.

"Kit, do not worry," he said, adopting a softer tone. "I know last night was not what we planned, but we will get there. We just need to think a little more and come up with a new plan. We now know Lady Ruskin really is at the heart of this. There must be a way we can use that to our advantage. Do not feel ye have let down Walsingham yet. There is much more we can do."

Kit nodded, though she was not convinced. She felt too deflated after the night before.

"If she is anything like her husband," Iomhar went on, "I warrant Lady Ruskin has another plan of how to get that gunpowder. Even if they did not get their hands on it last night, she will find a way."

"You seem to know quite a bit about her husband," Kit pointed out, earning a dark glare from Iomhar. "What? I tell you my secrets and you will not tell me yours? Is it unreasonable for me to ask?"

"Aye, I know," he sighed and pinched the bridge of his nose, evidently stressed. "We crossed paths, long ago."

"You said last night that you would never forgive him for what he did. What did he do to you?"

He dropped his hand from his nose and looked across the river, hesitating before answering her. "He betrayed me and my family, let us leave it at that," Iomhar said quietly.

"Must we leave it at that?" Kit pressed the point. "What did he do?"

"That is not relevant now," he looked back to her. "I've met him before, I know what he is capable of, how willing he is to let others suffer for something he has done."

"What do you mean by that?" Kit asked, watching him closely.

"Has it not struck ye as odd that his wife is here in London to help spearhead this plot and he is not?" he countered, turning to her with animation.

"Will he not lead their army to Sheffield Castle?"

"Aye, maybe." He shrugged with the words. "Yet there he would have an entire army with him to protect him. In London, his wife is left to control the plot against the queen. If we foil it, whose head will be taken to the Tower?"

Kit swallowed, her mouth feeling suddenly dry at Iomhar's words. "Lady Ruskin's," she said succinctly.

"Just so," he gestured to her, showing she was right. "Lord Ruskin has separated himself from being accused as being part of this plot. If something goes wrong, in Scotland he is arguably much safer than his wife is. It is hardly surprising when ye know the man like I do."

"Lady Ruskin…" Kit tarried over the name for a minute, thinking on it. "She still thinks I am her friend, does she not?"

"What are ye thinking?" he asked, his tone turning wary.

"Well, as far as she is concerned, her men were jumped last night when they went to collect the barrels. They were being watched, but she cannot be certain that I was involved. She may just think that it was her men who were being watched rather than the barrels."

"Or she may think that ye work for Walsingham after all and know exactly what ye were up to," Iomhar's voice grew louder.

"Yet if I went back to her and pretended innocence, as though I knew nothing about it, she would surely believe me. After all, why would an intelligencer go back there now?"

"Exactly! Why would an intelligencer go back there now?" he said wildly. "Ye would be walking into your death."

"Hardly. By going back there, it would be a statement of innocence."

"Nay, ye are not doing it, Kit."

"Why not?"

"Because I will not let ye walk towards your own death."

"Going back to Lady Ruskin may be the only chance we have of finding out more about this plot," she said, leaning toward him with her hands outstretched, pleading with him to believe her. "Who else do we have to go to? We have to do it."

"Nay, we will think of something else," Iomhar said firmly. "It is far too dangerous."

"Oh, and you are making that decision for us, are you?" she asked tartly, crossing her arms.

"Nay, I am stopping ye from making a foolish decision," he motioned toward her. "Ye want to live? Then ye are not going back to Lady Ruskin's house. Ever."

"You cannot tell me what to do, Iomhar."

"This is a partnership. We make our decisions together."

"Well, what if I decide we should go ahead?" she asked, lifting her chin in defiance.

"I could tell Walsingham what ye were planning to do. Ye may not listen to me, Kit, but I feel quite certain ye will listen to him." He had outfoxed her. She lowered her chin, giving up on the argument. "So, ye promise not to go?"

"Yes, I will not go," she relented quietly, though in truth she had no intention of keeping to her words. Going back to Lady Ruskin could be the only way of finding out what the plot was against Queen Elizabeth. That was worth any risk, including facing Iomhar's fury.

CHAPTER 23

Kit had to wait to the evening until she found her chance to sneak out of the house. She had agreed with Iomhar that they would go back to Walsingham the next morning, to reveal what had happened and discuss their options, but Kit had no intention of going to Walsingham empty handed, not if she could do something about it first.

When Iomhar retreated to the kitchen to discuss dinner with the cook, Kit poked her head above the wooden banister over the stairs, watching him retreat. Once she was certain he was gone, she pulled her own doublet, now fully dry, tighter around her body, tucked her hair under her cap and hurried down the steps. She glanced once at the painting of Iomhar and his family, feeling strangely watched by the eyes before she slipped out of the front door and into the street.

It didn't take too long to reach her own lodgings, where she hurried to change into one of the fine dresses from her wardrobe, transforming herself from Kit the intelligencer into Mrs Katherine Allaway. In the mirror, she could see her uncertain expression staring back at her. She felt as out of place now in the dress as she always did. This one was dark midnight blue, with a collar attached to the neckline, and bell-shaped sleeves around her elbows. The farthingale was smaller than in her other dresses, allowing a little more movement, if not much more.

Once transformed, it was time to make her way to Lady Ruskin's house. Without Iomhar to pose as her servant, she paid for a cart to drop her at the end of Lady Ruskin's street, and approached the house alone, moving between the people in the road and trying to pretend that she belonged.

A gentle knock on the door wasn't answered straight away. It left Kit to stand there for a little time, feeling her nerves grow until the fluttering sensation in her stomach grew to such an extent that she felt sick. She tried to reassure herself it was the right thing to do, that the risk was worth it, but the moment the door opened, she realised she may have been wrong.

"Mrs Allaway," the steward declared with surprise, his face revealing the full extent of unreserved anger. "We were not expecting ye."

"I am here to see Lady Ruskin," she said, adopting her Scottish accent once more.

"Then ye better come in." The steward opened the door wider and beckoned Kit to move inside. She walked feeling her legs tremble slightly beneath the large skirt of the dress. "Wait here," he ordered, bumping her shoulder until she was standing in the very centre of the tiled entrance hall.

Down the corridor, Kit still had a side view of Mary Stuart's painting. She purposefully looked away from it, unable to bear staring at it. The steward walked past this painting and into the drawing room. His announcement of Kit's arrival was met with an awful clatter. Kit flinched where she stood, listening as it sounded like someone dropped a tray full of china crockery. Seconds later, footsteps angrily moved across the room, before Lady Ruskin appeared at the end of the corridor. She paused there for a second, with one hand on the wall beside her to stand straight, her cheeks reddening visibly even through the ceruse paint on her cheeks, and her nostrils flaring.

"Ye. Ye dare to come back here after what ye did?" Her words echoed off the walls around them.

"After what?" Kit asked, figuring her best chance to seem innocent was to plead ignorance first.

"Ye betrayer!" Lady Ruskin marched forward, moving so quickly that the folds of her dress rippled behind her, as if caught in a wind. "Fraser. Grab her, now!"

Fraser? Kit only had long enough to realise it was the same surname as Graham Fraser's, the man who had thrown her into the river before she turned to see who Lady Ruskin was addressing.

It was the steward. He rushed past Lady Ruskin, going straight for Kit, with his arms outstretched. Kit had to quell her instinct to battle him. Instead, she held up her hands in innocence.

"What is going on? My Lady? Ahh!" Kit affected a yelp of pain as the steward, Fraser, grabbed her wrists and dragged her a little forward. She had a chance to look at his face a little longer, seeing there was a similarity between him and Graham Fraser, enough to suggest that maybe the men were brothers. "I do not understand. What is this?"

"Hold her down, now."

Lady Ruskin's order was dutifully followed. Fraser pushed Kit down to the floor, on her knees. She was only stopped from falling forward, face-planting the floor by the cumbersome farthingale that kept her in place. Another footman joined the steward. Together, they held her down.

Had Kit even wanted to fight them anymore to break free, it would have been futile. With Fraser bearing down on her, grasping one wrist behind her back and needling his elbow down on her shoulder, she could not move out of fear of her arm being broken. Beside him, the footman was placing equal pressure on her other shoulder.

"Lady Ruskin, stop this, I beg of ye! What is all this for?" Kit cried out the words, feeling the desperation of her situation bleed into her tone.

Lady Ruskin left the room for a minute, leaving Kit to let out a growl of pain, almost feral and animal-like. She tried to tug away from the steward and the footman, but it did no good at all.

She heard Lady Ruskin return as the shoes clicked against the floor, though she did not lift her head to see. She focused on the floor, gritting her teeth against the pain.

"Hold still, Mrs Allaway," Lady Ruskin's order was met by the tip of a blade that appeared under Kit's chin.

Kit froze, falling still in the men's hold as she looked down at the blade. It was a basilard, a long dagger, with the handle ornate and encrusted with jewels. Despite its ornamentation it was clearly lethal with the blade sharpened to a thin point.

The blade was placed against Kit's chin and then tipped her face upwards, forcing her to look up into Lady Ruskin's eyes that were glaring down at her.

"I want to see the face of the lass that betrayed her own kin," Lady Ruskin's husky voice emanated around the room, despite its quietness.

"I did not betray ye. Why would ye say I had —"

"Be quiet!" Lady Ruskin ordered. In emphasis to her words, Fraser pulled Kit's arm up more. She yelped at the agony, knowing she was inches away from her elbow being snapped. The movement grazed her chin against the basilard, and it cut her, not deeply, just enough to draw a little blood and remind her of the threat she was facing.

"At least tell me what I am accused of before ye slit my throat," Kit said, trying to hold onto some dignity as she felt tears prick her eyes from the pain of the steward grasping her arm. She could see Lady Ruskin tilt her head to the side, watching those tears that Kit was trying to blink away.

"Ye do not know? Ye pretend ignorance?" she asked, pressing the basilard closer to Kit's skin.

"Tell me what it is I am accused of."

"The gunpowder ye supposedly so kindly arranged. There were people watching it. Two intelligencers that attacked my men," Lady Ruskin said, her voice shaking with anger.

"That will explain why the barrels are still there then," Kit voiced her lie.

"What do ye mean?" Lady Ruskin asked.

"I received word this afternoon from my husband's contacts that the barrels were not collected. We could not understand why. That's why I came here today, to find out why the barrels are still there." Kit tried to keep her voice level to convince Lady Ruskin of the lie, yet it shook all the same because of the pain in her arm.

"What did ye say?" Lady Ruskin lowered the basilard a little. "Ye came because ye knew the barrels were not collected?"

"Aye, I assumed something must have gone wrong, but I did not know what it was," Kit said hurriedly. "How could I?"

Lady Ruskin lowered the basilard completely, though still the steward and the footman kept their tight hold on Kit, refusing to let her go. Lady Ruskin also still held the dagger downwards, threateningly, ready to raise it at a moment's notice.

"Then explain why my men were attacked. Two people tried to arrest them," Lady waved the basilard for emphasis.

"I do not know," Kit protested with feeling. "Who were they? Who attacked your men?"

"Intelligencers, we believe, that work for Walsingham. Elizabeth's guard dog," Lady Ruskin said. "One we know, the other, we do not. Though one of my men seems to think it was a lass dressed as a man." Her words made Kit freeze slightly, no longer struggling against the steward's hold. She was waiting for Lady Ruskin to accuse her of being the cross-dresser, but she didn't. Lady Ruskin turned away, using the base of the basilard to scratch the side of her head in thought. "Ye claim ye did not know any of this."

"Of course not," Kit raised her voice. "Ye asked for gunpowder, and I asked my husband to arrange it. All I had to do was pass ye the address of where to find it."

"Lower your voice a little, Mrs Allaway, I do not wish my neighbours to hear ye," Lady Ruskin said tiredly.

"Then ask your steward to release my arm a little," Kit warned.

Her words apparently surprised Lady Ruskin who turned back to her. "Ye do have spirit in ye," she spoke with a small smile.

Slowly, Lady Ruskin sank down, crouching to the floor so that she was at a similar level to Kit, though a little above. She lifted the basilard once more and drew the tip of it across Kit's cheek lightly, not hurting her in anyway, just threatening to do it. "Do ye give me your word that ye are telling me the truth at this moment?"

"I do."

"I am not done," Lady Ruskin said, lowering the basilard just an inch. "Do ye give me your word with God as your witness, so that ye may be punished in hell for any lie that ye may tell? Lie to me now and ye disgrace His name as well as yours. Tell me, in the name of God and our rightful monarch, Queen Mary, that what ye have just spoken is the truth."

Kit only hesitated long enough to lift her chin a little higher. After all, she believed the rightful monarch was Elizabeth, she was jeopardising nothing. "I have told ye the truth."

The basilard fell away and Lady Ruskin stood straight. "Fraser, release her." Despite Lady Ruskin's words, the steward did not move. "Are ye choosing which orders to follow now, Ross?" She had slipped to using his first name.

Kit tried to glance over her shoulder, up to the steward. Slowly, Ross Fraser released her arm, though his face was red as he moved, clearly angered with the decision. The footman followed suit.

Kit cradled her arm, bending forward and grimacing against the pain. She pushed up the bell-shaped sleeve to reveal a purple and dark blue bruise that was already spreading across her skin from where the steward had held her.

"I must say this is getting more and more confusing by the minute." Lady Ruskin stepped away and placed the basilard on a nearby table before walking up and down the entrance hall. Kit flicked her eyes toward the basilard, thinking of how she could use it as a weapon to escape if Lady Ruskin changed her mind and chose not to believe her. "If ye did not tell Walsingham and his intelligencers what we were up to, then someone else must have."

"Do ye have a turncoat in your men, my Lady?" Kit asked.

As Lady Ruskin snapped her head toward her, Fraser grabbed Kit's shoulder another time and shoved her back down to the floor. She yelped at the pain and struggled to set herself right, battling with the farthingale hoop to sit straight.

"Do not harm her anymore," Lady Ruskin ordered, waving at her steward. "It pains me to say it, but Mrs Allaway may be right. If she did not tell anyone of our plans, then someone else must have done, and the only others who know of it are within our own men."

Kit glanced at Fraser, seeing that he reluctantly backed up a little, increasing the distance between them. Kit had to fight her instinct to crawl away from him across the floor and grab the basilard from its place. If her plan was to work, she needed to be seen as someone who was not a threat to Lady Ruskin or anyone in that house.

"My husband will not be happy when he hears of this," Lady Ruskin said, clearly more to herself than to anyone else as she paced across the room. She came to a sharp halt in front of Kit and looked down at her, before throwing a handkerchief to her. "Ye need to clean yourself up, Mrs Allaway."

Kit snatched up the handkerchief and lifted it to her chin. After dabbing it a few times, she pulled down the white cloth that was embroidered with Lady Ruskin's initials, to see that she was still bleeding from where the basilard had cut her. She held firmly to her chin with the cloth, trying to stop the bleeding.

"Ye cannot believe her, my Lady," the steward spoke up.

Kit darted her head toward him, just as Lady Ruskin did.

"Ye dare to speak against me?" Lady Ruskin asked, her tone so dark that Fraser took a step away from her.

"I merely mean we cannot take her at her word."

To Kit's dismay, Lady Ruskin seemed to be debating his statement, thinking on it for a minute before she turned and looked back to Kit.

"Well, maybe there is a way we could test my new friend," Lady Ruskin entreated, her tone lifting with lightness that suggested she was pleased with herself.

Kit's gaze followed Lady Ruskin as she crouched down in front of her once more. "A test?" Kit tried to keep the worry out of her voice.

"A test of loyalty." Lady Ruskin elongated the syllables of the final word, emphasising her meaning. "Maybe we could kill two birds with one stone, if ye do not mind the pun."

"What pun?" Kit asked.

"I have two problems now, Mrs Allaway," Lady Ruskin said dramatically. "One is whether or not I can trust your loyalty, the other is that one of the intelligencers that went after my men last night is known to us. He has been a thorn in my husband's side before and we cannot give him the chance to be troublesome to us now."

Kit paused with pressing the handkerchief to her chin, realising that she must have been speaking of Iomhar, and that he had been recognised by Fraser and the others. They must have seen him somewhere before, back in Scotland, perhaps.

"Ye know this intelligencer? How?"

"My husband once knew him. Knew his father too, two of a kind they are. As long as this intelligencer is in town, we cannot be certain of our success," Lady Ruskin said then gestured toward her. "Which is why my predicament with ye is so fortunate."

"What do ye mean?" Kit asked nervously.

"To prove your loyalty to me, Mrs Allaway, ye will arrange a death for me," Lady Ruskin said with a smile. "Do the deed yourself or have one of your husband's men do it, I do not care, but see it is done. Can ye do that for me?"

"I can," Kit spoke with feeling, just as her heartbeat quickened and echoed in her ears. "What is this intelligencer's name?"

"Mr Iomhar Blackwood."

CHAPTER 24

"Ye said ye'd do what?" Iomhar demanded, his arms crossed as he stared at Kit across the room. The anger in his face was evident, his cheeks red and the sinews of his neck taut. It was the first time since she had seen him after sneaking out of his house the night before, and she didn't doubt he was angry at her for that by itself, let alone what she had just told him. "Say it again."

"Do you need to hear it again?"

"Clearly, because I am doubting the proof of my own ears," he said, motioning to his ears.

"As am I," a third voice joined them. It was Walsingham.

They were back in Walsingham's normal study, where the fire damage of the house was being attended to. Enough improvements had been made to allow Walsingham along with his secretaries to work there. Doris had moved back in too, and in the distance, carpenters could be heard at work on timber beams, and roofers were attending to the tiles on the roof. Walsingham was currently sat behind his desk, popping more pills from a glass jar as he looked up from the paperwork in front of him. He winced every now and then, gripping his lower back in obvious pain.

"It is not easy to explain," Kit said, shifting her weight between her booted feet, relieved that she was back in her men's clothes. She glanced at Iomhar and Walsingham, seeing that neither of them were happy with her. Unusually, Walsingham's anger was not the fiercest. He was too weak to be able to rise to such anger, unlike Iomhar, who seemed to reach such heights easily.

"Not easy? I think it is perfectly simple," Iomhar snapped. "Last night ye sneaked out of the house and went to see Lady Ruskin, going back on the promise ye made me —"

"I never made an explicit promise, I just said yes."

"That is beside the point and ye know it!"

"If you two are going to continue shouting at each other like a couple of adolescents, please leave my house to do it," Walsingham said, rubbing his temples with both hands.

"Can ye honestly blame me?" Iomhar asked, turning back to Walsingham and gesturing to Kit.

"Any other time, I would say no." Walsingham lifted his head, startling Kit with his words. "Yes, Kit took a risk."

"The greatest understatement I have ever heard," Iomhar pointed at Kit. "Have ye seen that bruise on her arm?"

Kit looked down to where she had rolled her shirt sleeve up to her elbow. Seeing the bruise plainly visible, she hurried to unroll the sleeve and hide it.

"What's the point in hiding it now?" Iomhar asked her.

"So you will not mention it again, I suppose," she said, masking it from view.

"What of the cut under your chin? Ye cannot hide that so easily." He pointed to the cut that had now scabbed over.

"Cut? What cut?" Walsingham asked, nearly standing from his chair.

Kit knew his eyesight was not what it once was, but she hadn't even considered that Walsingham might not be able to see it. She crossed toward him, standing on the other side of the desk so he could see it clearly.

"It is just a nick. It is nothing to worry about," Kit assured him. He looked at it for a long time before he nodded in agreement with her and retook his seat.

"Nothing?" Iomhar asked from where he stood by the windows.

"Iomhar, listen." Kit had had enough of his anger. She marched toward him, stopping in front of him when she could be sure she had his gaze. "Whether or not I chose to risk going back there was my decision, not yours to make."

He said nothing, apparently registering her words as his gaze flicked down to the cut on her chin again. "Ye lied to me," he said plainly.

"Well, it is hardly the first time," she shrugged. "I wish I could say I'm sorry for it."

"But ye are not."

"It got results, did it not?"

He revealed the smallest of smirks before it vanished. He lifted a hand to her chin, bringing it higher. She gasped at the touch, not having expected it.

"What did this?" he asked, his hand lingering on her for a moment.

"A basilard," she explained, watching as his eyes widened in surprise. Realising she hadn't yet walked out of his grasp, she did so quickly, stepping away from him.

"Your argument can wait for another time," Walsingham called from his desk where he sat back in his seat further. "Kit, tell me again what you promised Lady Ruskin you would do."

"She wants me to prove my loyalty, so she has set a test," Kit explained, looking toward Iomhar. "If I can prove my loyalty to her, then maybe she'll let me in on the details of her plan."

"That's still only a maybe," Walsingham said nervously, tapping the hard tip of a quill on the edge of his desk. "And to prove your loyalty?"

"She wants Iomhar dead." Kit watched as Iomhar shifted on his feet, altering his stance and ruffling his hair with stress.

239

"She said her husband knew you. That you were just like your father, and they had to be free of you."

"She said that?" Iomhar asked, turning to look at her with his eyebrows quirked.

"She did," Kit nodded. It was on the tip of her tongue to ask him yet again why he had crossed paths with Lord Ruskin before, but the wish to ask it died. He had already evaded that question often enough with her. He was hardly going to tell her the answer when in the company of Walsingham.

"Great, so I have to die for this cause," Iomhar shook his head with a sigh.

"What of a ruse?" Kit asked him, watching as he snapped his head back toward her. "Well, obviously I would not really kill you —"

"I'm relieved to hear it, but considering how we met, somehow I doubt ye could resist the temptation," Iomhar smirked at her.

"Give me some credit. I like you a little bit now," she said quickly, to which his eyebrows shot up.

"Ah, ye like me now, do ye?"

She felt a knot tighten in her stomach at the admission, especially when she could see him staring so avidly at her. "All I meant was that I can bear your company. Funnily enough, I am not eager to see you in a grave."

"How magnanimous of ye," he said with a chuckle that had no real humour in it.

"Think of it, Iomhar." She reached out to him with both hands, pleadingly. "What if we could convince Lady Ruskin that you were dead? We could put together the appearance of it easily enough. Then she would undoubtedly trust me. She would share her plot with me."

Iomhar said nothing for a minute. His green gaze held her own showing that he was slowly being persuaded of her thought, even if he wasn't jumping at the idea.

"Surely it is worth a try," Walsingham said from his desk. "You could hide here for a while, where no one would see you."

"Aye, I suppose so," Iomhar nodded, turning in a small circle and breaking eye contact with Kit for a minute. "If we do this though, it has to be orchestrated carefully and Lady Ruskin will have to see it with her own eyes, otherwise she would have cause to doubt it. If any of her men saw it done rather than her, she would always be uncertain, willing to believe they had been deceived. She will have to see me die herself."

"Die?" Kit repeated.

"Well, appear to die," he added with a small smile. He reached down to the crossbow that hung off his belt beneath his dark cloak and held it up. "For how we accomplish that, I have an idea."

"It involves that, does it?" she asked, pointing at it.

"That depends."

"On what?"

"On how good a shot ye are."

Kit was hovering in a building on London Bridge. Stretching far across the Thames and filled with over two hundred timber houses, each one bore a shop on its lower floors and housing up above, with the thatched roofs stretching high into the sky and the yellow colour masked by chimney smoke.

From where Kit was leaning her head out of a window, she had a view of the centre of the bridge. Here, there were no buildings, only a wide expanse, encased with white stone walls either side that looked over the water. Far below, the bridge consisted of a myriad of arches, each one built out of stone and elm poles.

Kit looked away from the dizzying height. If all went according to the plan Iomhar had formed, he would be falling off this stretch of bridge and down into the wide River Thames below within minutes. She knew well enough her own basic swimming skills would mean she would struggle to survive such a feat, but Iomhar might well be able to manage it.

She tried to focus elsewhere on the bridge and look around for the other pieces of their puzzle to fall into place. It was a busy day, with lots of people walking between the shops on the bridge with an air of purpose about them. Ladies in farthingales and big skirts were being followed by servants carrying boxes of garments, piled so high that they could only just balance their noses over the tops of the boxes. There were gentlemen wandering to and fro too, with ruffs so large that it was as though their faces had been served up on trencher dishes for a feast.

On the opposite side of the clearing between the houses, Kit had her eyes trained on an archway where she was waiting for Lady Ruskin to appear. Just as Iomhar had said, they had planned carefully for Lady Ruskin to witness the event. Kit had dropped a message to Lady Ruskin that morning, signed Mrs Allaway, bidding Lady Ruskin to come to the bridge today and wait in this very arch if she wished to see her test of loyalty completed. She had received no reply.

Kit was growing nervous, fidgeting within her position on the windowsill as the archway stayed empty, but eventually, someone appeared.

Lady Ruskin's face was not visible, but the grand cloak and hood she wore suggested it had to be her. She was draped with fine jewellery too, and at her side walked the same steward who had forced Kit down to the ground and nearly broken her arm. At the memory, Kit found she rubbed the bruise around her elbow, trying to bring some kind of soothing comfort to the dull ache there, but it did little good.

With her audience in place, watching the clearing relentlessly, Kit stepped off the windowsill into the room and prepared herself. She had the crossbow ready to go, down by her feet. Slowly, she slipped the bolt in place, and lifted the hat on her forehead a little, the better to aim, then she lifted the crossbow and held it partly out of the window, ready to take her fire. So high up on the fourth floor of the building, she hoped none of the shoppers had cause to look her way, but with the shadow caused by the adjacent building, it masked her mostly from view.

Now, she had to wait for Iomhar to approach.

Through the heads of the shoppers, she could see more than one person gasping and looking behind them, all eagerly trying to get out of the way of something approaching them. A cart drove through the middle of the crowd, parting them all as it went about delivering goods to shops. Behind the cart, a familiar face appeared atop a steed.

Kit looked up from the crossbow for a minute and down to where Iomhar was riding. He was clearly making a point of not looking toward the archway where Lady Ruskin was hiding, not wanting to show he knew she was there. He rode on, right to the very edge of the bridge, through the crowds until he stopped beside the wall. Compared to people who were on foot, the wall was high, but atop a horse, the wall was quite low, dangerously so.

"I hope you are as strong a swimmer as you think, Iomhar," Kit muttered as she lined up the crossbow toward him, beginning to take her aim. He made a point of pulling on the reins and keeping the horse in check, then looking about the people nearby, as if he were waiting to meet someone. Not once did he glance up in her direction.

Kit lined up the shot, ready to fire it, when people walked in the way. There were two ladies, with not only large dresses, but headdresses and French hoods so grand that they masked her shot.

"God have mercy," she muttered, lifting her head up from the crossbow. They decided to stay where they were and talk between themselves for a minute, blocking her view completely. "Maybe this was a bad idea," Kit murmured as she looked back to where Lady Ruskin was standing with her steward.

Lady Ruskin was appearing quite impatient to Kit's mind. Where she had been standing perfectly still before, she was now shifting between her feet, restless, and fiddling with the hood around her face.

One glance back to the two ladies blocking Kit's view showed they had no intention of moving anytime soon.

She backed away from the window, looking into the room where she was standing. It was a storeroom for the confectioners down on the bottom floor, and they had no idea she was there. She had crept in more than an hour ago whilst the shopkeeper was busy with customers. Another window further along the building was blocked by sacks of cubes of sugar, and a table lined with marchpane.

She hurried toward it, lowering the crossbow on the marchpane just long enough to slide the table backwards and drag one of the sacks of sugar out of the way. Once done, she knelt upon the second sack, grabbed the crossbow and leaned out of the window.

Squinting down to where Iomhar was standing, she could see that he was getting restless too, enough to even glance up to try and see her position in the windows, clearly wondering why she hadn't yet taken the shot. Seeing her aim clearly now the ladies were out of the way, she took her fire, pulling tightly on the lever trigger. The bolt snapped away from the crossbow, whistling through the air before it found its target, right at a bag of hay that Iomhar had dropped by the horse's feet.

On cue, the horse reared back, startled and whinnying loudly into the air. Others around, including the chatting ladies veered away, terrified as to who had shot the crossbow. Iomhar affected his part — scrambling with the horse as though he could not get control and then falling backward toward the wall. He released the reins, tipped out of the saddle and fell over the wall completely.

There were shouts and cries for help, even a scream from one of the ladies, all terrified for the gentleman that was now falling into the water.

Kit snapped the crossbow inside and dropped it nearby, craning her head out of the window to try and get a glimpse of Iomhar in the water, but it was no use. She heard the splash, it was much louder than she had expected, suggesting Iomhar had hit the water with his face and body planted toward it. She cringed at the sound.

One man ran forward, trying to get control of the reins of the spooked horse, whilst another hurried toward the edge of the wall, searching for Iomhar.

"Do you see him?" a voice cried up from the crowd.

"Is he there? Is he alive?" another shouted.

"I cannot see him," the man called back before bending his head fully over the wall. A minute or so passed with everyone

245

exchanging cries of fear and wonder before the man lifted his face and shook his head. "He's not coming back up."

It was all he needed to say. The crowd around began to disperse, all horrified with their hands over their mouths at what they had seen, a life lost so easily, now plunging to the depths of the Thames and drowning.

Kit turned her eyes to the archway where Lady Ruskin stood. She said something to Ross Fraser before nodding and the two walked away, leaving the archway empty. Kit spun back into the room, sinking further down onto the sack of sugar as the fear began to make her shiver.

She tried to persuade herself that Iomhar would be fine. She had already seen he was a strong swimmer after all, but it was a long way to fall, and he may well have gone into shock, making the task of swimming impossible. What if something did actually happen to him and their ruse went wrong?

The fear made her jump to her feet. She snapped up the crossbow, latching it onto her belt, and then threaded a cloak around her shoulders to hide it from view before she retreated toward the door, about to make her escape. She was ready to leave when she stepped back into the room, pinching a small amount of marchpane off the table to eat. As she left, chewing on the sugar and almond paste, she felt the prayer repeat itself over and over again in her head.

She prayed Iomhar survived.

CHAPTER 25

"Mrs Allaway! At last, I have been looking out of the window for ye every few minutes since luncheon," Lady Ruskin said with a much more charming tone than she had adopted the last time that Kit had come by.

Straight after shooting the crossbow at Iomhar, Kit had run home and changed. Now she had come to see Lady Ruskin, as proof of her loyalty.

"Did ye see it, my Lady?" Kit asked as Lady Ruskin beckoned her inside.

Lady Ruskin glanced up and down the street, evidently checking there was no one nearby who was suspicious to her before she closed the door firmly. "That I did." She looped arms with Kit. "I can see I was a fool to ever doubt ye, Mrs Allaway," she said as though she and Kit were suddenly the closest of friends. "Come, share a drink with me. There is much I need to tell ye, and one more way in which ye can help our cause."

Kit affected a smile though it was strained as she hurried alongside Lady Ruskin. As they passed the portrait of Mary Stuart, Kit's gaze lingered there, thinking of all the bloodshed and violence that had been done in this one woman's name. It made a dull ache bloom in Kit's chest. She wanted to retreat from the house, run from it and head back to the River Thames, to see if Iomhar truly had made it out alive, but that was not an option.

"First, ye must tell me all about it," Lady Ruskin spoke with something of a childish giggle as she drew Kit into the drawing room.

Today, Lady Ruskin had none of her visitors that had been there before. In the centre of the room, wine had been set up on a table, beside two crystal glasses with the stems twisted, and on one side was a small ornate box, made of dark mahogany wood, inlaid with mother-of-pearl that was shaped to form tiny dancers moving across the surface. With eagerness, Lady Ruskin pushed Kit into the chair nearest to the table.

"Tell ye all?" Kit asked, startled. "Did ye not see it?"

"Aye, of course," Lady Ruskin said. "My steward and I watched from the archway, just as ye sent to us in your message. Oh me." She clasped a hand to her breast as she took a seat beside Kit. "I cannot tell ye the joy it gave me to see that man plunge to his death."

"Truly?" Kit asked, feeling her body stiffen in surprise. "Had he wronged ye and your husband in some way?"

"Aye, ye could say that," Lady Ruskin hurried to pour wine for the two of them. "To start with, he betrayed his kin when he turned his back and supported Mary Stuart's son for the throne, rather than Mary Stuart herself. Just as his father did too."

Kit spun in her chair toward Lady Ruskin, the better to hear Iomhar's tale, but something about it riled her. It felt a betrayal to hear the story told from anyone except Iomhar himself. "Well, ye are rid of him now," she said with a smile.

"Thank our lord." Lady Ruskin paused with the wine and cast her gaze to the sky. "He once vowed to kill my husband, so ye can imagine the comfort it brings me to know he is dead."

"To kill him?" Kit repeated, her voice hitching higher than she had intended.

"Aye, I know, what a shock it was." Lady Ruskin shook her head in clear dismay. "That is why I am so delighted to see he is gone. Now, tell me all about it. Who was handling that crossbow?"

"Someone I trust more than any other," Kit answered, figuring her words were not a lie. She would only trust herself to do such a thing. Yet her mind was still on the last thing Lady Ruskin had said. For some reason, Iomhar had vowed to kill Lord Ruskin someday, but why?

"I see ye will not give me their name," Lady Ruskin said with a laugh as she pressed the wine glass into Kit's hands. "I said before ye keep your cards close to your chest."

Kit tried to smile, though she struggled with it. She chose to mask the effort behind the glass instead.

"What do ye say to a celebration?" Lady Ruskin asked, reaching for the mother-of-pearl lid on the box beside the wine tray. She tipped the lid back, revealing inside a glass pot of dried leaves and the two long ivory smoking pipes Kit had seen before.

Remembering the effect that they'd had on Kit the last time she had partaken in Lady Ruskin's habit, made her throat tighten. Iomhar's words and his worry for her when she had stumbled down the steps of the house too made up her mind.

"I am afraid I have somewhere to be after this," Kit eagerly made the excuse. "I will pass for today."

"Ah, what a shame," Lady Ruskin said, closing the lid with a tight click. "Well, to business then." She lowered her glass and turned fully in her chair to face Kit. "Now I know I can trust ye, Mrs Allaway, I will need your help another time. I presume ye still have access to the gunpowder ye tried to set up for us before?"

"Aye," Kit nodded, deciding it was best to continue the lie as much as possible.

"I need ye to organise it to be brought to an event for me."

"What event?" Kit asked, lowering her wine glass.

"In three days' time there is to be a river parade that the queen will take part in. All her privy councillors will be there, her courtiers, every affluent and influential lady and gentleman ye can imagine will be in attendance, and crowds will watch from the riverbank as the pretender queen sails down the river and waves at everyone to see." Lady Ruskin mocked the queen and mirrored the way in which she would wave.

Kit's hand tightened around the glass, thinking of the woman she had seen at Hampton Court Palace a few days before and the fear that had been in her eyes when the plot against her had been revealed.

"I need ye to bring a barrel of gunpowder to the event."

"In three days?" Kit asked, startled by how near it was. They had known the attempt on Queen Elizabeth's life would be within the week, but so soon she had not figured.

"Aye, is that a problem?" Lady Ruskin arched a single eyebrow.

"Nay, not at all," Kit said hurriedly. "I will make the necessary arrangements." She watched as Lady Ruskin smiled, delighted with her assent. Kit placed the wine down on the tray, thinking how odd it was to be discussing things like gunpowder over a glass of wine. "How will the gunpowder be a part of the plot?" She waited to see what else she could find out.

"Let's just say that when the pretender queen's boat leaves Hampton Court gardens, one of my men will be there waiting with a wheellock pistol to ensure that the gunpowder in question will be put to excellent use." Lady Ruskin giggled as she knocked back what was left of the wine in her glass.

"Ye mean…" Kit trailed off and made a hand gesture, splaying her fingers out to illustrate an explosion, just as Lady Ruskin had done once in the past.

"Aye, just so. *Boom*!" Lady Ruskin laughed at her own dramaticism as she flung an arm into the air. "Not only will the queen drown in the river, or die in the flames, but her followers and councillors will too. Do not ye think it is poetic, Mrs Allaway?"

"Aye, quite excellent," Kit said stiffly, pushing the wine glass as far away from her as she could and trying to conceive a way to leave Lady Ruskin's house fast.

CHAPTER 26

"Slow down, Kitty! You are running like the flames of hell are at your heels." Doris's voice followed Kit through the house as she ran towards the stairs.

"I feel as though they are," Kit muttered as she took the stairs, as quickly as she could. When she reached the top, she didn't even bother knocking on the door first, she pushed straight in.

"Who is — wait, Kit?" Walsingham's voice went from initial anger to shock as he whipped his head round from beside the desk. He was half leaning on the desk, evidently struggling with the usual pain in his lower back. "It's some time since I've seen you dressed like that."

Kit glanced down at the dress she was wearing. She had come straight from Lady Ruskin's house, even though she had been certain to take a less than direct route, just in case anyone had been watching her.

"Where have ye been hiding all these dresses?"

The Scottish voice made Kit stumble as she walked forward. Practically hidden behind the door and sat on the opposite side of the room to Walsingham, Iomhar was sat in a wooden chair, damp with his hair brushed back off his forehead with water dripping down slowly forming a puddle around his feet.

"I do not like dresses, I prefer to keep them hidden," she said, unable to keep the small smile off her face from the relief to see that he was alive and well. "Besides, what is wrong with the clothes I normally wear?"

"Hose and doublet? They're hardly usual fair for a young lady, Kit," Walsingham's voice was low from the other end of the room.

"I never said I did not like them," Iomhar said with a growing smile as he leaned back in his chair. Kit tried to keep the smile off her face. What she had to impart was hardly any reason to smile. "I hope me jumping into the Thames was worth it."

"You seemed to have survived fine," Kit said, gesturing to him.

"Aye, though the river is filthy. I would not wish a swim through there on my worst enemy."

"Not even Lord Ruskin?"

"Aye, I may make an exception for him."

"My God, what has happened to you two?" Walsingham's cut into their conversation made Kit jump. "I think I preferred it when you were arguing all the time. Laughter aside —" Walsingham's words forced the two of them to turn away from each other to face him — "do you have a reason Kit for running into my house like a madman?"

"Lady Ruskin's plot is to attack the queen in two days' time at the Summer River Parade. She wishes me to bring a barrel of gunpowder to be placed on the queen's boat. One of her men will be waiting nearby with a wheellock pistol, to ensure the powder blows at the moment she wants it to." Kit finished reeling off what she had learned, watching Walsingham with great attention.

Walsingham still had half his hands bandaged from the burns to his palms. He banged his fists down on the flat of the table, creating a loud thud before retracting them instantly and wincing, realising what he had done to himself. "God have mercy! She wishes to blow up not only our queen, but everyone who would attend her on her boat at the parade? All the ladies-in-waiting? All the councillors? Burghley is to be on that boat. I was to be myself." Walsingham stood quickly to his feet, walking away from the desk in apparent energy and anger.

"Lady Ruskin thinks naught of the other lives that will be lost," Kit explained as she looked between the two men in the room. "It's almost like watching a child talk about life and death. It seems not to matter to her."

"At least that explains how she can take it away so easily," Iomhar muttered, resting his elbows on his knees as more water dripped off him onto the wooden floor. "Back home we call such people Kelpies."

"Kelpie? What's that?" Kit asked, turning to face him.

"Old myth of a creature that lives in water and draws men and women down to their deaths in lochs. It seems to find … amusement in the idea of ending lives."

"That's awful." Kit scrunched up her nose in repulsion of the idea. "Sounds very much like Lady Ruskin."

"I cannot get used to the way you two are now," Walsingham's tart words made Kit take a step away from Iomhar, self-consciously. "Kit, what did you say to Lady Ruskin? About the gunpowder?" Walsingham was animated on the other side of the room.

"I told her I'd have the gunpowder ready that morning," Kit explained, watching as Walsingham tried to pace the room. He gave up halfway, reaching out for a nearby armchair that he clutched at with one of his bandaged hands before falling into the seat with a heavy flop.

"Then we'll have to prepare an empty barrel," Walsingham said decisively. "You two can watch the boat. When did she intend for it to be blown?"

"As the queen leaves Hampton Court gardens." Both Walsingham and Iomhar stiffened in their chairs. "What? Have I missed something?"

"Aye," Iomhar agreed, ruffling his hair and casting some of the droplets around him. "For that to happen, Lady Ruskin must be confident that one of her men can get access to the palace gardens."

"That kind of permission is not easy to obtain," Walsingham's tone was sombre as he steepled his hands together over his nose, hiding his cheeks with the bandages across his palms for a minute. "You two will have to watch the boats, be there to arrest whoever pulls out the wheellock pistol. I will send more men to arrest Lady Ruskin."

"Can we not arrest her now?" Iomhar asked, nearly moving off his chair in his sudden enthusiasm. "She has confessed to plotting against the queen."

"To one of my agents only." Walsingham gestured to Kit rather dismissively. Her spine straightened and she locked her hands together. "Lady Ruskin is a respected name. To accuse her of treason it would have to go to court, and then whose name is going to be believed by a jury of twelve gentlemen? The fine Lady Ruskin, wife of a Scottish Lord, or a woman who lives in an attic?"

Kit looked away, feeling the burn of the words. "You make it sound like all I have done is of no use," she said bitterly, placing her hands on her hips and keeping her eyes on the floorboards.

"It is not that, Kit. It is that the commission is not finished yet. If we are to accuse Lady Ruskin in a court of law, we need her proven to be guilty. We need to capture her men and have them testify against her. This has to be done with such attention to detail that there can be no doubting the woman's guilt." Walsingham had lowered his hands and was staring at her. Kit could feel his eyes on her though she refused to return it. "Now, you two are cluttering up my study. Not to mention there's a puddle," he said, gesturing toward Iomhar who stood from the chair. "You, go dry yourself off, you can hide here until the parade. Kit, go home, prepare yourself. Meet back here tomorrow to discuss the particulars."

With a wave of his hand, they were both dismissed.

There was a tightness in Kit's throat and chest as she walked out of the room, feeling the burn of Walsingham's implication that all their hard work up until this point had been for nothing. Together, she and Iomhar walked down the stairs, with her heels clicking on the floorboards, and his boots squelching. Once they were far away from the study above, wandering away down the corridor, Kit felt a firm hand take her elbow, stopping her walking away.

"Ah, that's damp!" she complained, turning round as Iomhar released her, holding up his hands innocently.

"Are ye all right?" he asked, to which she shrugged.

"I am fine," she said simply.

"There's that word again."

"What word?"

"When my mother and sisters say they're fine, it does not usually mean that everything is fine. The word that means ye merely wish me to stop asking."

"Then stop asking!" She went to turn away another time, but as he lifted a hand to her elbow, she jumped away, out of his grasp.

"Will ye at least tell me how it went at Lady Ruskin's house? She did not hurt ye again, did she?"

"No, she believes Mrs Katherine Allaway is now her closest friend." Kit smiled smugly with the words, trying to brush over her disappointment. "Now, if you will excuse me, I'm going to go home and take this ridiculous dress off."

"Ye are not running away from me asking how ye are then?"

"No," she lied as she walked toward the door, with Iomhar following her all the way.

Doris emerged from the kitchen and hurried to undo all the locks. Kit waited patiently by her side, trying to fix her focus on the door and not look at Iomhar who was gazing at her.

Once the door was unlocked, Doris opened it, only Iomhar stepped in the way, stopping Kit from going any further.

"What are you doing?" Kit asked, waving at the doorway.

"Trying to get an honest answer out of ye."

"Ha, good luck with that," Doris giggled at their side, earning a sharp glare from Kit. The housekeeper duly looked admonished and turned away, pretending interest in some of the fire damage to the doorway outside of the kitchen.

"Ye do know what will make ye happier, do ye not?" Iomhar asked, lowering his voice and stepping toward Kit.

"What will?" she whispered.

"Giving up trying to please Walsingham all the time."

Kit widened her eyes and balled her hands into fists, tempted to push Iomhar out of the way rather than plead with him to step back. "You do not know me, Iomhar. Do not pretend to."

"I know ye a little," he said with a stern expression.

"No, you do not," she lifted her voice, feeling the anger spike within her. "You do not know me, and you have no right to tell me what to do with my life. In fact, I'll be very happy when you and I no longer have to work together, and this commission is over. Now, get out of my way."

"Ye going to pull out one of those daggers again if I do not? I have not seen where ye have been hiding them in that dress."

"Out of my way. Now." She kept her voice dark.

This time, Iomhar stepped away. Gone was the humour between them and any trace of a smile at all. He merely stepped back, giving her the chance to leave with a rather angered expression.

Kit tried not to think why it riled her the whole walk home.

CHAPTER 27

Kit walked between the crowds, checking the weapons at her belt. Her daggers were there, ready to be used if needed. More comfortable now she was back in her boy's clothes, she pulled her hat a little higher on her head, giving her a view of the area around her.

People were gathering at the side of the river, having made their way through the formal knot gardens, pebbled with yellow stones and bordered with green bushes and white speckled flowers. So many people had come to see the start of the River Parade that Kit kept bumping against shoulders as she reached the edge of the river and trying to walk round large skirts.

Today, the gentry of the queen's court had put on their finest garb. The sight of them pulled Kit's lips into a reluctant smile, finding the sizes of some of the ruffs so large that men struggled to move their heads back and forth. The women too had such large farthingales that they could barely reach their friends' hands to clasp in greeting.

Kit looked away from the display and moved toward the edge of the river, turning her gaze out to the parade that was ready to begin. In the centre of the boats that were preparing to leave, there was the largest boat pulled against its moorings. The boat was laced with decorations, including red and white roses, to signify the Tudor rose. Between the flower heads, green leaves were draped along the bows of the boats and bells were hung on ribbons.

Kit frowned peering at the bells, remembering something Walsingham had once told her. *"It's said when a bell is rang, it signals that danger is near."*

She prayed today the bells did not ring.

A ripple went through the crowd, anxious whispers as clearly the main event of the River Parade made an appearance. Kit looked away from the smaller boats, where singers, and musicians with pipes and lutes were prepared ready to accompany the queen down the river. She turned her focus instead through the crowd to where people were bowing and curtsying, moving to the side of the yellow pebbled ground and creating a path.

Within seconds, Queen Elizabeth appeared, her face impassive. Kit offered a curtsy along with everyone else, though she kept her eyes up, examining the features of the queen a little longer. The lead paint on her face was so thick today that she looked more like a ghost to Kit's mind, as though she walked this earth on borrowed time. The illusion wasn't helped by the white dress.

The queen turned her head, talking to one of her ladies-in-waiting, before offering her hand to a footman who helped her onto the boat. As the queen's foot touched the bow of the boat, Kit felt her stomach tense. The time was drawing near, it had to be. One of the bells along the edge of the boat tinkled with the movement of the boat rocking on the water surface.

Kit's eyes darted from the boat to the river water. It was practically green today in the clouds that gathered overhead, far from the glistening blue it should have been. Remembering what the Thames had been like the last time she had taken a tumble into its depths, Kit stepped back from the river edge, putting the pebbled path beneath her boots rather than the riverbank.

"Have you seen anything yet?" The familiar voice made Kit look to her side. Walsingham was there with a cane in his bandaged hand, darting his head back and forth.

"No, nothing," Kit answered, taking another look around her at the crowds. It was true, for she had seen nothing suspicious; there were only happy delighted faces, with some of the ladies throwing flower petals toward the queen on the boat.

"The barrel?" Walsingham asked, not needing to say any more.

"It's in place," Kit whispered, nodding her head toward the boat.

At the very front of the boat, a good distance away from the queen, was a barrel that she had placed there earlier that morning. Dressed in more flowers and some of the decorations for the summer event, it would not draw attention to itself, but Kit didn't doubt Lady Ruskin's men would see it there and believe it to be full of gunpowder.

"Be ready," Walsingham warned.

"When am I not?" Kit asked, though she didn't look back to him as he said the words.

Slowly, Walsingham walked away, struggling with his cane. Kit stayed in position, watching out of the corner of her eye as he climbed onto the back of the boat with the other members of the privy council. Behind them, there was a second ship, not quite so grandly decorated, that was filling up with gentlemen and ladies of the court.

In the front boat, the queen stood in the centre of her ladies-in-waiting. Around her, the ladies were all happy and smiling, but the queen said nothing. She merely stared forward at the river, clearly aware of the risk she was about to take.

Preparations were being made for the boats to depart. With the time nearing, Kit took up her position. She moved to the very edge of the riverbank once again, level with the front of the boat and looked to the far end of the garden, searching expectantly for where Iomhar should be.

"Where is he?" she muttered, waiting for some of the gentry to board the second boat, hopefully revealing where Iomhar was standing guard. The gentry moved away, revealing a space behind them.

Iomhar wasn't there.

Kit took a sharp step forward, squinting and searching again, but there was no sign of him. She flicked her head back and forth, frantically trying to find him in the crowds, but there was no sign of him, not on either of the boats, nor in the crowd that had gathered to wave the queen off.

"All set!" a shout went up.

Kit flicked her head back around as the ropes were taken off the ship. This was the moment Lady Ruskin had been talking of. When the queen left Hampton Court gardens, someone would be here to shoot the gunpowder.

Yet, the shot didn't come.

"What is going on?" Kit said, louder to herself this time. She backed away from the boat, keeping her head on the crowd, looking for any sign of someone pulling a gun.

This was not the way it was supposed to go. Iomhar was supposed to be keeping guard on the other side for starters, then someone was supposed to take a shot. The plan was for her and Iomhar to tackle the shooter together, from either side, to ensure that he could not escape.

Kit turned her gaze to the boat where Walsingham was standing at the very edge, looking at her. The boat was moving further and further into the middle of the river, moving down the stream and setting off. He was waving an arm madly at her, communicating across the vast space to ask what on earth had gone wrong. She didn't know.

With shouts going up from all around, people cheering and calling the queen's name, Kit pushed through them all. It was difficult, with so many people scrambling to the very edge with the chance of one last view of the queen, Kit had to bend her head round capes and ruffs, as well as kicking through farthingales and large skirts.

Once at the back of the crowd, she jumped up onto a low-lying wall, searching for any sign of Iomhar or a shooter. Neither of them were there, only happy faces.

She jumped down off the wall and made her way back toward the crowd. If she could get herself on one of the smaller boats following behind the parade, then she could at least keep the queen in her sights, surely then she could stop anything that was to occur. She only managed to take two steps forward when something clattered against her temple.

She stumbled on her feet, her hands going to her head, cowering at the pain. With blurry eyes, she looked at the crowd, hoping for help, but they all had their backs to her, all much too busy looking at the River Parade. When the second blow came across her temple, everything turned black, all she was aware of was the pebbles pressing into her cheek.

"Kit, if ye can remotely hear me, now would be the time to wake up." Iomhar's voice came from somewhere, but it was as though Kit couldn't move toward it. There was too much darkness enshrouding her, impossible to fight her way through. "Kit!" the voice snapped at her.

This time, she managed to flutter her eyes a little, before she felt a thump in her side.

"Oomph!" Kit exhaled loudly, opening her eyes properly this time. Beyond the pain in her head, she grew aware of her surroundings. She was lying on some floorboards, hard beneath her, with her wrists bound together in front of her. Lifting her head, Iomhar was sat beside her, with his wrists bound too, tied to hers, before they were both fastened down to the floor, tied to some metal hoops in a trapdoor beneath them.

"Kit? That's her name then?" Lady Ruskin's voice tore through her confusion.

Kit sat bolt upright, so sharply that she jumped against Iomhar's side.

"Ye're bleeding," Iomhar said. Kit tried to lift a hand to her temple to touch the sore spot on her forehead, but she couldn't get her hands very far, not whilst they were bound to his as well as the floor.

"About time ye woke up, we're running out of time," Lady Ruskin declared, commanding attention.

Kit looked up, seeing Lady Ruskin standing a little distance away, her arms folded, dressed in a deep red gown. Behind her, Ross Fraser was standing there, staring at her.

"For what?" Kit asked.

"For killing the queen," Lady Ruskin said, bending down so that she was at Kit's head height. Kit frowned, remembering no shot had been fired at the queen's boat. "What was in the barrel in the end. Sand? Rocks?"

"Nothing," Kit sighed with the word, not seeing the point anymore in adopting the Scottish accent.

"Ooh, English too. I should have seen that coming," Lady Ruskin said as she stood straight.

"I do not understand," Kit looked at Iomhar at her side. Her eyes darted up and down him, seeing that there was not only a large purpling bruise on his jaw, but others too, across his forearms.

"Mrs Allaway, do you remember telling me that he was dead?" Lady Ruskin asked, pointing directly at Iomhar.

"He could be a ghost," Kit offered up, feeling a little dizzy thanks to the strike to her head.

"Ye cannot tie a ghost up!"

"How did you know he wasn't dead?" The more conscious of the situation Kit became the more she began to panic. She and Iomhar were fastened to the floor, in what appeared to be some kind of attic room, with timber beams overhead and slanting windows in the rooftop. They had to be a distance from Hampton Court Palace now.

"I had someone watching Walsingham. Imagine my surprise when he mentioned seeing Mr Blackwood here walking into his house, soaked to the bone." She pointed at Iomhar again.

"Could you not have sneaked in?" Kit asked Iomhar.

"Oh aye, ye're right, completely my fault," he said, with a shake of his head. "We did not know he was being watched, did we?"

"So, we knew ye were lying, Mrs Allaway." Lady Ruskin's words made Kit's lips flicker into a smile. "Why are ye smiling?"

"No reason," Kit let the smile falter. There was something amusing to her that after all this, Lady Ruskin still called her Mrs Allaway.

"Let me put things into perspective for ye," Lady Ruskin said, her voice so dark and deep that Kit was not the only one to snap her head up to the woman, Iomhar did too. "Ye have stopped nothing today. Thanks to seeing Iomhar alive, we changed our plan. One of your soldiers' stores was robbed just yesterday. A box of gunpowder was taken by Fraser here and his brother. Now ye two can look out of that window —" she pointed behind them to the window slanted in the roof — "and watch for the explosion."

"Ye still got your hands on gunpowder then?" Iomhar's voice was tight.

"Fortunately some of our kin are loyal, ye turncoat," Lady Ruskin spat at him. "It was easy enough for the Frasers to break in once they had talked to a few more of our friends."

"I am loyal to our actual monarch. King James —"

"He usurped his own mother!"

"He was a bairn, he could not usurp anyone to become king. It was the court's choice," Iomhar said the words as though it had been argued all before.

"Yet not God's choice!" Lady Ruskin snapped. She took a step forward, threateningly toward Iomhar who veered his head back a little. "Do not go anywhere, Mr Blackwood, I'll write to my husband to let him know ye are still alive."

"I wonder what he will want to do with me then?" Iomhar muttered sarcastically.

"I could not believe it when Graham Fraser described ye to me. I have heard my husband speak of ye so many times. With that scar he gave ye, I knew it had to be ye." Lady Ruskin gestured to the scar upon his cheek. Kit darted her head toward Iomhar, frowning at the tale. "I expect ye're right. My husband may well enjoy taking your life himself."

Lady Ruskin offered one cruel smirk before heading toward the door and pushing the steward out before her. She hesitated just long enough to look back at Kit. "Enjoy watching your queen's death." The door closed behind her as she walked out.

CHAPTER 28

Kit felt her stomach drop as she whipped round, angling her head toward the window, half expecting the explosion to happen any second.

"Ah — watch it," Iomhar warned. In her turn, she had wrenched their joint hands behind him, tugging on his arm.

"What?" She turned back round. He held up his arm for her to see. She parted her lips in shock as the bruises she had spied before travelled even further than she had expected, stretching under his arm practically black in colour. "What happened to you?" she asked, a little breathlessly.

"What does it look like?" he said, turning his focus to the ropes around his hands and trying to pull them apart. "I took a step outside Walsingham's house this morning and was attacked. I did not have time to pull a weapon. That steward has a strong hit on him," he muttered, rearranging his jaw.

"The steward is Ross Fraser. Graham Fraser's brother."

"That explains a lot." Iomhar focused on pulling his wrists apart, making little headway beyond growls of pain.

"You'll hurt yourself," she said pointedly.

"Ye think I have not noticed that?"

"The sarcasm is hardly helping. Did she say any more?" Kit asked, twisting her head back to the window in panic. Her heartbeat was thudding hard in her chest, practically making her ache. "What their plan was?"

"Nay more than she said already. Just an explosion."

"The queen cannot die like that!" she cried in panic.

"Then help me with these ropes," Iomhar said decisively.

She turned back around and tried to prise her own wrists apart, hoping to tear the ropes, but she could quickly see it was of no use. The rope was thick, of the kind often used for boats on the Thames, her strength would hardly be enough to break it apart.

"Give me your wrists," Kit motioned at him.

"What?"

"You cannot break them apart like that. Our best chance is to try and undo them."

"Good luck with that," he said tartly as he pushed his wrists toward her.

"Any idea where we are?" Kit pulled on the ropes around his wrists.

"Och, that's just tightening them," he said, glaring at her, before she returned her focus to the ropes. "Nay idea where we are," he answered her question. "I did not see much after they put a bag over my head."

She winced at the idea, trying to undo the knot around his wrists, yet it was too tight. "Your weapons?"

"Gone, as are yours."

At his words, she looked down, seeing that he was right, her weapons belt and the daggers were gone. She cursed. Without a blade nearby to cut through the ropes, trying to undo them could be futile. "How long have we got?"

"I do not know," he sighed. "But I'd bet anything Lady Ruskin will want to be at the river to watch it happen. She wanted to watch me die, did not she?"

"I remember," Kit said. "God have mercy, they tied this tight," she said as she moved to her knees, pulling on the ropes.

"Ah, ye're tightening it again," Iomhar growled against the pain.

Kit could see the way the rope was cutting into his skin, drawing it tight, but with her wrists bound together too, getting hold of the knot around his wrist was beginning to feel impossible. "On that subject," she said hurriedly, "want to tell me now why Lord and Lady Ruskin are so keen to see you dead?"

"Is this actually the moment?" He snapped the words.

"When else would there be?" She looked up sharply and met his gaze. "Let's face it, you and I could be dead soon. Quite frankly I would like to know before I died."

"We're not going to die."

"Really?" She broke off from trying to prise open his ropes and waved her bound hands around the room. "What about this situation is giving you hope right now? The fact the queen's boat is about to blow up at any moment? The fact we're trapped? Or maybe that Lady Ruskin's steward may well be back any time to kill us both?"

"I'm beginning to see what ye mean about sarcasm."

"What about it?"

"Not always nice to hear."

"Exactly," she said, returning her attention to the ropes. "So, come on. Why does Lord Ruskin want you dead?"

"I want him dead too," Iomhar spoke darkly. The tone of his voice made Kit glance up, just long enough to see the fury in his eyes that coupled these words.

"Go on," she urged.

"My father was one of the ones charged with moving Mary Stuart out of Edinburgh after she was deposed in favour of her son." Iomhar's words made her stall slightly with the ropes. "Hurry up, or ye do not hear the tale." She frowned at him, but carried on, nevertheless. "From that time on, whenever she was moved between homes, my father was one of the men to escort her, to make sure none of her followers could find her. Ten years ago, Lord Ruskin put an end to that.

"Lord Ruskin was supposed to be my father's friend. He took advantage of that. When my father was moving Mary Stuart out of Loch Leven Castle, Lord Ruskin attacked with his men," Iomhar said, his voice turning huskier than normal. "Someone in that regiment killed my father."

Kit snapped her gaze up to him. An image of the man she had seen in the painting at Iomhar's house flashed in her mind.

"Do not stop," Iomhar said hurriedly, shaking the ropes at her. She carried on, though she kept glancing up to his face. "Lord Ruskin knows exactly who took the life of my father and he would not tell me. He protects the man who did it, claiming it was war, soldiers' rules. It was not war. It was murder, pure and brutal. Either Lord Ruskin did the deed himself, and refuses to confess to his crime, or he is protecting the man who did it. Believe me, Kit, I know well enough that finding out whoever did it will not be easy, but I have made sure to cause a lot of trouble for Lord Ruskin ever since."

"Why do I have a feeling there is more to this tale?" she asked. "Such as how you received that scar?"

"Because there is, but we hardly have the time for it now. Are ye making any progress?"

"No." She gave up, seeing that she had merely frayed the rope. "We need to think of something else." She looked away from him, seeking another idea. "That does not really explain why he wants to kill you." She moved toward the trapdoor where their ropes were tied down. From how they were fastened together, her sudden movement dragged him forward too. "He has more reason to feel guilty, surely?"

"He does not feel guilt like an ordinary man," he said tartly. "He wants to kill me, because believe me, I have caused enough trouble for him to want it."

"I will want to hear more of this at some point."

"Ye may do. If we get out of here."

Kit made a grab for the trapdoor iron rings that their ropes were tied too as an idea dawned.

"Ye have thought of something?" he asked, staring at her.

"We cannot break the ropes, but…" She paused and lifted the trapdoor. "We can break this door." They'd still be fastened together, but it would release them from the floor and given them the freedom to move around at last.

"Step back," Iomhar took the trapdoor from her.

She backed away, giving him space.

He lifted his foot high and rammed it down into the centre of the trapdoor, it fractured beneath the kick into fragments of wood, until all that was left in his hand was the iron hoop to which their ropes were fastened. "It worked."

"You are surprised?" Kit asked, jumping to her feet and running to the door. "Come on."

"Ah!" he yelped as she dragged him out of the room. "Tied together here, try not to pull me flat on my face."

"Tempting," she said, earning a scoff from him as she hurried out onto a set of stairs, high and pokey, with wooden walls caging them in. As she descended, she had to hold her wrists high in the air, from where she was still tethered to Iomhar, so that she didn't pull him down the stairs.

When they reached the bottom, Kit came to a skidding halt and Iomhar nearly fell over her from where he stopped on the step above her.

"What is it?"

Kit looked around her, realising just where they were. "It is Lady Ruskin's house," she whispered to him as she walked out across the landing, dragging him with her. Peering over the banister, she could see down into the entrance hall that was flanked by portraits, with Mary Stuart's painting amongst them.

"We are near the river then," Iomhar followed behind her. Together, they leaned over the banister into the entrance hall below. It was empty. "Aye, there could still be staff in the house."

"Then we go quietly." Kit didn't wait to discuss the matter. She headed toward the staircase, pulling him sharply behind her. He cursed a couple of times under his breath, but he made no further complaint.

On the stairs, they both crept down, using the very edges of the stairs to avoid creaking floorboards. The whole time they were glancing back and forth, checking for anyone who might still be in the house to come and discover them. When they reached the ground floor, Kit's eyes went straight to the painting of Mary Stuart.

"All for you, isn't it?" Kit muttered angrily.

"What?" Iomhar asked distractedly, bumping her side as he stopped moving. She gestured to the painting. He looked up, following her hand before his expression settled into a frown. "Well, it looks a little like her."

"You have met her?" Kit spoke a little too loudly.

"Shh!" Iomhar said, as a sound came from nearby in the house. Someone was walking about. He tugged on their ropes and dragged Kit through the nearest doorway. It happened to be into the same drawing room where she had visited Lady Ruskin more than once.

With their backs against the wall beside the door, Kit strained her ears, listening for more sounds.

Footsteps padded across the floor through the entrance hall, heading somewhere. It was followed by the sounds of metal clanging together, as though of sword blades bumping. Iomhar peered his head around the corner of the doorframe at the sound.

"What is it?" Kit whispered to him.

"Our weapons," Iomhar turned back to face her. "Ready for this?"

"For what?"

"We're going to get our weapons back."

"How are we going to do that then? You have not told me a plan yet. You like a plan."

"Well, we do not have time for a plan right now, so I'm taking a leaf out of your book." He offered one smile before striding back through the doorway, pulling her sharply behind him. She had to stifle a yelp of surprise as she followed.

Two steps into the corridor, Kit crept behind Iomhar. Ahead of them, the same footman who had held her down to the ground with the steward was standing there, with their weapon belts in his grasp. Kit's belt was slung over his shoulder, with the two daggers still in their small scabbards. In his hands, he was examining the crossbow and the rapier that Iomhar usually had attached to his belt, turning them over, with his back to their approach.

Soundlessly, Iomhar took hold of a brass candelabra that had been resting on a nearby table, shaped into an angel standing aloft a platform, with her wings outstretched and her palms carrying two tall white tallow candles.

"Lift your hands when I say," Iomhar whispered to Kit, yet the small sound in the room was enough to grab the footman's attention as they approached, now just a step behind him. He snapped his head up, about to turn round when Iomhar elbowed Kit, signalling now was the moment.

She lifted her hands into the air at the same time Iomhar did, he held the candelabra aloft in the air and brought it down sharply onto the back of the footman's head where it met his neck. The footman was stunned, his head tipped back for a second before he dropped to his knees and fell forward, his nose and cheeks slapping against the tiled ground.

Kit grimaced at the sound, looking away from the figure. "I hope you didn't kill him."

"He'll live," Iomhar said, stepping forward over the figure and snapping up their weapons. He reached for Kit's daggers first and cut through the ropes that fastened them together, before passing her the belt. As Kit fastened the belt around her waist, Iomhar added the crossbow and rapier to his own belt. "To the river?" Iomhar asked quietly, moving toward the door and darting his head back and forth just in case anyone else approached them from the corridors of the house.

"We need to get the queen off that boat," Kit reached for the door and pushed it open. She jumped down the front steps that led to the porch, not even bothering to take them two at a time, then looked about the street.

They were not far from the river, but at this distance, with a few streets and lines of houses between their place and the riverbank, it would be difficult to push through the throng of people to catch up with Lady Ruskin and her steward on foot.

"Any ideas?" Kit asked, gesturing to the busy street around them.

"Aye, one," Iomhar said, moving forward to the street. He stepped straight into the road.

"What are you doing?" Kit cried, just as a cart came to a skidding halt. The horses complained, whinnying loudly and clomping their hooves down onto the cobbles, struggling to stop in time. "I thought you said you didn't want to die for this cause?" Kit shouted after Iomhar as he turned and shrugged.

"They were going to stop in time." He moved round the horses and eying the driver. He lifted the crossbow from his belt and pointed it straight at the poor man. "Off. Now."

"You can't do that, this is my cart, this is," the man said obstinately, gesturing down to it.

Iomhar flicked a switch, taking the safety off the crossbow. No more words needed to be said and the driver scampered off the cart, practically falling sideways as he hurried away.

Iomhar jumped up and took his place as Kit climbed up the other side.

"You will get it back, I promise!" Kit called to the man as they pulled away in the cart.

"If we live to bring it back," Iomhar added to her in a whisper.

She didn't respond with words though she glowered at him as they travelled through the streets, overtaking single horses trotting along and smaller carts that could not gather such speed across the cobbled road. When the river came into view, Baynard's Castle stretched out to the left of them, tall, with towering turrets all bricked up in yellow stone with a red-tiled roof. To the right-hand side, the riverbank appeared, leaning along the side of the green Thames.

"Where are they?" Kit said, jumping to stand on the back of the cart that was filled with hay. She had only just turned to have a proper look at the Thames when the ground shook beneath them and a rumble echoed through the air.

Iomhar brought the cart to a halt as above the river, a cloud of black smoke plumed. "We're too late." Iomhar's words were quiet.

CHAPTER 29

Kit fell still as her eyes settled on the explosion. Beneath the pluming smoke, half the royal boat was visible. Part of the bow was shattered and ladies-in-waiting were falling into the water. Councillors at the back of the boat were screaming, each one scrambling to try and get to safety on the part of the boat that remained intact and was slowly tipping upwards.

The queen was nowhere to be seen.

Kit jumped down off the cart and ran along the side of the river.

"Kit!" Iomhar shouted after her, but she didn't listen. If the queen wasn't there, then there was only one place she could be: in the water. With that dress, the farthingale, the petticoats and the corset, she would be dragged quickly down the depths, and drown within minutes.

Kit sprinted along the riverbank until she was level with the boat. There were others there, all had gathered to see the queen and were now gasping with horror. Above them the smoke hovered, masking the other side of the river and all the crowds that had gathered there. All Kit could see was the carnage on the boat. Other sloops from the parade were moving toward the wreck, trying to pull councillors to safety.

Amongst them, she could see Walsingham. He was pulled from the water onto another boat, waving his cane wildly in the air.

Kit moved one boot toward the river edge, pushing through the crowd, feeling her palms grow clammy and her stomach knot tightly. For a second, the image of being beneath the water when she was little flashed in her mind, along with the fear of never being able to reach the surface, yet the image quickly left her.

She couldn't let her queen suffer that fate.

Kit jumped into the river. The cries of surprise from the people around her she ignored. The coldness of the water against her skin was a shock — for a minute, her body wouldn't move, frozen, then the sight through the water of women and gentlemen scrambling to swim kicked Kit into action. She swam forward, up to the surface, remembering everything that Iomhar had taught her. As she broke through the top, she took a deep breath and crossed the distance toward the wreckage, shortening the gap between them.

Once she reached the others, she trod water for a minute, searching back and forth, looking desperately for any sign of the queen. Still, she wasn't there. There was no sign of that bright red, practically orange hair, nor of the grand white dress she had been wearing, only others trying desperately to swim, with ladies struggling against the weights of their dresses.

Taking a deep gulping breath to hold, Kit dived under the water, turning her body downward. She had to fight all of her natural instincts that made her want to swim back to the top, to save her own life. She had to save someone else's first.

The deeper she swam the more she felt a pressure against her chest. Debris floated past her in the water, fish swam far away, and the intense green murkiness blurred things in the distance. Kit was about to give up and swim back to the top when a blur of white caught her eye. She kicked toward it, reaching through the water. A few seconds later a figure came into view — a woman with orange hair and a white dress.

Realising who it was, Kit increased the speed of her kicking legs, reaching forward. The queen couldn't fight the weight of her dress, it was too heavy, dragging her downward. Her eyes were practically closed and her body convulsed against the pressure of the water.

Kit grabbed the queen's arm and tugged her upwards. At first, nothing happened. The weight of having to swim with another person carrying such a large dress tugged her back down toward the bottom of the riverbed.

Kit snatched one of the daggers out of her belt and reached for the queen, whose eyes fluttered open, realising someone was touching her. Those same eyes widened when she saw the dagger, though she didn't have the strength to swim away. Kit reached forward with the dagger, cutting the skirt, the kirtle, and the farthingale away, leaving the queen in just the petticoats and the shift beneath. With the dagger safely back in her belt, Kit reached this time for the queen's waist and kicked upwards. At last, she began to make progress.

With her head turned up to the surface of the river, the memory came back. The distinct moment where the figure who had been watching her in the water walked away cut through her, making the swim to the surface feel like an impossible height to climb. She kicked harder, feeling her lungs burn without breathing for so long.

When her head was near the surface, she reached one hand up, touching the air with her fingers first before her head broke through. She took deep lungful's of air as the queen coughed in her arms, choking on the water. Kit slapped her back a few times, trying to clear it.

"Kit? Kit!" A voice she knew was shouting her.

She turned her head in the water, spitting out some dregs as Iomhar came into view. He was in the water too, swimming toward her, having helped others out of the exploded boat and into others nearby.

"Ye got her?" he called.

Kit moved her body to the side, revealing the queen who she was holding up. The smile that spread across Iomhar's wet face made a happiness burn within Kit's stomach.

She had done it. She had saved the queen from Lady Ruskin's malicious intent.

Iomhar reached her side and together they began to tow the queen toward the edge of the river. Up onto the riverbank, the crowds that had gathered were shouting. Some of the other councillors had made it to shore too and were shaking off their excess water.

Kit pushed the queen up onto the riverbank ahead of her. There were cries of panic at the queen's state of undress, as councillors took off their cloaks and threw them around her, covering her up.

Kit then felt a pressure against her own back. She was shoved up onto the bank, before she had chance to look back and see that Iomhar was the one to push her forward. After that, he climbed up himself.

"Still afraid of the water?" he asked her quietly.

She glanced behind him, down at the watery depths, feeling the same fear that always dwelled there. Her body was shaking, the trembling fingers beyond her control. "Terrified," she acknowledged, but at least this time, she had not been beaten by it.

A cry went up from the crowd, first there was a scream, then shouted words.

"What is that?"

"It's a pistol!"

Kit whipped her head round, seeing the throng cower down as the familiar face of Ross Fraser strode forward, with a wheellock pistol in his hands. The silver barrel underlined with cherry wood was pointed in their direction, straight at the queen.

Kit moved forward, pushing the queen behind her. The other councillors jumped out of the way as Kit turned her focus on the pistol. There was the spark of a flint and a massive bang as the gun went off. With the steward's eyes on her, Kit didn't doubt he had changed his aim from the queen to her.

Only the view of Fraser was quickly blocked by something black moving in front of her, then a growl of pain followed the bang. Kit clutched to the black mass, realising it was Iomhar's doublet, sodden from the dip in the Thames.

There were more cries of panic as Kit's eyes went from Iomhar's pained face down to his arm — it was bleeding.

"Iomhar, are you mad?" Kit cried, shoving him in his back.

He didn't seem to notice her question. He gritted his teeth, lifted his head and turned his focus back on the steward. He took the crossbow from his belt and fired straight at Fraser. More panicked shouts went up as Fraser dodged the bolt, using the pistol in his grasp to bat the arrow away.

"In the name of the wee man," Iomhar muttered and ran forward toward him.

Kit looked back just once to see the queen was safe in councillors' arms, staring at her, with those coral lips trembling and the colour that had been applied to them bleeding down her chin, then Kit turned and hurried after Iomhar.

Fraser tried to flee, running with the pistol in his hands that he was hurriedly trying to reload. Iomhar was close behind him, followed by Kit.

Iomhar reached the man first at the edge of the grassy bank before it met the towpath along the river. One tackle with his shoulder and the steward was down on the ground, having dropped the pistol. Fraser stretched out a hand to grab the pistol from where it had landed amongst the grass blades, but Kit reached them in time and kicked the pistol away, stopping him.

Iomhar grabbed hold of Fraser's wrists, trying to force them together. "Kit? Rope?" he called.

Kit looked down at her weapons' belt, but she had no rope, nothing that could use to tie the man up.

Before she could even answer, Fraser angled his body up, allowing him to elbow Iomhar in the bullet wound in his arm. Iomhar let out a guttural cry of pain, something that belonged more to a wild animal than a human. Fraser used the moment of freedom to roll away and try to crawl to fetch the pistol.

Kit stepped forward and tackled the steward, driving her elbow down into the middle of his back with her full bodyweight. He crumpled beneath her, with his face buried in the soil under their feet.

"Keep him down," Iomhar said.

Kit looked round to see he was back on his feet, with his arm bleeding even more than before. He was hurrying away, back toward the river. "This is not the time to leave!" Kit cried after him, just as the steward attempted to break free from her grasp. She had to crawl on top of him, pinning him down as she drove an elbow this time into the base of his neck.

"Do ye think I would?" Iomhar called back over the crowds that were squealing in fear. He appeared a moment later with one of the ropes in his grasp that he had taken from the boats. Thick and heavy, the steward would have as hard a time breaking free from it as she and Iomhar had earlier that day.

Iomhar bent down by her side as she wrenched Fraser's arms behind his back, tying them together. Kit gave Iomhar the control, looking around at the carnage that had ensued.

More and more people were being pulled from the water, with many ladies who had been struggling to fight the weights of their dresses being towed up to the bank with their gowns in tatters. Some people were hanging on the very edge of the bank, coughing and spluttering. In the centre of it all, the queen was surrounded by people, her face no longer visible, though the orange wig was a little more lopsided than usual, falling down across her forehead. Kit flicked her gaze away as she stood from the steward, looking for one person that should have been watching in the crowd.

"Where is she? She should be here," she muttered to herself. Iomhar didn't seem to notice, he was still wrestling Fraser into submission as he finished tying the ropes.

"Kit, help me get him up," Iomhar begged, though Kit didn't respond.

Her gaze had fallen on the far side of the crowd. On the other end of the riverbank, where the towpath led up to the main streets of the city, there was a woman. Her black hair was moving back and forth, as though the person couldn't stop shaking their head, in a kind of despair. The red gown was exactly what Kit remembered seeing when she was tied down in the attic room of Lady Ruskin's house.

Kit took a step forward, waiting for the woman to turn around to show her face.

"Kit?" Iomhar said, but she persisted in ignoring him. She kept her focus on the woman who spun slowly around. It was Lady Ruskin. Her lips were parted in panic and her eyes were darting frantically about. When those eyes landed on Kit's position, her cheeks paled.

"She's here," Kit muttered.

"What?" Iomhar asked, looking up from Fraser.

Lady Ruskin fled. She ran up to the city streets, grabbing the skirt of her gown to aid in her sprint.

Kit didn't wait to explain to Iomhar what was happening, she ran forward, chasing after Lady Ruskin, even though Iomhar was still shouting her name.

CHAPTER 30

Kit cursed the heaviness of her clothes as she ran. The doublet was so sodden that it stuck to her arms and her chest, whilst the shirt beneath was cloying and scratching at her throat. Her shoes too were slipping on the cobbles as she chased through the street. Her hat was gone, probably lost somewhere in the Thames, and her auburn hair stuck to the back of her neck in wet tendrils.

"Lady Ruskin!" Kit bellowed the woman's name.

Lady Ruskin didn't turn back. She continued to run ahead, reaching the edge of the road and turning into Whitefriars and the narrow pokey streets that meandered through the medieval buildings. As she took a turn down the street where an old monastery once stood before the Reformation, Kit followed a few seconds later, having to jump around clergymen and passers-by that were walking the streets.

Turning into Temple Street, the gap between them began to narrow. Kit may have been hindered by her wet clothes, but she was chasing down a woman who was much older and even more inhibited by the gown she wore. With her hose and boots allowing Kit to run with great striding leaps, it wasn't long before she was within an arm's length of her quarry.

At the end of Temple Street, Lady Ruskin dived to the side, nearly falling in her heels. The sudden turn jerked Kit, forcing her to drop a little behind as she hurried to catch up. Far ahead, at the end of the road, she saw the buildings become taller, with the old side of the monastery that was now just a carcass of what it used to be, with the stained-glass windows smashed through.

"Alsatia," Kit mumbled to herself, recognising it as she tried her best to kick up her speed, breathing even faster. "Stop! Now!" she shouted at Lady Ruskin, desperate for the woman to give up. She knew that if Lady Ruskin reached the square known as Alsatia, she would have reached an area of sanctuary. A place supposedly free of the law, where someone could hide from their crimes.

Lady Ruskin glanced back when she neared this wall. Seeing Kit evidently much closer than she had anticipated, she panicked, and in her haste managed to trip on the cobbles. It was the few seconds Kit needed.

Ignoring the cries of clergymen that were walking the streets, come to see the old monastery ruins and pray in the temple, Kit barrelled into Lady Ruskin, tackling her to the ground.

"Fetch a constable! A lady is being attacked," one man cried from nearby.

Kit almost laughed at the idea as she took hold of the back of Lady Ruskin's dress and used it to turn the woman round on the floor, up so that she faced Kit and the sky.

"You didn't make it," Kit said, nodding ahead to Alsatia, and the wall of the old monastery.

Lady Ruskin's eyes flashed with anger. She reached out with both hands, aiming for Kit's throat. Only one clasped around Kit's neck. She managed to push Lady Ruskin's other hand away before clawing at the fingers on her throat. There would be a bruise as Lady Ruskin's fingers tightened, but the grasp didn't last long. Kit was the stronger woman and prised them away.

"Let go of me. Ye betrayer!" Lady Ruskin cried. Kit saw a flash of a weapon as she lost track of one of Lady Ruskin's hands.

The basilard, the long dagger that Lady Ruskin had held at her throat before appeared between them, removed from its hiding place within the folds of Lady Ruskin's skirts. Kit managed to dodge the blow aimed at her, rolling away as the blade sliced through the air. Having released Lady Ruskin from her trap, the woman tried to move to her feet. Kit only had to reach out and grab her skirt to stop the escape, dragging her back down to the ground with a firm grip on the farthingale.

Lady Ruskin called out, asking for help, but the clergymen walking nearby in black smocks all stayed away. As she was the one to pull a blade, Kit rather thought the clergymen were confused as to who the attacker now was.

With Lady Ruskin down on the ground again, Kit climbed over her and snapped the basilard from her grasp, throwing it away, where it clattered across the stones. Placing a knee into the woman's back, hearing the way it flexed the horn within the linen of the corset, she shoved Lady Ruskin into the cobbled road and pulled her wrists behind her back.

"Lady Ruskin," Kit tried to catch her breath. "It is with pleasure I can tell you that you will be charged with treason. I will take you to the Tower of London, where you will await your court sentence."

Lady Ruskin appeared to give up fighting, falling limp in the grasp with her cheek pressed down to the cobbles. "What good do ye think that will do? Hmm?"

Kit didn't want to engage in the conversation. She pressed the woman's wrists together more firmly and turned her head to one of the clergymen nearby. Dressed head to toe in black, he watched on with quivering hands.

"You there," she called to him. "Go to the river, find the councillors attending to the queen. Tell them the woman who plotted to kill our queen has been caught."

He bowed his head and ran off. Around them, other clergymen backed off, hearing that the woman pinned down was guilty of treason, they all looked away, as though looking at her was a sin in itself.

"Ye think it was all my idea?" Lady Ruskin laughed, despite the situation. It was harsh, and without any real humour in it. "Well, at least I can take comfort in that. Arrest me if ye like. Take me to the Tower, but ye will not find out who is really to blame here."

"Blame? You are to blame!" Kit said, leaning forward and pushing harshly into the woman's back. "I had to sit in your house as you talked of our queen's death as though it were nothing more to you than a flower dying in a vase. Do not talk to me of blame. I know exactly who to blame for today."

"Foolish girl," Lady Ruskin abruptly fought against Kit's hold, trying to rear upwards. With Kit's full bodyweight in her back she didn't get far and struck her chin back on the ground as she collapsed. "Ye have stopped nothing. Enjoy your queen while she's still alive. Ye think this was the only plot? Ye think I have not thought of this possibility?"

"You are about to be taken to the Tower, you didn't do much to stop it if you feared it, did you?" Kit practically spat the words, so angry was she that Lady Ruskin was still talking, even as she was defeated.

"The one who gave me the orders will simply order another tomorrow," Lady Ruskin said.

This time, the words tore through Kit's haze of anger. She struggled to her feet and pulled on Lady Ruskin's arms, keeping them firmly wrenched behind the woman's back, then used them to steer her back down the street, through Whitefriars.

"Who gave you the order?" Kit shoved Lady Ruskin in the back.

"Ye want me to talk now?"

"You seem particularly keen on talking," Kit said drily, "might as well hear you say something useful. Who gave you the order?"

"Ye think I'll tell ye that?" Lady Ruskin laughed a little.

Kit wasn't sure what made her do it. Either it was the fear of seeing Queen Elizabeth and all those innocent people nearly die, or it was hearing Lady Ruskin laugh about death, but it happened anyway. Kit grabbed one of the daggers from her belt and brought Lady Ruskin to a stop in the street, holding the dagger to her throat.

Lady Ruskin tipped her head back, over Kit's shoulder, trying to rear away from the blade.

"Who gave you the order?" Kit seethed, whispering in Lady Ruskin's ear.

"Ye think ye will get the name out of me if ye cut my throat? Tongues do not work very well then."

"There are other things I can do." Kit moved the dagger to Lady Ruskin's arm. The woman flinched, feeling the blade press against her skin. "Tell me. Who gave you the order?"

"I will never tell," Lady Ruskin said, turning her head to the side so that Kit could see her expression. The face was malicious, not quite a smile, but almost pleased with herself. "I do this for God, and for my queen, ye think I would betray them both?"

"You are not loyal to the real queen."

"I could say the same for ye!" Lady Ruskin shouted the words. The noise shook Kit's eardrum as Lady Ruskin moved within her grasp. The movement was abrupt as Lady Ruskin veered forward, snatching one of her arms out of Kit's hands. She turned and took hold of the dagger.

"No!" Kit roared, trying to hold onto the weapon. In the tug of war over the blade, she was unable to keep her hand on the blade properly. Lady Ruskin elbowed her in the chest. The winding pain that took Kit's breath from her was enough for the woman to prise the weapon away. Kit stood straight, expecting the weapon to be turned on her, but it never came.

She looked up, hearing a whimper of pain, to see that Lady Ruskin had turned the blade on herself.

"What … have you done?" Kit asked, struggling to get the words out.

Lady Ruskin was standing in the middle of the cobbled road with the dagger in her stomach. Her lips quivered and her cheeks trembled too as the defiance in her face that had been there a minute ago vanished. "I will not let ye torture the information out of me. Ye wished to take me to the Tower?" Lady Ruskin pulled the blade out of her stomach, tossing it to the floor. Kit flinched as the blade struck the ground. "Ye lose, Mrs A-Allaway." The words were stammered as Lady Ruskin's body went into shock.

She stumbled backward, losing balance as the blood began to pool through the dress, turning the red gown a darker shade of crimson.

"No. No," Kit murmured to herself, as though she could deny the proof of her own eyes. She reached forward, catching Lady Ruskin as she fell, stopping her from hitting her head on the cobbles.

The woman was unconscious, barely breathing with her eyes firmly closed.

289

"You cannot escape that easily," Kit said insistently, moving the woman on the ground until she was flat. "No. Give me a name. Who gave you the order?"

Kit remembered back to the letter she had stolen from Fraser, that first referred to the plot. She had been so certain that when the letter spoke of number Eighty-Two, the codename referred to Lady Ruskin, yet she had never discovered who the letter was addressed to. Number Twenty-One had remained a mystery.

"Was it number Twenty-One?" Kit continued to ask the unconscious Lady Ruskin. "Speak to me. Wake up. The codename — is it them? Did they give you the order?"

Still, Lady Ruskin did not move. Remembering how Iomhar had brought Walsingham back after he had blacked out from the smoke inhalation, Kit bent over the unmoving form of Lady Ruskin and placed both hands in the centre of the chest. She pressed once, but nothing happened. She pressed a few more times, becoming harsher and harsher in her movements.

"Wake up. You cannot die yet!" With one more thump to the chest, Lady Ruskin's eyes fluttered open, and she breathed deeply, the breath sounding strained and croaky. "Who is it?" Kit demanded, grabbing Lady Ruskin by the collar of her dress and holding her off the cobbled ground. "Who gave you the order?"

"Y-ye will never know." The words were so quiet that Kit had to bend even further down to hear her. "He is under your nose all the time, constantly. Close to your precious queen, one of her trusted men, and still, ye have not found him. Ye think ye will ever find him now?"

"Give me a name. A name!" Kit ordered, shaking the collar of the dress, but Lady Ruskin's eyes closed again, and her head lolled back. "No. Wake up."

No matter how many times Kit pressed into the middle of Lady Ruskin's chest, she did not move. The blood pooled out of her wound, creating a puddle that sat in the lines of the cobbles, but no words passed her lips, and the eyes remained firmly closed.

CHAPTER 31

Kit felt hollow as she walked back to the river. By the time she reached the bank where the crowd was beginning to disperse, her body was numb. She moved through the crowd, inching slowly toward the edge of the river, searching back and forth for a face she knew.

Queen Elizabeth was surrounded by her councillors, her lips now pursed together, refusing to speak to anyone as all the men fussed around her, deciding what was best to get her safely to Hampton Court Palace. Kit strained her eyes, seeing that Walsingham was amongst them, his focus purely on the queen as he shook his cane high in the air, arguing with Lord Burghley over what was the best plan.

Kit looked away from them, searching for another face, but she heard him before she saw him in the end.

"Ye're covered in blood." Iomhar's voice came from behind her, before a hand took her elbow and spun her round. "What happened? Are ye injured?" He reached out, taking her other elbow in his hand and turning her back and forth, analysing her.

"It's not my blood," she answered numbly, unable to lift her voice very loud.

"What?"

"It's not mine," she said again, louder this time.

"Then whose is it?"

"It is Lady Ruskin's," Kit spoke tightly, watching as he frowned.

"Where is she?"

"With a priest," she answered, thinking of the moment when one of the passing clergymen had come to her side and placed a hand on her shoulder, urging her to give up trying to revive Lady Ruskin. "She's … she's gone."

"Did ye…?" Iomhar trailed off.

"What? No!" Kit refuted loudly. His question shook her out of her dazed state, and she stepped out of his arms. He had a habit of coming into close proximity with her these days. It left her unsettled. "She did it to herself. She took my dagger and then she…" She broke off and covered her eyes, praying she could somehow remove the memory of what Lady Ruskin had done from her mind, but it couldn't be done. It was firmly there, as though it had been burned on her memory with a hot branding iron. "She could not face going to the Tower. There was something else too."

Kit was about to tell Iomhar of what Lady Ruskin said when her eyes flicked to Iomhar's arm, seeing the blood trailing there. "God have mercy, why did you do that?" she cried, stepping toward him and grabbing the injured arm.

"Och, careful!" he complained, though she ignored him, wrenching back the now torn doublet to see the wound.

"You stepped in the way of a bullet, you fool," she snapped, reaching out and slapping him around the other arm.

"Ow, am I not injured enough as it is?" he asked, gesturing to his wound.

"I cannot believe you were so great a fool. What was it you called me before?"

"Bampot?"

"Yes. You bampot! Why did you do it?" She reached down to her belt and removed it.

"I am not answering that," he said, looking up, away from her. Kit tossed her daggers down to the ground, freeing the belt completely then wrapped it tightly around Iomhar's arm. "What are ye doing?"

"Stopping the bleeding." She threaded the leather through the metal hoop. She could remember one of the intelligencers teaching her once when she was young about the bodily humours, and how to protect the body. What she could remember from the lessons told her how to tend to a wound, or to at least staunch blood flow before seeing a physician. "Brace yourself," she warned Iomhar.

"For what?" he asked. Before she could answer, she pulled the leather tight, closing the wound. "Ah! Ye…" he broke off.

"Were you about to curse my name?"

"Aye, strongly indeed."

Her lips quirked into the smallest of smiles as she released the belt. "That should see you through to seeing a physician," she stepped back. He looked down at his arm, shaking his head a little before he lifted his gaze back to her. "Why did you step in front of a bullet? Any fool would realise it could kill you."

"Aye, then ye would be dead," he said tartly. "Would ye rather I had let that happen?"

"He might have missed. You said yourself the pistols are not accurate."

"Clearly not as inaccurate as I hoped!" he said, waving his arm in the air.

"Kit! Iomhar!" a voice called. It tore into their bickering argument and made them both look up.

Through the crowd that was dispersing, Walsingham was approaching them. He was wet, with water dripping off his black cloak and the cane struggling through the boggy bank. Behind him, there were other gentlemen, and between their heads the distinctive orange wig could be seen.

"Why are you covered in blood?" Walsingham asked as he stopped in front of Kit.

"It is not mine," she assured him, watching as his lips flickered into the smallest of smiles. Kit glanced once to Iomhar, thinking of what Lady Ruskin had just told her before she died. *'He is under your nose all the time, constantly. Close to your precious queen, one of her trusted men, and still, ye have not found him.'*

Could this person be a privy councillor? One of the men walking toward them, surrounding the queen, one of the men that Walsingham called a friend?

Kit couldn't utter the information now. She flattened her lips together, determined to keep it to herself for the moment. With so many privy councillors nearby, she couldn't risk being overheard at this time. The very man Lady Ruskin had spoken of could be amongst them, ready to hear her whispers.

"I suppose I should congratulate you on a task well done, but…" Walsingham trailed off and looked at the carnage on the riverbanks. "It was not quite the end I had in mind."

Kit swallowed nervously, looking to the riverbanks and the people gathered. Some were still being lifted out of the water, so drenched that their hair and wigs were plastered to their skin. Others were tumbled together on the banks, somewhat sick judging by the pallor of their skin.

"She is alive," Iomhar whispered. "Aye, that is what is important."

"You are right, Iomhar. It is." Walsingham smiled at Kit. It was a full smile of the ilk she had not seen for some time. "Your task is accomplished for today."

"At a cost." Iomhar grimaced with the words, holding onto his wounded arm.

Kit felt awash with relief. A smile leapt to her cheeks and her hands fell loose at her side. The Queen was safe. For now.

"I have someone who wishes to see you both," Walsingham said, stepping to the side.

Kit's spine straightened as Queen Elizabeth was revealed, standing between the councillors with more than one gentleman's cloak wrapped around her shoulders.

She looked even more lacklustre than Kit could remember. The wig was almost sideways on her head, the collar around the neckline of her dress was skew-whiff and hanging down at an odd angle, with drips trickling off the lace. Her white make-up was smeared and patchy across her skin, her dress was still in tatters too, though most of the damage that Kit had done with her dagger was now covered by the cloaks.

"I suppose I should be upset that you ruined my gown."

Queen Elizabeth's voice made Kit flinch. Standing slightly behind the queen, Walsingham made a gesture with his hand, urging her to curtsy. At once, she curtsied and Iomhar bowed at her side.

"My apologies, Your Majesty," Kit said before lifting her eyes back to the queen. "The dress was too heavy. It was the best way to get you free of the water."

"So I saw." Queen Elizabeth's hand flicked in her direction, urging her to stand straight. "You dived into the water to pull me out, then stood in front of a bullet. A bullet that was taken by *you*," she turned her head toward Iomhar. "I owe you both my gratitude. Had you two not been here, I may well have lost my life to the Thames."

Kit shared a glance with Iomhar, startled by the vulnerability once again displayed by Queen Elizabeth. The glimmer of that weakness was gone in the next moment as she lifted her chin higher, trying to appear regal despite her dilapidated state.

"Do we know who was behind the plot?" the queen asked.

"We do," Kit said, wishing she could believe it. Maybe Lady Ruskin was the commander of her little army rebellion, but she had been given the order by someone else, it seemed. It hardly felt the right moment to declare this, with still so many pairs of ears able to listen into the tale Kit had to tell. For the moment, it would have to be her secret. "Lady Ruskin. She is dead, Your Majesty."

Walsingham flinched at this news, as though Kit had physically hurt him with her words. "Dead? What happened?" Walsingham asked.

"She did it herself."

"Well, I will pray every day that you two will not be needed again, but Walsingham tells me weekly that my life is in danger," Queen Elizabeth said. With these words, she sent a resentful look toward her councillor, who offered her a sad sort of smile in answer. "So, I hope you two will be there the next time I have to see death standing by my shoulder."

"I will make sure they are always there," Walsingham affirmed pointedly, looking between them.

Kit frowned, glancing back to Iomhar, curious at what these words meant.

"Burghley!" Queen Elizabeth snapped his name and the small councillor stepped forward. "Take me back to the palace. This was adventure enough for one day."

Kit curtsied and Iomhar bowed beside her, as the queen walked off. Once Kit stood straight, she found Walsingham standing in front of her, staring at the two of them.

"What did that mean?" Kit asked, pointing after the queen as she left.

"I think Her Majesty was pointing out that you two work well together," Walsingham bore a small smile.

"Oh nay," Iomhar held up his hands hurriedly. "Ye're not going to make me work with her again, are ye?"

"Was I that bad?" Kit asked, spinning round to face him with her hands on her hips.

"For starters I have picked up multiple injuries since I met ye." Iomhar pointed to the new wound on his arm.

"That one was your own fault. You should not step out in front of a pistol."

"I would not have done had ye not already done the same thing!"

"I'm going to interrupt the two of you from arguing any further," Walsingham held up a hand between the two of them. "I think it is a good match."

"A good match?" Kit repeated in horror. "He second guesses everything I do."

"I rather liked that about his approach. It reins you in a little," Walsingham said, pointing at her.

"I am not that bad."

"Ye are," Iomhar muttered, earning another sharp glare from her.

There was a sound far to her left on the riverbank, someone was shouting, trying to argue with another. Kit turned her head toward the argument, seeing Ross Fraser was being pulled to his feet by two soldiers, with his arms tied behind his back with the rope from the boat. He was shouting loudly, turning purple in the face from the sheer effort he was putting into his words. "Do you suppose we'll find his brother?"

"When he hears of this, Graham Fraser will probably run before we can arrest him," Iomhar answered her.

"Someone want to tell me what went wrong with our plan?" Walsingham asked.

Kit's smile faltered. She looked away from Walsingham, up to Iomhar.

"Lady Ruskin has someone watching your house," Iomhar took up the explanation. "They saw I was alive and knew we had deceived them. They smuggled some more gunpowder onto the boat another way."

"Yes," Walsingham said gravely, lowering his hand from Kit's shoulder. "When the gun went off, I saw the explosion. It came from a box at the front of the boat. At least they did not win. We did not have a death today after all. Thanks to the pair of you. Your next commission will be one together." Walsingham took a step away as though the matter were decided upon already.

"I do not suppose my complaint against the idea will do any good?" Kit asked, prompting Walsingham to glance back at the two of them.

"Ye said not that long ago ye liked me now," Iomhar pointed out with a smirk.

"Be quiet." She waved her hand in his direction.

"No good at all," Walsingham answered her last question with a smile. "Before I send you both home for the night, is there anything else I should know? Anything that passed with Lady Ruskin, Kit?"

"Actually…" Kit faded. There was something Kit needed to say now after so many of the privy council had departed, but a grain in her gut niggled her. Lady Ruskin may have said someone on the privy council plotted against the Queen, but she had offered up no more clues as to his identity, and Walsingham was on that council.

"Yes, Kit?" Walsingham prompted her on.

She stared at him, unsure if her suspicion were a mad one, or if a doubt had simply been placed there by Lady Ruskin to cause trouble. She dismissed the idea yet found herself lying by omission regardless. "I was thinking we need to get Iomhar to a physician, urgently."

"That you do," Walsingham nodded. As he stepped away, Kit considered what she had done and why. She trusted Walsingham, yet a seed of doubt had been sown, and she couldn't pull it out again. Not yet.

"Kit?" Iomhar whispered, elbowing her in the side to get her attention as Walsingham walked further away from them. "Are you well?"

"Perfectly."

"Nay, you are not. Something is amiss."

"I will tell you later." Kit quickly waved a hand at him, urging him to be quiet as Walsingham stopped a little distance from them and looked back, speaking to them again.

"Best hurry to that physician, you two. I want you both well for Monday. Another task awaits you both."

HISTORICAL NOTES

When researching for the *Kit Scarlett Tudor Mystery Series*, there is inherently a challenge. The world of espionage in Elizabethan England is in many ways very secret, because that is of course the way Sir Francis Walsingham wished it to be. I became fascinated with all the information I could get my hands on. Whether it was in the National Archives, or research in looking at biographies and other books written by historians, I devoured it all, only to find there is a limited amount of what we do know.

While I found hints of women spies, most of the time male intelligencers are the ones spoken of when we talk about what we do know about this period. It raised an important question as to what could have happened in the shadows, in the area we know little about. What if there was a woman spy, who is virtually unknown?

So, this book is a woven text of fact and fiction. The fact is used to inspire, and the fiction used to create something that is entertaining.

We begin Kit Scarlett's story in this book in 1584, the time period that leads up to the historic events of 1587, the execution of Mary, Queen of Scots, and 1588, the invasion of the Spanish Armada. It is a significant and crucial period in the history of Queen Elizabeth I's rein, for so much could have changed depending on what the intelligencers could and could not find. The research into this era could not have been accomplished without the traditional foundations of the National Archives and the British Library, plus the research of valued historians, Suzannah Lipscomb and Lucy Worsley. As always, though, the more you research, the more you uncover.

Aside from the changing world of politics, this is an era where much social change occurred. On the ground and with those who weren't sat in royal palaces, we see a revolution in weaponry during this period, a shift in behaviour, and a challenge to the religion that divided the people. There are many places and historians I have to acknowledge for illustrating this world so far away from royalty. There's Ruth Goodman, and her book on *How to Behave Badly in Renaissance Britain*, and Ian Mortimer's *A Time Traveller's Guide to Elizabethan England*. Only so much can be achieved in the written word though, and the places which bring this past to life are a big part of creating Kit Scarlett's world: Montacute House in Somerset, the Fashion Museum in Bath, Beaulieu in Hampshire, Hampton Court Palace in London, Bishop's Palace in Wells, and Great Chalfield Manor in Wiltshire, to name a few of the places that have helped create the fabric of Kit's adventure.

A big thank you to them all! They'll be taken forward with all the more research that needs to be done for the next Kit Scarlett adventure.

A NOTE TO THE READER

Dear Reader,

Thank you for taking the time to read the first in the series of Kit Scarlett's adventures.

The inspiration for Kit's tale comes from a longing to see more stories where women are at the centre of a tale that is truly adventurous. We know from hints of this time period that there was the occasional woman doing espionage, but with Kit, I've taken that idea and thrown her completely into this world. Not only is she a spy, fighting to defend her Queen in one of the most turbulent times of history, when there were often assassination attempts on the Queen's life, but Kit is in the deep end. It is her responsibility to see that the Queen stays safe.

Naturally, at times, fact is played with a little and people are invented. The purpose of this book is to entertain after all, so I hope I have indeed done that, and you have enjoyed this story as much as I did writing it. This is a created world, where a woman walks freely dressed as a man, saving lives and even the country, but who knows? This is a world of shadows, where intelligencers operated in the dark and, for all we know, a woman like Kit may have truly existed.

Reviews by readers these days are integral to a book's success, so if you enjoyed Kit's tale I would be very grateful if you could spare a minute to post a review on **Amazon** and **Goodreads**. I love hearing from readers, and you can talk with me through **my website** or **on Twitter** and follow my author page **on Facebook**.

I hope we'll meet again on Kit's next adventure.

Adele Jordan

Sapere Books is an exciting new publisher of brilliant fiction and popular history.

To find out more about our latest releases and our monthly bargain books visit our website: **saperebooks.com**